Brand New
Human Being

Brand New Human Being

Emily Jeanne Miller

Houghton Mifflin Harcourt • BOSTON • NEW YORK • 2012

For information about permission to reproduce selections from this book, write to Permissions, Houghton Mifflin Harcourt Publishing Company, 215 Park Avenue South, New York, New York 10003.

www.hmhbooks.com

Library of Congress Cataloging-in-Publication Data
Miller, Emily Jeanne.
Brand-new human being / Emily Jeanne Miller.
p. cm.
ISBN 978-0-547-73436-1
1. Househusbands—Fiction. 2. Parenting—Fiction. 3. Families—Fiction.
4. Domestic fiction. I. Title.
PS3613.I5356B73 2012
813'.6—dc23
2011036973

Book design by Brian Moore

Printed in the United States of America
DOC 10 9 8 7 6 5 4 3 2 1

For my grandparents:
Jeanne, Arnold, Roz, and Sy

Brand New
Human Being

Part I

1

MY NAME IS Logan Pyle. My father is dead, my wife is indifferent, and my son is strange. I'm thirty-six years old. My life is nothing like I thought it would be.

The three of us plus one dog, Jerry, live in my childhood home, a sweet and sturdy Craftsman-style bungalow on a quiet block in a tree-lined section of a small Western city that was until the end of the last ice age the bed of a glacial lake. We sit at the confluence of three rivers, two of which – the Clark Fork and the Blackfoot – come together just east of town. A few miles downstream they receive a third, the Bitterroot, and the three persist across the Idaho panhandle and into the great Northwest as one. The scenery – the natural world in general – gets a lot of attention here. We're ringed on all sides by mountains, and the sugar maples that line our streets turn outrageous shades of red and orange and gold every fall.

So here we are, autumn. Another early morning, this one a Saturday, which means swimming lessons at Owen's school. I'm up in his room, digging through his top drawer with one hand, balancing him awkwardly on my hip with the other.

"Where's the blue, Jules?" I shout in the direction of the stairs. "It's a blue day, but I only see red. *Julie*," I shout once more. A sudden pain clutches at my spine. "Fuck. Four is too big to be carried," I tell Owen, depositing him a little roughly on the bed. Right away, his thumb is in his mouth.

"You sure it's blue?" asks Julie, rather dreamily, from downstairs.

"It's the twentieth," I shout back. "Odd, red, even, blue."

3

"Four and three-quarters," he says, showing me the fingers of his free hand.

"Exactly my point. Now come on. Take that thumb out and help me look."

He frowns. "I don't want to."

"*Julie*," I shout again. I give up on the top drawer and start in on the middle. "Sometimes in life we have to do things we don't want to do," I tell Owen. "It builds character."

"What's character?" he asks, around the thumb.

"Pardon? I can't understand you with that thumb in the way."

He takes the thumb out and says, "What's *character?*" then pops it right back in. Flipping over, he buries his face in the pillow and sticks his rear end in the air.

"Sit up like a big kid, please," I say.

He shakes his head, squeezes his eyes shut. "Shh. Baby sleeping."

"Christ, Owen, now? We have to go."

"Baby *sleeping*," he says again. I sit down next to him and rest my hand on his rump.

He's been carrying on this way for weeks now — "regressing," according to one or another of the myriad parenting books Julie's perpetually reading half of, then quoting to me. Besides the thumb, he's gone back to the bottle and climbing into our bed in the middle of the night, and he even insists on wearing a diaper some days under his pants. And now and then he'll slip into an odd, German-sounding baby talk it pains me to hear. Julie insists it's normal, or at least common — "'a phase many children experience,'" she read aloud to me last week, while we were getting ready for bed. "'It's incumbent that the parents of the distressed child recognize his or her behavior as expressing a critical emotional need and react accordingly,'" she said, laying the book down. "What that means is that we have to act like whatever Owen does is okay."

"But it's not okay," I said, right before she turned out the light.

Now I reach up and pluck his thumb out of his mouth. "*Julie*," I shout once more. "Could I get a hand up here?"

"Just give me a sec, babe," she calls back.

I hate yelling between floors; it's no way to communicate. I tell Owen to stay put, but he follows me down the stairs anyway and into the kitchen, his bare feet slapping the terra cotta tiles. Julie is not here. She's not in the living room, either, or at the built-in desk we share under the stairs, where she sometimes works in the mornings, before Owen and I get up.

I find her in the dining room, standing in a square of sunlight by the picture window, braiding and unbraiding her hair, looking out. I pause in the doorway. I can see she's deep in thought, and I wouldn't be hard-pressed to guess about what. She's a lawyer, and to say the case she's working on at the moment takes up all her time is a gross understatement of the facts.

I watch her take her braid in one hand and reach for the teardrop-shaped prism that hangs in the window with the other. She gives it a spin, sending shards of colored light racing around the room. Bennie, my father's widow, hung it twenty years ago, when she first moved in. She used to say that the way the sunlight went into a prism and came spilling out in every direction was like God's love in our hearts. Bennie is always proffering this brand of hokey/deep spiritual wisdom, which doesn't bother me but drives Julie up the wall. After Gus died, Julie wanted to take down the prism and everything else Bennie left here, but I said no. I'm not a sentimental man, per se, but some things you just don't feel right tossing in the trash.

"Earth to Jules," I say. "Come in, Jules."

"Mm-hm?" she says.

She's a knockout, my wife — by far the most attractive woman I've ever been with. I thought so the very first time I saw her. She was twenty-four then, an intern at my father's firm, and she was hiding behind some holly outside the offices of Mayfield and Pyle, sneaking a cigarette. I watched her through the window while I waited for Gus. She's a petite woman, almost a whole foot shorter than me, with long red hair that tends toward the wild, and dark, lake-water-blue eyes. And when she smiles — something she used to do regularly — she shows the sexy, sweet gap between her two front teeth, a feature she loathes no matter how many times, or in what manner, I protest.

Watching her now, though, I'm mostly aware of how thin she's gotten. With her hair pulled to the side, I can see the outline of her shoulder blades perfectly through the thin cotton of the old T-shirt of mine she wears, and her formerly snug Levi's hang off her hips. When I've told her how skinny she looks, she smiles and says flattery will get me nowhere. "*Too* skinny," I say, but she just rolls her eyes and says with everything going on with the case, she forgets half the time to eat. Meanwhile, I seem to be remembering for the both of us. Last week on the scale in the men's locker room at the pool, I had the pleasure of learning I'm pushing two hundred pounds.

Her mug of green tea rests on the windowsill, its paper tag hanging down one side. She picks it up to take a sip.

"The suit?" I repeat.

"What about it? Did Stan call back?"

"The *swim*suit, Jules, Jesus," I say.

"Right, of course." She takes a Mayfield and Pyle pen from behind her ear and, leaning over the dining-room table, scribbles something on a yellow pad. When she finishes, she taps the pad with the pen, which she tucks back behind her ear. From the doorway Owen says, "Morning, Mama," and holds up his arms.

"Morning, baby," she says.

I wish she wouldn't call him that. I shoot her a look, but it's lost on her as she scoops him up under the arms and sets him on her hip. She may be scrawny these days but she's still very strong. I forget how strong, sometimes. She carries him through the kitchen into the laundry room, saying, "Who's my favorite little boy in the whole wide world?"

Stepping into the sunny spot she abandoned, I pick up her mug and look out at the yard (*my* yard, I keep having to remind myself). It's November, but you'd never guess. Not only are the mountaintops around town still bare, we haven't had a single hard freeze

6

yet — barely even a frost. Fall crocuses are blooming, birds are singing. Julie takes her morning power walks in shorts. I'm not a superstitious person, I never have been, but sixty-five degrees and sunny, five
days before Thanksgiving, in this part of the world? It's just not right.

From upstairs I hear Jerry migrating from Owen's bedroom to the
hall, his nails clicking on the hardwood floors. You know those dogs
who stay right by their master's side, every minute of the day? Who
follow you from room to room, sleep under the table with their head
on your feet, never let you out of their sight? Well, Jerry isn't one of
those.

I watch a squirrel chase another up the old crabapple tree's trunk.
When Julie first moved in, five falls ago, she was *enchanted* (her
word) with that tree. She grew up in the city and always fantasized,
she told me, about having a yard with a giant apple tree. She used
to talk about hanging a swing from its branches, baking pies with its
fruit. But she used to talk about a lot of things. That very first October, when she actually went out and filled a bucket, she found the
apples were sour, like I'd told her, and a nightmare to peel, and every
year since we've let them fall to the ground and rot.

This morning, I notice what a disaster the yard (*my* yard) has become: a muck of dead leaves and fallen fruit atop unmown grass
that should have turned brown by now but has not; my father, Gus,
would be appalled. He was a fanatic about the yard. If he wasn't
working, or in his workshop building or fixing things, then he'd be
out here — mowing, weeding, mulching, planting vegetables every
spring, waxing philosophical about the value of dirt under one's nails.

A not-so-minor celebrity in these parts, Gus spent the first twenty
years of his career as a wunderkind systems engineer, designing and
building state-of-the-art gold mines all over Montana, until one day
he shocked everyone — including me — and quit. He'd been getting
a law degree on the sly, and he set up shop with his old friend Stan
Mayfield. Together they spent the next twenty years working to shut
the gold mines down.

My middle name, Augustus, comes from him, but that's where

the commonality ends. I'm nothing like Gus. I have no aptitude for science or math, I don't garden, I'm no good at fixing or building anything, and most of all, I have no interest in fame. I always wanted to write. I was supposed to live a life of the mind. I was going to be a professor; when I met Julie, I was just a couple hundred pages away from my American history PhD. But then she got pregnant with Owen and, like I said, here we are. Now, instead of hallowed halls, fawning students, and microfiche, my days consist of folding laundry, shuttling Owen to and from his pricey private school, and spending what's left of the money Julie makes, lawyering, on cruelty-free cleaning products and organic food.

I turn away from the window just as Julie emerges from the kitchen with Owen still on her hip, only now he's wearing his blue swimsuit, goofy yellow rain boots, his Superman cape from Halloween, and nothing else. I glance at him and quickly look away. Though he's had it his whole life, his scar, a ragged, dark red S that runs from sternum to navel, still has the power to catch me off-guard. I'm ashamed of my squeamishness, but thankfully neither of them is focused on me.

She puts him down and squats to his level. "Now scurry upstairs and get your backpack, quick like a bunny. Mama's got to make a stop on the way." Once he's gone, she stands, smoothes down her jeans, rests her hands on her jutting hips, and looks at me. "You coming with?"

"I can't. I have to go to the store first. Fall inventory's three weeks late, and we can't open back up until it's done."

"Mm," she says, and turns to check her reflection in the ornate, gilt-framed mirror that's been hanging on the dining-room wall since I was a kid. "Isn't that Bill's job?" She pulls back her hair, inspecting one side of her face and then the other. "I hope he's paying you overtime," she adds — a barb, since we both know Bill doesn't pay me at all. Technically, I pay him. Bill Hawks is my oldest friend as well as my business partner; together, we run an outdoor-equipment store called The Gold Mine, though I'll admit that in the four-plus years it's been open, it's been anything but.

"Time and a half," I say, to lighten the mood. I don't tell Julie that I haven't spoken to Bill in days — that Bill and I seem not to be speaking to each other — because then I'd have to tell her about the most recent offer to buy the store and the land it sits on (both of which, as of Gus's death, belong to me), and then we'd have to devote a portion of the increasingly paltry slot of time we spend together these days not arguing, to argue about that.

"Can you be back by noon?" she says. "Stan and I have to do phone interviews this afternoon and I haven't prepared anything yet. I'm totally swamped." She goes to the counter, leans on her elbows, and starts thumbing through a thick file. Her hair falls forward, hiding her face.

That I'm not jealous, by nature, has served me well these past two months, because the fact is there's another man in my wife's life; or rather, there are upwards of thirty-five other men — the plaintiffs in *Thomas Edgar Kowalski et al. v. Holliman Industries,* some of whom are alive and many of whom are dead. Since September, when Stan promoted Julie to the case, these men have ruled our lives, or ruled Julie's life, which in turn rules mine. I've tried to make her understand what it's like, taking a back seat to these admittedly unfortunate vermiculite miners, but she isn't particularly sympathetic. She tells me sometimes people need to put their own needs aside for a greater good, and that Stan thinks this might go all the way to the Supreme Court. It's not only me I'm worried about, I explain; Owen's suffering, too. "You know who's suffering? Those poor men. This is about getting justice for them," she says. And her ace in the hole: "Causes like this one are why your father founded Mayfield and Pyle in the first place." The fact that her long hours mean more money, in which we're not exactly awash these days, does little to bolster my case.

When Owen comes back downstairs, he's got his Mickey Mouse backpack over his cape, and he's changed into sneakers, but still no shirt. I want to tell him to get one but a stern glance from Julie stops me cold. "Say bye to Dad," she tells him, digging for her keys in her purse.

"Bye to Dad," he says, and comes over to hug my legs.

"Give 'em hell, champ," I say, palming the top of his head. He has Julie's blue eyes and fair skin, everyone says, and my mouth and disposition, but his dark gold curls came straight from Gus. "Remember, paddles," I say, holding my hands up and pressing my fingers together.

"Right, Dad, paddles," he says, and does the same.

2

HALF AN HOUR later, I'm at the old silo that serves as The Gold Mine's warehouse, sitting by the window watching a couple of wet-suited kayakers mess around in the deeper water, where the river bends. It's a clear, sunny day, rare for this time of year — rare for this valley, actually, most of the year — and I spend a minute or two resenting Bill. *I* should be outside, enjoying the sunshine, or at the library, working, or at Eden, watching Owen swim; it's Bill who should be here. One of the kayakers flips over, then rolls back up, shaking the water from his hair like a dog.

The silo and store sit directly on the bank of the Clark Fork River, on one of the only parcels of riverfront property left not owned by a conservation trust or by the U.S. government or by the town, which is why, every so often, an offer to buy comes down the pike. The most recent comes from an investment group whose name I don't even recognize, and though I haven't asked Bill, I'd bet money they're from out of state: another cohort of rich carpetbaggers who don't care about the river, or the town, or the valley — who care only about making a quick buck. They'd have a hotel or condos or a strip mall or worse up on this spot within minutes, given the chance, and in my view (as I keep telling Julie, and now Bill) there are special spots in hell reserved for people who'd willingly facilitate that.

Plus, it just so happens that this rocky rhomboid of earth is my inheritance from Gus. He bought the silo, the storefront (formerly a bustling meth lab), and the 3.75 acres on which they sit for a song at a police auction in 1989, when downtown was a wasteland of boarded-up buildings and For Rent signs, and the river was basically a garbage dump, a toxic soup of mine tailings and urban refuse so foul kids were warned not to get too close with open cuts, and everyone agreed he was throwing his money away. But Gus never put much stock in the opinions of other people, and in the intervening years, things turned around. By the time I moved back home, five years ago, our previously desiccated town center had undergone a major revitalization campaign ("Live It Up, Go Downtown!"), and with the copper mines upstream closed for good and even some of the old dams being taken out, the river was clean and clear and teeming with trout. Needless to say, by the time Gus died, in July, the lot made a valuable gift. But it came with a hitch. The taxes he owed on the parcel were enormous — more than Julie and I could ever possibly afford.

Right off, there were offers, and Julie wanted to sell. The proceeds would pay off our debt and then some, she said, and float us until I got my dissertation done. She reminded me (as she had before, and has since) that I was running out of time, and of our paucity of funds. But I said no. "Gus didn't leave me this land by accident," I explained. "He wouldn't want me to turn around and unload it for cash."

"He would've wanted you to be smart," she said. "To do what's best for your family. You and Owen and me."

"He meant for me to be a steward over it. He *entrusted* it to me. I don't think you understand," I told her, and shaking her head a little sadly, she agreed.

The kayaker is still turned over, and I wait for him to flip back up but he doesn't. After a few more seconds, I see two pale hands sliding up and down the sides of his boat, the signal for an Eskimo rescue, which the first paddler provides, positioning his boat perpendicular to his partner's so he can right himself on the bow. They complete this maneuver successfully and paddle back to the bank, where they both pull their skirts' tabs and step onto the dirt. The second paddler's just a kid, I see now, maybe twelve or thirteen. He sits on a stone hugging his knees while the first one, whom I take to be his dad, stands over him. While he goes through the motions of an Es-kimo roll, the boy shivers and nods his head.

I turn away from the window and go back to my desk. I've resolved to finish the fall inventory — which should have been done weeks ago, and by Bill — but before I get started, I take a look around. The place looks like a tornado came through; Bill is a loyal friend and all-around high-quality individual, but neat and tidy he is not. I gather up some Coke cans and fast-food wrappers from God knows when and add them to the overflowing trash, and when the desk is clear of garbage, I attack the mass of paper that's threatening to overrun it: receipts, bills, invoices, pay stubs, and so forth. I read each one, mark it "Paid," "Unpaid," or "To file," and after the better part of an hour, I've corralled everything into three satisfying piles.

Cleaning up after Bill is not what I came here to do, though, and I curse him again and stand up. As I do, my knees pop. This is new. But for those few extra pounds, I'm healthy as a horse and in great shape — or fine shape, anyway. I lean a hand against the wall and stretch one leg, then the other, pausing when I'm finished to look at the eye-level picture hanging in a fake-wood frame. It's of me and Julie and Bill and his then-girlfriend, Amanda or maybe it was Mi-randa, taken five Fourth of Julys ago, just a couple of weeks after Julie and I met.

The four of us spent that Sunday drinking and pretending to fish, floating the fast-flowing river in one of Bill's refurbished boats. In the photo, we're all wearing sunglasses, the wraparound plastic kind ev-eryone wore then, smiling stupidly on the sandy bank, happy fools in flip-flops and shorts. Bill and whatever-her-name-is hold up gold-col-ored cans of beer, and her bikini top looks like an American flag. I'm lanky from being a grad student, wearing a maroon Harvard T-shirt and a Red Sox cap, and my face is flushed from the beer or maybe the sun. Julie wears a white oxford of mine, which nearly swallows her. She has the sleeves rolled to her elbows, and a pair of cutoff jean shorts just barely peek out from under its hem. She looks so young and pretty, with her hair in two thick braids and her feet in white sneakers, her head resting against my chest. Chances are, she was already pregnant — that Owen, or the beginning of him, already existed. Of course, we didn't know that then. Chances are, Gus's cancer existed, too. But we didn't know that, either. We didn't know anything. I look closer. We look so happy. We *were* happy. I kind of hate looking at this picture. I always kind of have.

I check my watch. It's already almost ten. I decide to start where I left off last weekend, which was counting the life jackets. There should be eighty-six: fifty rentals and thirty-six new ones that didn't sell during the season. I'm at forty-three, reaching for forty-four, when the phone rings. Nobody knows I'm here except Julie, and nobody knows the number for the back room except her and Bill.

I pick it up. "Honey? Everything okay?"

"Honey, how sweet," says the gruff voice I've known as long as my own. "It's Saturday, kiddo. What are you doing in the mines?" It's Stan Mayfield, good old Uncle Stan. He's not really my uncle, I don't have any of those, but he was my father's lifelong friend — and now, of course, he's Julie's boss. This morning, as usual, he skips over the small talk. "There's a matter of some significance we need to discuss. Are you sitting down?" he says. I can hear him drinking something, probably Diet Pepsi, and his TV is on in the background, CNN or MSNBC. I picture some of those plastic-looking pundits, talking just to talk. Stan's a rabid newshound — he never turns the stuff off. I don't know how his wife, Marirose, stays sane.

I hang the life jacket I'm holding on a hook on the wall and say *forty-three* a few times in my head so I won't forget, and that's what I'm doing when he tells me that he's filing a petition to have my father's body dug up, for tests. *Disinterred* is the word he uses.

I pause, holding the life jacket midair a few stunned seconds before I decide he's messing with me. He's been making bad jokes since I've known him — they're sort of his thing. "Not funny, Stan," I say, and hang the jacket on the hook.

But he says no, not this time, he'd never joke about such an important case. "Did you sit?"

14

Now, I take his advice and sit on a steamer trunk full of unsold river shoes, and I try to focus while he tells me he has groundbreaking news. My father's cancer may not have been caused by smoking, as we all assumed, he says, but there's a good chance it was asbestos from Galaxy, Holliman's vermiculite mine, instead — same as the plaintiffs in *Kowalski*, his and Julie's case.

This makes absolutely no sense. First of all, I know for a fact Gus never set foot in that mine, and I don't know what Stan's up to, but I've known him long enough not to jump at the bait. I take a deep breath and look out at the kayakers; the father is out in the middle now, the son still on the shore. "Gus didn't work at Galaxy," I tell Stan, calmly. "You know that." Gus — and Stan — grew up in Tobey, the company town near the mine in question, but it was Gus's father, Paul, who spent his days underground. Gus studied his balls off and went to college instead — the first Pyle ever to do so. He'd be the first one to tell you that. "And Dad smoked for years, until Bennie made him quit. You know that, too." This is something of an understatement. Stan knew my father longer and perhaps better than anyone else on Earth. They met in grade school, shared a dorm room all four years at Tech. Stan used to get drunk and urinate on Gus's laundry, and Gus would change the answers on Stan's problem sets to wrong ones while he slept. Like brothers from the start, so the story goes.

"Kiddo, you're not listening," he says. "What I'm saying is maybe we *don't* know. Maybe it wasn't smoking. Maybe there's more to it than that."

It's too warm, suddenly, in the silo. I push up my sleeves and tug at the collar of my shirt. Embarrassingly, a lump has risen in my throat. I swallow to push it down. "I don't understand why you're telling me this. I mean, what difference does it make what killed him? He's gone, either way."

"It could make plenty of difference. Considering he didn't work in the mine, if he's got asbestos in his lungs, it would be hard evidence of secondhand contamination from Galaxy — miners coming home with asbestos all over their clothes and boots. What that means is a whole lot more folks getting sick from the mine than we thought. To those folks, an autopsy could make all the difference in the world."

At the word *autopsy*, my ears begin to ring. It's hard to get enough air, and my vision is going dim around the sides. I move onto the floor, close my eyes, and rest my head between my knees.

Stan says, "You there?"

"I'm here."

He clears his throat. "The thing is, there's not a whole lot of time."

With my eyes closed, I say, "Why? Is he going somewhere?"

Stan makes a laughlike sound and says, "That's funny. You're a funny kid, you always have been. But the truth is — How do I put this? The truth is, he is going somewhere." His voice sounds a little strange, now. "It's his lungs we're after, and they're made of soft tissue, and it's been four months already, and, well, soft tissue doesn't exactly linger through the ages, if you catch my drift. Ashes to ashes, all that." I swallow again, hard. "We have a window of opportunity now, before the ground freezes. But we have to act."

I don't say anything. The feeling in my chest, like someone's standing on it, is getting worse, and I breathe through my nose while he keeps hammering away, telling me about all the good, hard-working Americans who put their lives on the line for Holliman, and how Holliman fucked them over in return. "It's about getting justice for those good, patriotic men. Justice and nothing less," he says.

Maybe it's the word *justice*, which is tossed around our house with such abandon these days, but as he talks, I begin to understand: I've known Stan too long to swoon over his holier-than-thou, I'm-one-with-the-people, Woody Guthrie song and dance. This is about business, for him. It's this understanding — more than breathing through my nose — that gets my blood flowing again. I open my eyes and sit up, stretching my legs out in front of me. Sunlight slants through the window in a thick bar of gold that collects in a pool around my feet. "And by 'justice' you mean money," I say. "Just so we're straight on our terms."

"If you want to be cynical, then sure, kiddo, there's money involved."

"How much?"

"A lot, all right? Are you happy? A hell of a lot. That's our system. That doesn't mean it's not goddamn important. We'd be having the exact same conversation if there wasn't a nickel on the line." I hear him take another drink. When he speaks again, his tone is gentler. "Listen. I know how you must feel, hearing this. It's the pits for me, too. He was my best friend in the world. You think I relish the idea of digging him up? Well, I don't. But here's the thing, kiddo — it's what he would want. It's what he would choose, if he could. You know it and so do I."

I don't respond.

"Listen. I'm offering you something here: a chance to do something big in the world. To make your mark."

I'll admit, this stings. "You think I haven't done anything?"

He says, "That's not what I mean. You know it's not."

"Because it sure sounded like that's what you think. Is that what Gus thought? That I haven't made a mark?"

"Whoa, kiddo, whoa. Slow down. I know you miss him. I miss him, too. We all do."

"No, I don't. I mean, I do, but that's not why I —" I pause to breathe. "Look, this just doesn't seem right. He went through hell to get where he is, you don't even know. He deserves to rest in peace, doesn't he?"

At this, Stan makes a kind of clucking noise. I can almost see him shaking his head at his TV.

"I need some time to think it over," I say. "Do I at least get that?"

"How much time?"

"A few weeks. Until after the holiday, at least."

"And I want a pony, kiddo, a fat white one with big brown spots. That's not going to happen, either. Take a day. Two days, max. You have to trust me here. Kiddo?"

I don't know how many times I've asked him not to call me that. "I don't *have* to do anything," I say.

"Christ," he says. "You can be a petulant little shit when you want to. Anyone ever tell you that?"

As a matter of fact, someone has; I'm pretty sure it was Stan. I say nothing.

"Julie said you might get upset. She said you haven't been yourself. I should've listened."

I sit up straight. "Julie knows? Since when?"

"Oh, crap," he says insincerely. "I guess I've stepped in it now."

"What the hell, Stan? How long have you two been plotting this together, behind my back?"

"I've got another call," he says. "You think. We'll be in touch."

We hang up, and for a few moments I sit there, trying to process everything Stan just said, but mostly I come back to Julie: How could she keep something like this from me? It doesn't make any sense. We used to tell each other everything. We used to lie in bed at night and whisper things nobody else in the world knew into each other's ears.

My chest still feels tight, and now it sort of aches. I get up slowly and put the phone back in its cradle on the desk, making it officially the only item in the entire room that's in its proper place. I look around: somehow, despite my earlier efforts, the place looks even more disheveled, and more discouraging, than it did before. I glance over at the pile of uninventoried life jackets in the corner. I've lost count, and I'm going to have to start again from scratch.

But I've lost heart, too. I sit down at the desk, in front of my piles, and look outside. The father and son kayakers are gone, and a bum pushing a shopping cart full of soda cans and glass bottles has taken their place. At a green-painted garbage bin he stops and bends over to rifle through the trash.

That Gus has refused to go gentle — into that good night, or anywhere else — should hardly come as a surprise. The man never did anything gently; he charged through his life like a bull. His career change (and the dog shit in our mailbox, the death threats, the dead rats on the front stoop that ensued) was just one example. Marrying Bennie was another. As far as I could tell, he lived exactly as he pleased, never considering the consequences of his actions, or what anyone else thought, or the impact his decisions had on those around him (namely, me). "Fuck 'em if they can't take a joke" was something he liked to say.

Don't get me wrong: I'm not saying I didn't love the man. I did. I mean, he was a good father, maybe a great father, and I loved him very much. But like I told Stan, he's dead and buried, and he went through hell to get there. The cancer took four long years to finish him off, attacking his body and his mind in tandem and destroying them both just slowly enough for him to know exactly what was going on. The only part of him that stayed immune, it seemed, was his pride, and early on he swore us to secrecy. This meant Bennie was the only nurse allowed in the house, and Julie and I, because we lived there, the only other adults. He even tried (and succeeded, to a degree) keeping Stan and Marirose away.

As the cancer progressed, he became less and less the man we all knew and loved. His appetite ebbed, as did his ability to sleep, and gradually he lost control of his bodily functions. Eventually he quit eating altogether and, not surprisingly, grew depressed. Each evening at sundown, he hallucinated, talking to relatives long dead and mistaking us — the living — for monsters, throwing tantrums like a child. I'm not ashamed to say it was relief and not much else that I felt when he died — even at his funeral. Even when the priest sprinkled dirt on his casket, even as they lowered him down. Does this make me a bad person? A bad son? If so, then okay, maybe that's what I am.

Through the window I watch the bum wrestle his cart back up the uneven, pebbled bank. When he reaches the top, I turn around and take one last look at the room. It's a pigsty, and one on which I owe, as of my last statement, eighty-six thousand, four hundred fifty-nine dollars and seventeen cents.

The feeling starts again in my chest. I need to get out of here. I need to see my son.

3

AT EDEN MONTESSORI, I park on the east side of the lot, by a mound of lumber half hidden under an opaque plastic sheet. They're in the midst of a massive renovation, whose progress is chronicled by an oversize, smiling thermometer, painted on poster board beside the door, its red mercury having stalled, apparently, just shy of halfway up. Considering the parents we've met at Eden so far, I have a hard time believing they've actually come up short on cash, but that's their story, and right after Thanksgiving, to raise the rest, the Eden Parents Association is holding an auction which, in a burst of well-intended if irresponsible enthusiasm, Julie volunteered to chair. This basically means she volunteered me, and the thermometer's grin serves as an unwelcome reminder of all her auction-related duties I have yet to complete.

And where is Julie? A quick scan of the parking lot for her pea-soup-colored Subaru tells me she's not here, even though my watch says ten fifteen, and there's still a good half-hour of swimming to go. I make my way into the spanking-new Donna and Tom Zilinkas Jr. Aquatic Complex, which as far as I can tell is just an excessively fancy pool, and in the observation deck I take a spot down in front, among mainly dads and just a few moms (it is Saturday, after all) on the lacquered-wood bleachers overlooking the shallow end.

The deck is separated from the swimming area by a glass partition, but the air in here is steamy and permeated with the smell of chlorine, which reminds me of when I was young. It makes me think of high school — in a good way. I swam varsity all four years, made All-

State the second two. Five-hundred-meter crawl was my race. I set the record junior and senior year, held on to it until 1996.

I take off my jacket and sit in the front row, watching the four-, five-, and six-year-olds flail around in the lanes. These are beginners, I know — "Guppies," in official Eden parlance — but still, to call any of what's going on down there *swimming* is a stretch.

It takes only a few seconds to spot Owen. In this cadre of bad swimmers, he may be the worst. His splayed fingers drag along the water's surface when he lifts his arms, and he raises his head too often, sputtering between strokes and looking around. He looks disoriented and scared, and much of the time he's panting and hanging on to the blue plastic lane divider or the wall. It's painful to watch, and after ten minutes or so I'm having trouble sitting still. I stand up. I'm not one of those obsessed sports parents, like Earl Woods or that maniacal hockey dad in Canada who tried to strangle the ref, but it's not easy, watching my boy in distress, and after just a few more minutes it's all I can do not to bust through the door that says No Entry, jump in the pool, and finish out his lesson myself.

"Ever heard of decaf, Logan?" says a woman's voice.

I turn around. A few rows up sits Jennifer Huber-Green, the mother of one of Owen's classmates and a woman Julie says was put on Earth to make all other mothers feel bad. She's wearing an oversize T-shirt with her son Arturo's photograph on it, of all things, and waving at me enthusiastically, kind of doing a little dance, shaking her outsize bosom back and forth. I force a smile and wave back. Next to her is another Eden mom, Donna Zilinkas, of Aquatic Complex fame. Donna's a petite, pretty blond who's always dressed to the nines. I'm not sure where she's from, but I can say with confidence it's not Montana. Dallas, I'd hazard, or maybe L.A. Today, she's wearing a fox-colored fur jacket over a denim miniskirt and high-heeled black boots with no tights.

"Hey, Donna," I say, and she nods without smiling. "The pool looks great," I add, and she nods again. Her husband, Tom, is older and, guess what, filthy rich. He's a real estate developer and class-A jerk from what I've heard, and I don't think I'm projecting when I say Donna looks miserable most of the time.

When I ask them if they've seen Julie, Donna shakes her head, but Jennifer nods yes. "She got a call and had to go. Something for work, she said. She asked me to take Owen home, but now you're here. So nice to see a daddy pitching in." Julie's not wrong; she is deeply annoying. I thank her, turn back around, and refocus my attention on the pool, where Owen clings to a green Eden kickboard, moving at a snail's pace in the direction of the opposite wall.

I've watched Owen from behind glass before. He was born six weeks early, with a congenital defect in his grape-size heart. His great arteries were transposed, which means the aorta and the pulmonary artery were switched, and his body wasn't getting enough oxygen from his blood. It could've killed him — it *would* have killed him, without the surgery they performed when he was only six days old. After that, it was touch-and-go to say the least. He spent twelve weeks in the St. Patrick's NICU, in a heated, clear plastic box — an *isolette*, they call them — fighting to stay alive. I'll never forget the sight of him in there: a human being the size of an eggplant with sensors attached to his chest and hands and feet, tubes coming out of everywhere. He wore the smallest diaper imaginable and a tiny blue hat, and a tiny blindfold with even tinier sunglasses drawn on it to protect his eyes from the light.

My hands are in fists again. I straighten out my fingers and wedge them under my thighs, and I'm far more relieved than I should be when the coach blows his whistle and the kids start popping out of the pool.

Owen takes forever, as usual, his skinny arms shaking as he climbs the chrome ladder, pausing halfway up to rest. His scar is dark red, almost purple, which happens when he gets cold. Shivering, he turns, sees me in the bleachers, and smiles, lifting one hand off the ladder to wave.

A few minutes later, I meet him in the lobby and hold his backpack while he ties his shoes. His hair is still dripping, plastered to his forehead, and his goggles have left red raccoon rings around his eyes.

"You were great out there," I say.

He says, "I was not." When he stands up, I reach out to touch his head but he steps away.

In the car on the way home I fight the urge to give him pointers and instead, as Julie's instructed, ask him if he had fun. I look in the rearview mirror for a response, but none comes. He's sucking his thumb again, looking out the window, a sullen expression clouding his heart-shaped face.

"Hey, bud," I say. "I asked you a question."

Nothing.

"Did you have *fun?*" I ask again. "A simple yes or no will suffice."

This time, he shrugs.

"Why not?" I ask next, to no avail. "Do you not like swimming, or is it something else?"

He doesn't answer me. It's maddening. I try once more. "Is it the coach?" Still, nothing. "The other kids?" He shrugs. This is futile. I decide to back off, let him speak up when he has something to say.

But it's not long before the silence gets to me. I've never been great with silence. I just don't *like* riding around with my own child, not talking, as if we're strangers on a bus instead of father and son, two humans who share, among a great many other things, DNA.

I try another tack. "You know, champ, I wasn't such a bad swimmer in my day," I say. Eyes still on the scenery, he nods. Then — because I can't seem to help myself — I suggest, as I have before, that he keep his fingers closer together, like paddles, and that he try keeping his legs straighter when he kicks. "It's all about efficiency," I tell him. "Here's an idea. How about next weekend, you try keeping your head down as much as you can? Don't pick it up out of the water to breathe, no matter what, just turn it to the side. It'll save you a lot of energy. Like this." I demonstrate as well as I can, considering I'm driving, but apparently I get carried away, because before I know what's happening I've drifted into the left lane, and a woman in a monstrous white Suburban is leaning on her horn.

"Crazy *bitch*," I say, swerving out of her way, slamming on the brakes, and flipping her the bird before I can control myself.

I have that prickly feeling all over my skin, from adrenaline. Catching Owen's eye in the mirror, I say, "Whew. Sorry about that, champ. You okay?"

"That's Connor's mom," he says.

I look over and see that he's right. I wave sheepishly at a perturbed-looking Donna Zilinkas, who doesn't wave back. "Now you've got something to say. Great." I look at him again. "You sure you're okay?" He doesn't answer. He is smiling now, though.

"Owen," I say.

Still, nothing.

"Owen."

The light is red at the intersection of South Street and Trellis Road, where they keep saying they're going to build a minor-league baseball field and never do. I turn around in my seat to face him. Locks of wet hair peek out from under his ski hat, and his lips look tender and chapped. There's still the smell of chlorine coming off his skin. "Could you please *say* something? Anything. For crying out loud, could you please, please *speak*?"

His eyes widen, but he keeps them fixed on the empty field. After a long moment, he says, "Crazy bitch."

My face burns, and I turn back around and study a crack in the windshield. What would Julie's books advise now? I say, "Okay. How about something else?"

"The light's green."

"Thank you," I say. "Thank you very much," and I put my foot on the gas.

The rest of the ride home, we don't talk. In the driveway, he unbuckles his seat belt himself and gets out of the car. "Hey, champ?" I say. He pauses on the bottom step.

I want to say something more but I can't think what. I'd like to erase the last half-hour, or the whole car ride — or really the whole morning — if I could. "You'll get the hang of swimming, don't worry," I say. "It's in your genes."

A weird, warm wind is blowing from the west, causing the maples' bare branches to shiver and shake and filling the air with the sweet stink from the paper mills upstream, which always reminds me of being a kid.

He frowns and looks down at his shoes, dark green Nikes with a yellow swoosh. Having lied to him twice now to make him feel better, I'm pretty certain we both feel worse. I know I do.

"Can I go inside now?" he says finally.

"Of course you can."

"Are you coming too?"

"In a minute," I say. A hollow place opens up in my throat as I watch him trudge up the brick path and then the front steps, where he stands on his tiptoes to reach for the bell.

4

IN MY KITCHEN, a man I've never seen before is standing in front of my stove holding a spatula, moving something around in a pan. Julie is getting Owen situated at the table, where a pitcher of orange juice sits beside a vase of tulips I did not buy. The juice appears to be fresh-squeezed, and their glasses are full. Jerry the dog is curled in the corner by the radiator, eyes closed.

"Hart's making omelets," Owen announces. "That's French for eggs."

"I'm familiar with the omelet," I say, "but not with Hart." I turn to the stranger, whose ponytail, I notice, is secured with a sparkly purple hair elastic meant for a little girl. "I'm Logan," I say, over-riding my instinct and holding out my hand. On the counter by the stove are small bowls filled with shredded cheese, diced tomatoes, mushrooms, and chives.

"Hart," this stranger says, shifting the spatula into his left hand and wiping his right dry on his jeans.

"Hart," I repeat. "Is that a first name or a last?"

"First. It's a family name," he says, glancing at Julie as if checking his facts. I look over at her too. She's wearing her glasses, and there's a manila folder marked "Tobey: Depositions" next to her plate.

"Hart's a journalist," she says, crossing her legs. She's changed out of her old T-shirt, I see, and into a plaid Western number with pearl buttons — one of her manifold thrift-store finds. That it's too big only makes her look more petite. "He just got in from Seattle. He's look-ing into the case."

"Huh. I didn't know this was national news."

"Turns out it just might be," Hart says, nodding earnestly. He glances at Julie again. It's like a tic.

I open the refrigerator—looking for what, I don't even know. There's a plate of leftover spaghetti with tomato sauce, a blue bottle of lemon-flavored fish oil, a bag of ground flaxseeds, something unidentifiable and green in a glass jar, a half-bottle of Chardonnay, organic this, sugar-free that. It depresses me. What happened to our regular food? For no particular reason, I think about Gus. His grave appears in my mind: "Heart of Gold," says the inscription on the stone. That was his idea.

"I need to talk to you," I tell Julie, closing the fridge.

"Now?"

"Yes."

"Can't it wait? We have company."

Hart says, "No worries," a phrase I hate, adding, "I just dropped by to tell Julie where we're at," a phrase I hate even more. "If I'm in the way—"

Julie cuts him off. "Don't be silly. Whatever it is can wait an hour. Right, babe?"

I look at Owen. He's using a toothpick to spear slices of banana like fish on his plate. I reach over and touch the top of his head. He pulls away. I look at Julie. She's waiting for me to answer. I say, "It can wait."

She nods in a measured way and takes a sip of her juice. Brightly, she says, "Hart's not just a journalist. He has a PhD in microbiology. He's doing research for a book on the case." She looks at him and smiles. "Some bigtime Hollywood agents are interested in the movie rights. One of them did *The Insider*, you know, with Russell Crowe?"

I say, "Hollywood. How impressive."

Hart shrugs, affecting modesty. "A *potential* book. And there's just one agent," he says. "And really, I'm not half as hard-core as Julie makes me sound. Basically, I've devoted my life to avoiding getting a real job. I'm just lucky I get to play around with bugs and microscopes

27

in the lab." He actually winks at me. "Don't tell the grownups."

I don't like this man.

He turns back to the stove and says, "Brunch is served," and I watch while he cuts the flame, removes three slices of toast from the toaster, and carries all of it quite deftly to the table. He pulls out the fourth chair for me, and I consider sitting down but decide not to.

I look out the window. In the yard, some starlings are going to town on the feeder Gus set out there for goldfinches.

"You sure you won't sit down?" Julie says, her mouth already full. I haven't seen her eat so enthusiastically in months.

"I'm sure," I say.

Owen says, "Da-da. I want my ba-ba."

"Come on," I say. "You're a big boy. Drink from your glass."

"I want my ba-ba," he says.

"I said no and I mean it," I say. His face darkens, and Julie frowns. "Fine," I say. I go to the cabinet, get down one of the baby bottles Julie brought up from the basement, transfer the juice, and screw on the top. He snatches it right up and starts sucking away.

"I didn't talk until I was almost three," Hart offers.

Julie looks down at her plate.

I go back to the window. "I need to do something about those god-damn birds," I say.

"Safflower seeds," Hart says. "Starlings hate them."

"Is that true?" I say.

He nods and says, "I hope everything tastes okay."

"Everything's wonderful," Julie says. The smile on her face is tight now. She's put down her fork. "Really," she says, "everything is just great."

5

"I MEAN IT," I tell Owen again, later that night. He's tucked in his bed and I'm in the rocker, Eugene Field's *Poems of Childhood* open on my lap.

"But why?" he whines.

"Because you heard that story last night, and the night before, and the night before that."

"But it's my *favorite*."

"No, Owen," I say.

"Please?" he says, clasping his hands together in supplication and making his eyes big.

What he wants to hear — so badly I worry he might pop a blood vessel — is the story of his birth. Lately, he's obsessed. But not to worry, I'm told: this is classic regressive behavior. According to one of Julie's books, learning about his or her own birth, or even imagining him- or herself inside the womb, can make a distressed child feel secure.

This was a week or two ago. I was in bed, and she was in the bathroom with the door open, brushing her teeth. "But the story isn't about his birth," I pointed out, recalling too vividly the impossibly tiny thing they took out of her belly. "It's about some make-believe child, whose birth story we made up."

I heard her spit into the sink. From the doorway she said, "But it makes him really happy."

"But it isn't *true*," I said, and I proposed the idea of telling him what actually happened.

"Tell him he almost died?" She'd turned on the water. "While we're at it, how about we tell him he was a mistake?"

"He's a fighter," I said. "I want him to know how tough he is. I think that would help." I laid down my book. "And for the record, he was an accident, not a mistake."

"Of course he was, babe," she said, patting her face dry with a towel. "You know that's what I meant."

"Was I not clear?" I say to him now. "No means no."

He crosses his arms over his chest and pouts.

"There are so many other stories in the world," I tell him. I hold Eugene Field aloft. "Like the ones in this book, for example. Did you know this was my father's book? And that he used to sit here, right here in this very chair, and read it to me? Is that cool or what?"

He stares straight ahead.

"Owen." I wait, but he won't respond. "Come on. This is great stuff. It's a classic." But I know I've lost this round. "How about both, then?" I suggest, and he sits up straight, suddenly all smiles and light. "But this is the last time. Agreed?" He nods eagerly, and I begin. "So Mom was feeling all sick." I hold my middle and stick out my tongue, making my obligatory sick-feeling-Mom face. Owen laughs too hard. "So I took her to the doctor."

"Dr. Root?"

"Yes, the good Dr. Root."

"Dr. Ro-oo-oo-oo-oot," he says, bouncing up and down.

"Okay. Yes. Dr. Root. And Dr. Root put his magical, mighty x-ray machine on your mom's belly, and you popped up on his TV screen."

"What did I look like?"

"What do you think you looked like?"

"Did I look like a bug?" he asks, gleeful.

"Yes, you looked like a bug."

"And did you love me anyway?"

"Yes, we loved you anyway. Very, very much. Okay? Now, Eugene Field." I glance down at the book, a musty maroon hardcover that actually was Gus's (I wasn't making *that* up), and I open to the poem I've marked, "Little Boy Blue."

"No," he says. Lines appear on his forehead, just like his mom. "That's not all."

"I can't remember the rest."

"*Dad,*" he pleads, stretching the word over two syllables.

"Nope. I think that's it."

"No, it's not. You guys couldn't wait to meet me, so you went to Dr. Root and he got me out of Mama's tummy early. And you and Mama were so happy, right?" I nod. His fingers wander to his sternum, the spot near the top of his scar. "And then they put extra sweetness into me. Double the regular amount. That's what the *S* is for, *sweet,*" he says. (Julie added this lovely little embellishment last summer, when he started asking about his scar.) "Right?" he says again, more urgently. I look away, at the dark windowpane on the opposite wall. I can feel his eyes searching my face. I notice my jaw is clenched, and I make an effort to relax.

"That's exactly right," I lie. "That's how it happened. Now, how about some Eugene Field?"

He nods happily. I could read him the dictionary right now and he'd be thrilled.

Though I am not thrilled, I smile, clear my throat, and begin. "*The little toy dog is covered with dust, but sturdy and staunch he stands. And the little toy soldier is red with rust, and his musket moulds in his hands.*"

"What's moulds?" he interrupts to ask.

"Decays," I say. He shakes his head, and his hand rises to his mouth, the thumb slipping between his parted lips. "You know, deteriorates. Gets yucky." He looks satisfied enough, so I start in again. "*Time was when the little toy dog was new, and the soldier was passing fair; and that was the time when our Little Boy Blue kissed them and put them there. 'Now, don't you go till I come home,' he said, 'and don't you make any noise!' So, toddling off to his trundle-bed, he dreamt of the pretty toys.*"

"Hey, guys," says Julie's voice, and we both look up. She's standing in the doorway in her fleece vest, her bulging messenger bag over one shoulder, a big black book and a stack of manila folders tucked under her arm.

"How was the library?" I ask.

"Sorry, I didn't mean to interrupt." She glances at the book in my hands and frowns. "I see it's maudlin Victorian poetry night at the old home." She deposits her book and the bag and the folders in the hall. She looks tired. Her eyes are bloodshot, and there are dark shadows under them. She comes in to sit on the edge of the bed. Her cheeks are flushed. I think I can feel the chill from outside coming off her as she brushes past.

"We're halfway through 'Little Boy Blue,'" I tell her.

Her frown deepens. "It's way after eight already. How about you wait until tomorrow to finish?"

Owen looks at me. I shrug. "You heard the woman. She's the boss."

Julie says, "Did you and Daddy have a good afternoon?"

He nods. "We watched a scary movie on TV," he says.

She takes a moment to frown at me.

"It wasn't scary. It was *The Wizard of Oz*," I say.

To Owen she says, "Mama missed you terribly all afternoon. Did you miss me?" He nods seriously. "Do you know what time it is?" she asks. He grins and shakes his head. She looks at her watch. "It's exactly two minutes past time for kisses." He lets out a delighted yelp as she leans over, lifts the top of his pajama shirt, and nuzzles her face into his belly.

"Stop, Mama, stop!" he squeals.

She sits up and tucks him in, dropping one last kiss on his nose. "Good night, sweet boy," she says, and turns on the night-light at the foot of his bed. I get up, too, and lean over to kiss him on the forehead.

"Good night, champ. I love you," I say.

"Good night, Dad."

I turn out the light and look up. The glow-in-the-dark constellations Gus stuck to the ceiling, years ago, are still doing their thing. "There's Orion," I say. "He's particularly bright tonight. See his belt?" But Owen doesn't answer me. Maybe he's already asleep.

6

JULIE STAYS UPSTAIRS to change while I put an organic, dairy-free frozen pizza (her pick) in the oven to bake. I shake some iceberg lettuce out of a bag, slice in a tomato, and toss it with some fat-free something from a bottle, then open a beer and sit at the table to wait.

This is new. Until recently, we always ate really well. When it came to traditions and to good food, Gus was at his most tyrannical, and almost every night of my childhood, come hell or high water, the two of us, plus an ever-changing assortment of friends, fans, colleagues, clients, students, and sycophants (many of whose categories overlapped), would sit at the dining-room table and break bread. Gus would be at the head, holding forth, boasting about whatever case he'd most recently won, lecturing about right and wrong, good and evil, refilling everyone's glass.

Julie's experience was different, to say the least. Her family was large, and chaotic at best, and survival generally meant fending for oneself, which included meals. She says this was the good news; her family never sat around the table together once, she claims, without somebody leaving in tears. When the two of us moved in, I worried she'd find Gus's institutions oppressive (as I often had) or, worse yet, traumatic. But I didn't need to fret. Not only did she love the family dinners, she assumed a starring role in facilitating them. She'd never learned to cook, and Gus decided he would be the one to teach her. Straightaway, the two of them were spending Sunday afternoons in the kitchen together pulling off ever more complicated culinary feats.

Then Owen came and of course that went out the window, along with everything else civilized and predictable and routine. For weeks, Julie and I ate our meals in the hospital cafeteria — chicken fingers, Jell-O, doughnuts with goo inside, literally whatever was there. But when we finally brought him home, that March, it happened to be a Sunday, and I remember the house smelling so good when we stepped inside, tears came into my eyes. Gus had cooked a leg of lamb with new potatoes, pureed fava beans, and fresh mint, and Bennie had set the table with his mother's good china and lit candles, and once we got Owen situated in his white wicker bassinet in the corner, we all sat down.

We kept the Sunday dinner tradition going for the next three-plus years; we clung to it kind of desperately, I guess, looking back. Bennie and I would help Gus down the stairs, and he would sit in his wheelchair in the kitchen while Julie cooked, and while she cooked, she would sing to him. She has a lovely voice, clear and high and perfectly pitched, and she learned all his favorites, Kris Kristofferson and Willie Nelson and Johnny Cash. It wasn't long before his appetite was gone, and he enjoyed her singing more than the food, which he'd mostly push around on his plate. The night he told Bennie not to bother bringing him downstairs, I remember, Julie cried herself to sleep. It was right around then, not coincidentally, that our collective eating habits went into a spin.

When Julie comes downstairs, tonight, she looks different. She's wearing a black V-neck sweater and some yoga pants, and she looks skinnier than a six-year-old, but it's not that, it's something more. It takes me a minute, but then I realize: she's cut her hair.

She's cut it a *lot*. The luxurious, ginger-colored cascade that used to fall midway down her back now grazes her chin, and complicated layers of different lengths frame her face. "Well, what do you think?" She turns this way and that, showing me her newly exposed — and quite lovely — neck.

"Wow," I say. "It's so, so — different. You look — "

"What? Ridiculous?" she says, and turns around to face the oven, fussing with the layers reflected in the black glass.

"I was going to say glamorous. Sophisticated."

She cringes. "You mean old?"

I tell her no, she looks gorgeous — actually, even more gorgeous than before. "Striking," I say, but there's a forced aspect to my voice that I wonder if she can hear. I *love* her hair — or I did — and somehow the fact that she's gone and chopped it off without consulting me — without even a word of warning — feels wrong. I watch her inspect her reflection. In the back, along the nape of her neck, I see the hair's been shaved, and I don't know why but this fills me with a sudden, plunging sorrow I have to look away to conceal.

She frowns into the glass. "It's just hair, right? It'll grow back." But there's color in her cheeks, two wide and spreading spots of deep pink, and I can tell she's pleased.

"You look wonderful, really," I say again. She smiles and blows me a kiss. In the hall her cell phone rings, and she says she'll be right back.

I get myself another beer, twist off the cap, and take a long swallow, heading into the dining room for silverware and mats. I gather what I need from the sideboard, but then I pause a minute. It's a hard room to be in and not think about Gus. For starters, an enormous portrait of him hangs on one wall. And of course there's the table: a big mahogany antique with lion's paws for feet that he allegedly won off the governor of Idaho in a bet. The chairs, too, eight of them, all of which every night, for so many years, were full.

Back in the kitchen, I set the table and take out the pizza, putting a slice on each of our plates, and I pour Julie some Merlot.

When she reappears, I ask her if she's ready to eat. She's got a funny look on her face and doesn't answer. I ask her what's wrong.

She's still holding the phone. "That was Stan. He said the two of you spoke."

"We did."

"This morning. Like twelve hours ago. Why don't I know?"

"You do, now."

"Come on, babe. Why didn't you say?"

"I tried to, this morning. You said it could wait."

36

"No, I didn't. I mean, I didn't know what you meant."

It's late by now, and I'm hungry. I don't want to argue. "All right, I'm sorry," I say. Sitting down, I take a bite of the so-called pizza, chew, and wash the bland, gummy stuff down with beer. Would some normal pizza, like the kind with actual cheese on it, really ruin anybody's life? I take another bite. It tastes terrible. I start to feel upset. "And besides, if one of us is going to be angry about my conversation with Stan," I tell her, "I'm pretty sure it should be me."

She looks down at her plate. "I would have told you," she says. "I wanted to, but – " She lifts her wineglass, then puts it down without taking a sip. "He thought – *we* thought, I guess – that it might be less upsetting coming from him. Since they were so close?"

"Well, you thought wrong."

"Maybe." She pauses, picking up her fork. "I'm sorry if that's true. But it doesn't change the situation. The fact is – "

"Please, Jules, not now." I put my fork down. "Stan was pretty clear on facts."

She sighs. "I know. It's just that it really is so important. Did he tell you how important it is?"

"He did."

"And there's a time issue. Did he tell you that? The medical examiner said – "

"Julie," I say again. "*Please.*"

She presses her lips together. "You're right," she says. "Not now." She takes a drink, a long, thoughtful one, and sets down her glass. "Can I say one more thing?"

I nod.

"I believe he would want us to go through with this. I really do."

I don't say anything, which seems to embolden her.

"He spent his whole career trying to help people," she says.

For a reason I can't quite pinpoint, the tone in her voice irritates me. "I know what he did," I say.

"And if he knew he had the chance to help this many people, and all at once, honestly, honey, I think he'd be ecstatic."

I think of his grave. Of his stone. Of his coffin. Of the baby-blue satin lining Bennie chose for the inside. And I think of him in it — of the too-pink pancake makeup the undertaker used on his face, and of the suit they'd dressed him in, his best suit, which was gray with pin-stripes and so big on him by then he looked like a kid in his father's clothes. "Ecstatic?" I say.

She starts to speak again, but I cut her off. "You said one thing," I say.

She nods and looks down, then picks up her fork and knife. Studi-ously she cuts her pizza into squares, then cuts those into triangles. She still doesn't put anything into her mouth.

For which I cannot blame her; the stuff tastes like salty cardboard. Nonetheless, I'm putting it in *my* mouth. Out of nervousness, I guess, I've downed three pieces already. I push my plate away. "This pizza's crap. Let's order Chinese," I say, but she's pretty focused on her cut-ting project and doesn't seem to hear.

I lean back in my chair. From this position I have a clear view right into the dining room. On the south wall, over the sideboard, is the portrait, which a Fish and Wildlife official — and amateur art-ist — painted for Gus as a thank-you for getting him out of a pinch involving beer, buckshot, and a neighbor's much-loved cat.

The painting's not terrible, but it's not great either. Something about the eyes is off. They're uneven, or maybe too even, and they give him a fierce, semi-crazed look he didn't have in life. He's sitting at his desk, or someone's desk, with an American flag over one shoul-der and a Montana flag over the other. *Oro y Plata*, says our great state's motto: "Gold and Silver." His hands are folded in front of him. I've heard before that artists are skilled at either faces or hands but not both, but in my opinion this guy was skilled at neither. Painted Gus's fingers look crooked and flat, and the nails look cartoonish, as if their renderer ran out of time or more likely talent at the wrists.

What I notice tonight, though, is Gus's watch. A gift from his fa-ther, Paul, when he graduated high school, it was one-hundred-per-cent Montana gold, so the story goes, and cost Paul three months' salary. He had Gus's initials, "AJP," and the date he graduated engraved on the back of the case.

"What happened to his watch?" I ask Julie.

"Whose watch?"

"Gus's. The gold one." Her wine is gone. I pour her more. "You know, the one he always wore."

She swirls the wine around, and we both watch it slide down the sides of the glass. "Bennie probably has it, along with everything else that should be yours."

I know from experience not to respond to this. "I take it you're finished eating," I say, reaching for her plate.

She goes to bed shortly afterwards, saying she has to be in Helena tomorrow first thing, but I stay downstairs, knowing it will be a while before I can sleep. I help myself to yet another beer and bring it outside, where I sit on the deck and try not to think about what Stan said, or what Julie said, or about Gus at all, while Jerry roots around in the pachysandra, pausing now and again to sniff the air.

Inside, he stands and watches while I wash our dishes and put them on the rack. I offer him the pizza we didn't eat, but he takes one whiff of it and backs away. "Come on. It's food," I say. He turns his face to the wall.

Jerry is caramel-colored with a white blaze on his chest, and he'd pass for a retriever if it weren't for his pit bull's pointy ears. Nine years ago, Gus found him in an alley, covered in ticks and tied to a Dumpster with a length of climbing rope. He was just a few weeks old then, and half starved, so Gus brought him home and he and Bennie cleaned him up and named him Jerry and nursed him back to health, after which he stuck to Gus like glue, following him everywhere — around the house and the neighborhood, to and from work, all over town. There were even a couple of judges who let Jerry accompany Gus to court. When Gus got sick, nothing changed. Jerry spent all day curled on the foot of the bed, his head resting on Gus's skinny shins.

Now, though, with Gus gone, it's like the Jerry we knew disappeared and a different dog has taken his place. This one is sullen and solitary and has to be coerced to eat. Julie says he's depressed; he's in mourning, she said — as if that's obvious — citing a piece she heard on NPR about animals experiencing grief. "That's patently ridiculous," I said, even though I know it's probably not.

"You're smarter than you look," I tell him now, and throw the remains of the pizza in the trash. Then I open the door by the pantry and make my way down the bowed, uneven stairs to the basement. It's cold as a tomb down there, as always. At the bottom of the steps, I turn on the lights.

In the far corner are my father's things: his clothes, his shoes, his books, boxes full of newspaper clippings and photographs, mostly of him. I brought it all down here the morning he died, planning to go through it with Bennie later in the week, but there was so much to take care of already, and then the funeral happened, and then what happened after the funeral happened, and that was the last time I spoke to her. Now almost four months have passed, and here it sits.

An orange Nike shoebox crowns the pile. I pick that up and sit on the old wooden church pew Gus bought years ago at the ranchers' auction but never found a place for in the house, and I lift the lid. Here, loose, are some of his dearest possessions: his two gold wedding bands, his grandmother's rosary, and a thick stack of family photos. I take out a few and look. One's a black-and-white snapshot of Gus as a small boy, flanked by his dour-looking parents, Paul and Marie. Another is of me as an infant, in the arms of my mother, Jo, a towering, dark-haired beauty who died when I was one. The last shot is of Bennie, alone. Somehow, I haven't seen this one before, and I take it out and hold it up to the light. She's wearing jeans and cowboy boots and a thick wool sweater, and she looks young and lovely, standing in front of a split-rail wood fence, hips pitched unevenly, black hair loose and blowing, arms draped over the highest rail. I don't know who took the picture, but from the look on her face — a private, suggestive smile — I have to imagine it was Gus.

Something churns deep inside me, like an engine turning over. I put the picture — I put all of the pictures — back in the box.

I sift through a few other boxes, but Gus's gold watch — the thing I came down here to find — isn't in any of them, and replacing the last one atop the pile, I sit again on the pew and start thinking about him, I mean thinking about his *body*, what he might *be*, now. How does a person look after four months in the ground? Not so great, is my guess. But he wasn't winning any beauty contests, either, by the time he died.

That happened early one morning at the very end of July, after a terrible night in a long string of terrible nights. Bennie and I would take turns sitting up with him, and if she didn't have an early meeting, Julie would take a turn. But that last night, it was just me.

He was sleeping soundly, for once, and I guess I dozed off myself, because I woke up in the dark to the sound of his voice. "Son," he was saying. "Logan. Son?" He sounded more lucid than he had in days.

I sat up. "What is it, Pop? What do you need?"

"I need to go," he said. "I'm leaving in the morning, and I haven't packed."

"You're not going anywhere," I said, but I felt alarm. He started to push himself up in the bed. "No, Pop," I said. "You have to rest." But he wouldn't listen. He brushed off the covers and swung his legs toward the floor. His feet were dark and swollen and covered with sores, the nails thick and beginning to curl. Before I knew it, though, he was standing up, something he hadn't managed in weeks.

"I have to tell you a secret," he said, teetering.

"That's okay. Tell me from bed."

He wasn't listening. He took a couple of tentative steps, over to the window, and looked out. The moon was big and bright white — a full buck moon, Bennie had called it. Gus lifted his arms. The light coming in made the sleeves of his pajamas look like wings.

"What's going on up there? Do you need a hand?" called Bennie, from downstairs. She was watching TV. She was a terrible insomniac. Even on the nights that were mine, she barely slept.

"We're all right," I called down.

He turned to face me. "I'm ready," he said. His voice was raspy, but his eyes were clear.

"You're not going anywhere, Pop, not tonight," I said. My heart had begun to pound. I took his arm and he let me, and I guided him back to the bed. A strange, sweet smell was coming off him, like new-mown grass or fresh hay. He lay down. I was arranging his blankets when he caught my wrist. His grip was surprisingly strong; it hurt. His eyes were fixed on a spot over my shoulder.

"It's Mother," he said. "And Dad. And the redhead, that's my cousin Lee."

His hallucinations weren't new, but I felt chilled nonetheless. Slowly I turned to look behind me. Of course no one was there. I said, "It's okay, Pop, you're confused."

"You're the one who's confused," he said.

"Okay, Pop. It's okay," I said. But it wasn't okay. It was the exact opposite of okay. His fingers were cold but my skin was hot where he held on to me. I knelt down. "You can't go, Pop," I heard myself say. At some point I'd begun to weep. "You can't leave us. Not yet."

He said, "You'll be okay." He tried sitting again, but he was too weak.

I said, "Please, Pop, just stay."

Bennie came into the sewing room then. She wore a robe and sheepskin slippers, and her hair was wet. She took one look at me and said, "What's the matter? What did he say?" She knelt beside me, her shoulder touching mine. I could smell her shampoo, and the wine she'd been drinking downstairs.

"I think he's okay now," I said.

She frowned and touched his forehead, took his pulse. She laid her head on his chest and stayed like that. I got up and sat in the chair. When she righted herself, she said, "I think it's time to call Father French."

It was close to six by the time Julie brought the baby-faced priest up the stairs. Gus was struggling to breathe by then, the air whistling through what was left of his lungs. He held his arms straight at his sides. The windows and the blinds were open, and as morning broke the white walls of the room turned pink.

Father French asked for some space. Julie stood in the doorway, crying softly with her hands covering her nose and mouth, and I stood in the far corner, using both walls to stay upright. At the foot of the bed, Bennie closed her eyes and made the sign of the cross once, then again. I wished I were a believer, too, if only so I'd have something to do with my hands, which shook. I put them in the pockets of my pants. French pulled the chair close to the bed. He leaned forward and whispered something into Gus's ear. Gus made a small nod. The priest smeared oil on his forehead and made the sign of the cross on Gus's chest, then his own. He took a flask from his pocket and with an eyedropper put a couple of red drops on Dad's cracked lips, then slipped a sliver of white wafer between them. Dad swallowed.

You hear about a "death rattle," some dramatic last breath they say is the soul taking its leave, but nothing like that happened with Gus. It got very quiet. We all held our breath. His hands, which had been balled into fists, released. That was all. In the next room, at that very moment, Owen began to wail.

Now, in the basement, I get up from the pew. I stretch my arms over my head, then side to side. From the shelf near the window I get down my bat, a 1930s Louisville Slugger, for which Gus reportedly paid a small fortune the year I was born. He had my whole name, Logan Augustus Pyle, and my birthday, September 13, 1974, branded into the barrel, and he gave it to me for my birthday, the year I turned ten. Because it was so valuable, though, I wasn't allowed to touch it. He kept it wrapped in special oiled paper, in a custom-made case, on a high shelf in the hall closet, out of my reach. When I turned thirteen, I could hold it, but only under his supervision. Never was I to get it down myself, or remove it from the house, or, God forbid, hit a ball with it. It was with a regular aluminum bat — one from the used sporting-goods store out on Reserve — that one Saturday morning when I was six or seven, he taught me to swing.

Now, in the middle of the basement, I do just that; I swing the bat as hard as I can, and then I swing it again. It feels great to move, and I swing again and again. I keep at it until my breathing is heavy and I've broken a sweat. By the time I put the bat back on its shelf, cut the lights, and head upstairs, my arms sing with fatigue.

It's past midnight, and all the rooms are dark. I open Owen's door a few inches, like I always do, and watch him sleep, his chest rising and falling steadily in the night-light's ghostly glow. He's on his back, one arm thrown over his head, the palm wide open, exposed. Something compels me, and I go over and fold his fingers down. He doesn't wake up. He's an excellent sleeper — another trait he inherited from his mom.

On my way out, my foot kicks something on the floor: *Poems of Childhood.* I pick it up, put it back on the shelf, and pull the door closed almost all the way but not quite.

In our bedroom I undress and slide into bed. Surprisingly, Julie stirs. "Hey, you," I whisper, moving next to her.

"It's so late," she says sleepily. "Your hands are freezing."

"Sorry," I say, and I take them off her, warming them between my thighs. We lie there a while not talking, but I can tell from her breathing she's still awake. "Hey. I'm sorry about earlier. I didn't mean to be a jerk."

"It's okay," she says. "I understand." My hands are warmer, now, and I slip them around her waist. She curls into me.

"I know it's different — easier — for you and Stan," I whisper. "More black and white." She doesn't answer. For a while neither of us says anything. I close my eyes, but sleep doesn't come. "Honey," I whisper, after a while, "why'd you stop me from reading to Owen, before?"

"The little boy dies during the night, remember? His toys wait and wait for him to come back, but he never does," she says. "They just keep waiting. It's horrible. Did you forget?"

"I guess I did," I say. I pull her closer, put my face against the back of her neck, and breathe in. Her scent is different tonight, floral and unfamiliar after the salon. My hand migrates down to her hip. She takes hold of it, folds my fingers into a fist, and positions it between her breasts.

"Is anything the matter?" I ask after a while.

She doesn't answer right away, and I'm thinking she's not going to, when she whispers, "I loved him too, you know, very much."

"I know you did," I whisper back. "You don't have to tell me that. I know."

She whispers, "Sometimes it seems like you forget."

I don't know what to say to that. I close my eyes again, and soon I can tell from her breathing that she's left me behind. I free my hand from her grip and turn onto my back. I lie awake a long time. I know it's silly, but I can't stop thinking that I'm really going to miss her hair.

7

SUNDAY MORNING, JULIE'S gone by the time I get up, and when I look at the clock on the nightstand I see it's late, past nine. I hurry into a sweatshirt and pants and head downstairs, where I find Owen in the living room, prone on the carpet, watching TV. A cereal bowl half full with bluish milk sits on the coffee table, and Jerry's curled in Gus's favorite chair.

"Morning, champ," I say, taking a seat on the sofa. He's watching that show, I think it's Australian, where drug-addled-looking adults in bright-colored clothes jump around and shout. Its appeal is unfathomable, if you ask me, but Owen can't seem to tear his eyes away, and he nods his head without turning around by way of a greeting.

"Did Mom go?" I ask. He shrugs. "Did she say what time she'd be home?" He shrugs again. "There are purple dinosaurs falling from the sky," I say. He doesn't respond.

In the kitchen I find her note. She's on her way to Helena, via Bozeman, and she didn't want to wake me, so call her when I'm up. It's signed "Yrs, J." I pour coffee into a black mug with "Mayfield and Pyle, Attorneys at Law," stenciled in gold, and I stand by the window looking out at the day. There's not a cloud in the sky. I take the dog out and wait while he sniffs around what used to be Gus's strawberry patch, then does his business off to the side of the shed. It feels less like November than May. I watch while some more starlings infiltrate the wooden box Gus nailed to a wood post for the purpose of attracting bats.

I feel a tug on my pants. Turning around, I find Owen standing there in his PJs and bare feet.

"Jeez, you're like a ghost," I say. "Boo!" which makes him smile, and when I ask him if he wants to come to the store and count camp stoves with me, he nods enthusiastically. "You've got some spunk this morning, champ," I say, which immediately generates a frown. "Hey, come on, don't hide those magnificent Pyle choppers under a bushel." He can't help it, he smiles again. I touch the top of his head and tell him to go upstairs and get dressed.

While I wait, I pour more coffee and try Julie's cell. It goes straight to voice mail, but reception's not great around here, especially outside of town, and I'm not concerned. I leave her a message saying we'll be at the store if she's looking for us, and I put my mug in the sink.

By the time we're good to go, the thermometer outside the kitchen window reads sixty-one degrees, and I decide we should walk, which I regret after about two minutes, waiting at the corner while Owen carves his circuitous, meandering path. When he finally catches up, I offer to carry him but he refuses. "You sure?" I ask, but he's adamant, and it's so nice to see him adamant about something, I say, "Excellent choice." We make our painfully slow way past the Food Farm, and the park, and the Exxon where Julie used to go, late-night, for emergency cigarettes. We cross Howard and then First. The closer we get to campus, the larger and better-maintained the houses become. On University Avenue, we pause to admire a particularly grand Victorian, one of the ones that used to belong to professors but that now none of the professors can afford. This one has a wide front porch and a turret with shingles that look like fish scales, and an elaborate color scheme involving several well-coordinated shades of paint. In the morning sunshine, steam rises from the manicured front lawn.

"Do rich people live there?" Owen asks, as if reading my thoughts.

"Yes," I tell him. "I think I can safely say they do."

"Are we rich?" is his next question, and I pause a moment before saying no.

"Why not?" he asks.

"Because we aren't," I say, starting to walk again.

"Mom says it's because Gus gave Bennie all the money in his will," he says.

I stop walking. "Mom said that?" He nods. "Well, it's not exactly true," I say as diplomatically as I can.

"Mom lied?"

"No, of course not. Technically, I guess it is true — he left her some money. But he left us other stuff — the house, and the land, and that includes my store. Those are valuable, too."

But he has more to say. "Mom says Bennie made out like a bandit, and that if she were anyone else in the world, you'd move a mountain to get Gus's money back. Is that true? You could move a mountain?"

I pause before answering. Like I said, Julie loved Gus dearly, but she and Bennie never really clicked. In the past, when I've asked her about it, she's shrugged and said things like "We're just cut from different cloth," and I've always let it go. But since Gus's death (and frankly, the distribution of his estate), her comments have taken an overtly hostile turn.

I try to conceal my irritation, now, but it's hard. "Mom shouldn't be talking so much about things she doesn't understand," I say. This appears to upset him — maybe it's my tone. I soften it. "Does a muffin sound as good to you about now as it does to me?" And we start to walk again.

At Elsie's Bakery, I leave him on the bench out front, where I can watch him through the windows while I buy two muffins — cranberry-corn for me, lemon–poppy seed for him. When I rejoin him, he's petting a brindled brown-and-black dog easily three times his size. The dog's owner, a middle-aged woman with magenta-framed eyeglasses, spiky, graying hair, and earrings shaped like feathers swinging from her ears, looks down at Owen, then up at me. I can tell she disapproves of something she's seeing, though I'm not clear on what. I stare right back.

Soon she leaves, trailing her dog, and we take her spot on the bench, sitting side by side in the sun to eat. Owen swings his feet and concentrates on his food, nibbling around the muffin's edges and then moving on to the top, saving the cakey middle for last. We're finishing up when he says, "Dad?"

"That's me," I say, hoping he's not going to ask about Bennie again.

"What's a will?"

This takes me by surprise. I swallow and put down what's left of my muffin. "It's a legal document," I tell him. He frowns, unsatisfied. "It's kind of a letter you write."

"To who?"

"To everyone. To the world, I guess, giving instructions about what you want done with your stuff after you die," I say.

He nods, but it's not long before his brow furrows again. He says, "Dad?" in an uncertain voice.

"Still here."

"What's *die?*"

I'd been balling up our muffin bag, preparing to take a three-point shot at the trash can, but I stop. Something about hearing the word *die* from a child is inherently unnerving. I take a deep breath and turn so I'm facing him on the bench. "It's what happens when you've finished living, when your life is done. You – " He looks petrified, and quickly I understand why. I correct myself. "A *person* dies. It means they go away forever."

"Where do they go?" he wants to know.

"Far away," I say, and briefly I consider saying heaven, invoking some saccharine scenario involving pink-cheeked cherubs and cloud chairs, but then I think about how vehemently I've argued, lately, for telling him the truth, and I resist. "Well, it depends if you mean the body or the spirit. What happens to the spirit is debatable, I mean nobody really knows that, but the body — well, in one way or another, the body goes back to the earth." His face darkens. "What I mean is, most people get buried in the ground."

"Is — " He looks down at the muffin refuse in his lap. "Is Gus in the ground?"

I nod.

"Really?"

"It's where he wanted to be. He said so himself. It's okay, I promise."

He's not looking so convinced, though, and I start wondering if I've made a major mistake. I try again. "Everything in the world dies, at some point. It's like the only truth of being human, the great irony of our lives, the great equalizer. No matter who you are, you can't escape death." From the look on his face, I'm only making things worse, but I can't seem to stop talking. "Gus knew he was going to die for a long time before it happened, which was awful in a way but also has its upside, because it allows you — I mean it allowed *him* — to make plans, to really give things some thought. What I'm saying is that he got to choose what happened to him. He got to think it over, and he chose being buried in the ground. He loved the ground, the earth. He spent practically his whole life working with it, in one capacity or another." Finally I manage to stop myself and take a breath. "Does that make sense?"

He looks like he might cry.

I put my hand on his knee. "Look. It's a hard thing to understand. Smarter men than I have spent their entire lives pondering what it means. But it's just part of life: eventually, everything living has to die."

Evidently, this isn't the balm I'd hoped it would be. His eyes widen. "*Everything?*" he says. "You mean, you? And Mama? And Jerry? And *me?*"

"No, no," I say, pulling him toward me. "No, honey, none of us. At least not for a very, very, very long time."

"How long?" he asks.

"Long. Years and years. Decades. Epochs. Eons. Longer than you can possibly comprehend."

Maybe it's just the big words, but this answer, finally, seems to assuage him somewhat. "Promise?"

"Years and years. Cross my heart." I wait a minute, but he doesn't say anything else. Giving his knee a squeeze, I get up. "You ready, champ?" He nods, and I breathe a sigh of relief. "Youth before beauty," I say, and let him walk ahead.

We pass Greeley Park and Mona's Beautiful You, and the Star Kitchen and the fire station and Casey's Secondhand Books. I pause outside McGarry's and touch Owen's shoulder. "You know what this place is?" He shakes his head. "It's where I first met your mom."

"Cool," he says.

"It was cool. It was at Gus's birthday party."

"How old did he turn?"

"Sixty."

"That's close to a hundred."

"Compared to four and three-quarters, sure," I say, standing on my toes to peer inside.

"Did Mama look pretty?"

"Oh, yeah," I say, remembering for a moment the black dress that showed her shoulders, and the white hibiscus flower she'd pinned in her hair.

It was a surprise party Bennie and Marirose had planned for Gus and Stan, who were born two weeks apart. Like I said, Julie had been interning for Gus, and when I saw her there, with her back against the bar, sipping a glass of white wine, I knew I had to talk to her. "You shouldn't smoke" was my opening line.

"Excuse me?" she said. The bar was packed with people – of course – and it was hard to hear over the noise they made, and the band.

"I saw you the other day, behind the holly. Smoking's bad for you. You should quit," I said, louder.

She smiled a little wickedly and thanked me for my concern. "Did you learn that in your doctoral program?" she asked, and I knew she'd been talking to Gus.

"I'm just looking out for you. My dad has a nose like a bloodhound. He used to smoke, and now he's on a crusade. I'm surprised he hasn't lectured you yet."

Her face turned serious. "I appreciate the heads-up," she said. "I basically worship your dad. I'm so lucky to work for such an amazing man," she said. The band finished its set then, I remember, and everyone began to clap.

"Take a number," I told her.

"What?" she shouted, leaning closer.

I said, *"You're hardly alone."*

She misunderstood. Nodding, she said, "I broke up with my boyfriend in March." She had freckles on the bridge of her nose, I noticed, and on her collarbones, and up and down her arms. I tried to concentrate while she told me she'd graduated from law school at the university the month before. She was working at Mayfield and Pyle again (her third summer there) and studying for the bar.

"Good luck, then," I told her, raising my drink.

"I don't believe in luck," she said, raising hers. Her dress was bare in the back, and when she turned to look at the stage, where Gus was clinking a knife against a glass, I saw she had freckles on her shoulder blades, too. When I asked if I could get her another drink, she said yes.

Up on the parquet stage, Gus was ready to make his speech, and I ordered us another round as he began cataloging for the gathered crowd all the blessings he had in his life. He talked about his work for a while, and then he called Bennie up. She was wearing a long, loose dress with a crazy pattern and silver sequins that flashed when she walked. "God, she's gorgeous, isn't she?" Julie said.

"I guess so," I admitted, feeling heat start up my neck.

On the stage, Bennie put her arms around Gus and he kissed her hungrily. This was a month or so before his first episode, so he was still very strong, and I remember her feet lifting off the floor a few inches, and that she wore gold-colored Converse high tops instead of high heels. Behind her back, Gus gave the crowd a thumbs-up, and everyone cheered. Next he asked me to come up. I shook my head. "I hate it when he does this," I whispered to Julie, behind my beer.

"What, tells two hundred people how wonderful you are? Get up there," Julie whispered back.

All night I stayed as close to her as I could, and later, when the crowd thinned out, I asked her if she wanted to take a walk. She said sure, and I took her hand and led her out of the bar and around the corner and into the alley, where I kissed her, her back pressed up against the fire station wall.

"I don't usually do this," she said, coming up for air.

"Neither do I."

She put her hands on my chest and pushed me gently back. "No. Really. I usually have tremendous self-control."

"I believe you," I said. I had my hands on the bricks on either side of her head. I kissed her neck, which smelled like roses. I said, "You should come home with me."

"I can't do that."

I touched her face. "Sure you can."

She was fingering one of the buttons on my shirt. She shook her head. "No, really, I can't. Your father is my boss, remember? He respects me, and that's like gold around here. Plus, we just met."

"Details," I said, and kissed her again. "Come on. Maybe this is fate."

She grinned. "I don't believe in that either."

"So what do you believe in?"

"Honestly, not very much." She pulled me closer, so there wasn't any space between us, and looked up at me.

I said, "We have to believe in something. It's what hearts are for."

She rolled her eyes and said, "Oh, boy."

"Listen. I don't want to say good night to you," I said. "Do you

53

believe that?" She laughed, and I kissed her again, and then she took me home. I saw her every day and every night for the next two weeks, and when the two weeks were over, I flew back east.

It was six weeks later, in the middle of my summer session C, when she called. We'd spoken a handful of times since I left, but the truth is I didn't know her very well. Still, right away I could tell something was wrong. I'd just walked into my apartment, and I was carrying an armful of library books. "Are you doing okay?" I asked, putting them down.

"I don't know how to answer that," she said, and in a shaky voice she told me she'd been to her doctor, and that he'd confirmed what she'd feared since July, when her period hadn't come.

"But I thought you were — "

"I was," she said. I heard a car honking in the background; she must have been standing on the street. "He said it could be the antibiotic I was taking, but it's hard to say for sure. Nothing's one hundred percent."

I had no idea what to say. "Are you — " I began. "What are you going to — " I couldn't finish the thought.

She finished it for me. "I don't know what I'm going to do yet. I'm trying to figure it out."

Like I said, we hardly knew each other. When I think about it, the idea that two people — Julie and me, for example — who happened to be in the same room one evening, by chance, can spend a little time together, some days and some nights, and produce a brand-new human being — produce *Owen?* When I think about that, and about all the people in all the rooms, producing all the brand-new human beings, more or less by chance — when I think about that, well, my head spins.

Now, he tugs at my pants. "Dad, the Preacher," he says.

And he's right; coming toward us is our local white-haired madman, who walks the city streets day and night shouting about the Lord. Usually he's all fire and brimstone, Christ bled for you on the cross, the end of days is nigh, et cetera, but this morning — maybe it's the warm weather — he's in an expansive mood.

"Love one another!" he bellows, swinging his arms wildly to and fro as he walks. "*Love* one another!"

I lift Owen so he can pass.

Two blocks north and three blocks east is the river, and I take Owen's hand as we venture out onto the bridge. In the middle we stop and look down. The water is low this time of year and clear as glass, and we watch it slide over stones worn smooth by knocking into each other for what — a thousand years? A million? Ten? I spot a beaver and we watch it slip into the dark water beneath its dam. A few yards off the southern bank, a man in waders catches a tennis shoe, removes his hook from the tongue, and throws it back.

"Can I fly, Dad?" Owen asks.

When he was smaller, I would hold him up over my head and he'd put his hands out at his sides and, well, "fly." I shake my head no, and he asks why.

"You know why."

"But I'm not too big. I'm a *baby*," he says, putting his thumb in his mouth.

"I have a better idea," I say quickly. I reach into my pocket, fish out a penny, and hand it to him. "Now that you're a big boy, you get to make a wish," I say. He holds it up for examination but instead of making a wish, he puts it between his molars and bites down. I lunge at him, snatching the penny away and praying it's before he's cracked a tooth.

"What the hell?" I ask, wiping the penny on my pants.

"It's how you tell if it's real gold," he says. "I saw it on TV."

"That's TV," I say. "And this isn't gold. It's a penny. Christ." I hand it back. "Come on. I used to do this when I was a kid." Without ceremony, he pitches the penny through the metal bars so fast I don't even see it fall. I try not to look disappointed.

"What did you wish?" I ask, with all the cheer I can muster, but he won't say, so I take a second penny out of my pocket and hold it in the air, closing my eyes. Silently, I wish first for Owen — that he'd snap out of whatever "phase" he's going through and start having fun, like a normal kid. My second wish is for Julie: that she'd stop working so much, and that she'd eat something for God's sake, and that one of these nights she'd reach for me, like she used to. And finally, I wish for cold; I wish for the temperature to plummet, and for the ground to freeze so hard and so deep that nobody can even think of digging anybody up until July at least.

"What's your wish?" Owen asks.

"I wished we'd have hamburgers for dinner," I say, knowing full well *that* wish isn't likely to come true. Julie, for reasons not entirely clear to me, has banned from our home all meat that someone we know, or someone who knows someone we know, hasn't killed, and as far as I know none of our friends — or their friends — has recently taken down a cow. But I flip my penny into the air anyway, and it spins and catches the sun, and there's a tiny, satisfying flash on the flat water right before it disappears.

8

I DIDN'T SLEEP at all the night of Julie's telephone call, and first thing in the morning I called my adviser, Carlos Pearl. Notoriously gruff, and a vocal cynic on the subject of the academy, Pearl was a long-faded star in the field, who'd made his name in the seventies and — as far as I could tell — coasted on fumes ever since. Not only did I like him instinctively, he took an unexpected shine to me. He helped me find my dissertation topic (the legacy of Catholic missionary schools in Montana), and over the years he'd written letters and called in favors from colleagues on my behalf. That morning, instead of disappointing him, which I figured the truth of my situation was sure to do, I lied.

I told him that my father was sick (though he wasn't, then, or I suppose he probably was, but we didn't know it yet), and that I had to go home to Montana right away. He frowned at me over his glasses. "You have a prodigious talent," he said. "Use it, or it will turn inward and cause a great big mess." I was as ashamed of my lie as I was flattered by his praise, and a lump rose in my throat I couldn't push down. I stood up, shook his hand, and told him another whopper: that I'd do as he said.

That same afternoon I packed my things, loaded them into my car, slipped my keys through the mail slot, and drove west. I drove all night and into the next morning, stopping to close my eyes at a shitty motel outside of Aurora, Illinois. I called home from a rest area somewhere in North Dakota.

Bennie answered. "You sound funny," she said. "Is anything wrong?"

I paused. I'd lived away from home for more than a decade by then, but somehow her voice still had the power to make me feel exactly like I had when I was seventeen.

"What happened? Are you okay?" she asked, when I told her I'd left school.

I paused again. Julie had asked me not to tell them. She'd passed the bar in July, and now, as a first-year associate at the firm, she feared that if Gus found out she was pregnant, she'd lose not only his respect, but her job. "Gus would never do that," I told her. "And besides, it's against the law."

But she made me swear. "I've never worked so hard for anything in my life," she said. "I can't just throw everything I've accomplished away." I assured her I understood, and of course I did understand, but something in Bennie's voice made me want to bare my soul — or at least not lie.

"Actually," I said, and standing at the pay phone, I filled her in.

I don't know what I expected, but when she said, "Do you love her?" my eyes filled with grateful tears. Something shifted between us, then. "I barely know her," I said. "But I think maybe I could."

"It's wonderful, just wonderful," she said. She spoke quietly; Gus was napping in the next room. "But you sound so sad."

Uneasily, I confessed that Julie hadn't decided whether she wanted to have the baby or not. Bennie didn't speak right away. She didn't have children of her own (the possibility was one she'd pretty much relinquished, marrying Gus), and though I'd never dared ask, intuition told me it was a decision with which she hadn't necessarily made her peace. Plus, she was a devout Catholic, and I thought I could imagine her view on these sorts of things. But when she spoke, her voice was gentle and kind. "What do *you* want, honey?" she asked. Every once in a while she called me that.

"I want her to have it." And as I said it, I knew it was true. I'm sure it sounds far-fetched, but standing there, I thought I could feel the spark of a seed of a new kind of love — the love for my child — sprouting in my chest.

"Then that's what I want, too," she said. I looked out across the Interstate, where a dark wall of weather was sweeping across the prairie, west to east.

"I better get back on the road," I told her.

"Logan, wait," she said, before we hung up. But then she said, "You know what? Forget it. You drive safe."

Late the next night I pulled into the driveway, which was empty. It was fire season in Montana, one of the worst in years, and on the phone Bennie had told me they were going to the cabin for a couple of days to get a break from the smoke, so I used the spare key to let myself in. I carried my boxes of clothes and books up to my old room, made my bed with the same bird-printed sheets I'd slept on as a boy, and lay down.

I slept like the dead, and in the morning I went to Julie's apartment with a bouquet of tiger lilies, which I remembered were her favorites, and a box of sticky buns, no nuts, under my arm. "Professor," she said — a nickname she'd appropriated from Gus. She wore a sky-blue bathrobe, and pajamas with dogs on them underneath. The whites of her eyes were cloudy, her face puffy and pale. Even so I thought she looked beautiful. I wanted to take her in my arms, but I wasn't sure whether I should.

"I can't believe you're actually here," she said, turning the sash of her robe around her arm. "Actually, all of this still seems pretty surreal."

"I couldn't stay in Massachusetts," I told her. "Not with you and the — not with you out here."

Her hands went to her face. "You should have called. I must look terrible. I know I do. I'm sorry. I can't seem to stop throwing up." She tucked some uncombed hair behind one ear and looked down. Her feet were bare, and her toenails were painted dark wine red, almost black. "My sister says that will let up after a few weeks. She promised."

I stood still while what she was saying sank in. "Does this mean — ?"

She nodded and raised her head. It was almost as if she was afraid to look at me. "It does. But listen," she said. Her voice shook. "You don't have to be here. I want to make absolutely sure you know that."

"I want to be here. More than anything."

A smile spread over her face then, and she came over, stood on her toes, and kissed me on the mouth. "In that case, it's really nice to see you, Professor," she said, then stepped back. I was still holding the pastries. "Elsie's, my favorites," she said. "Sweets are practically the only thing I can keep down these days. How did you guess?" She took the box and started toward the tiny galley kitchen she shared with her roommate, a law-school friend named Brandi Cosette. In the hall she stopped and turned around. "Aren't you going to come in?"

From their small, octagon-shaped living room, I watched while she transferred the sticky buns onto a plate. Extracting a knife from a wood block on the counter, she started to cut one in half but stopped abruptly. Setting the knife down, she leaned on the counter with both hands and closed her eyes. "Shit," she said. I put the flowers down and I went to her. Her eyes were still closed and I put my hand on her back and moved it slowly up and down. "Maybe don't do that," she said, not unkindly. When she opened her eyes, she said, "Damn it," and pushed past me. I heard the bathroom door close and the faucet open, and the unmistakable sound of Julie throwing up.

When she came out, she'd washed her face and brushed her teeth and put her hair up in a knot. She stood in the doorway in her PJs, arms crossed, one foot on top of the other. She looked so beautiful to me then, and my heart was so full, I wanted to cry. She said, "Are you okay? You have a bizarre look on your face."

"Come here," I said, opening my arms to her. And she did.

That night, when I got home, I found Gus sitting on his plaid chair in the living room, wide awake. This was strange. I hadn't seen a car in the driveway, and usually Bennie was the one up late.

"There he is," he said. "The Professor. Come give your old man a hug." He looked like something of a madman himself, with what was left of his hair going in every direction, and wearing sandals and socks with running shorts and a preposterous purple smoking jacket he'd been given as a gift. A hefty drink sat balanced on the sofa's arm.

"I thought you were at the cabin," I said when he released me. "Where's Bennie's car?"

He was at the bar already, pouring me a drink. He handed it to me. "We were at the cabin. She dropped me off and turned around."

This sounded unlikely. "Did you two fight?"

"Don't you worry about that," he said, sitting back down. "To what do we owe this pleasant surprise? Bennie said you weren't very forthcoming on the phone."

I didn't like the way he wouldn't really look at me, and I wondered if she'd told him more than he was letting on. "Did something happen between you two?"

"Ach," he said.

"Did you do something, Pop?" (What he'd done, I would learn months later, was cough up blood; Bennie wanted him to call his doctor, but he'd refused.)

"I mean it, kiddo," he said. "Back off."

I didn't know what was going on, but I knew better than to press. I put my drink down and showed him my palms.

He raised his glass. "To my son, the Professor," he said.

Now I was the one who looked away. It was no secret he was proud as hell of what I was doing; I'd be the first Pyle in history to have the word *Doctor* in front of his name, he told everyone who'd listen. I hated — really hated — to let him down. But I thought of Julie, and of the tiny life inside her, the life that was partly me, and what choice did I have? With an unsteady hand, I held up my glass, too. "I have something better to toast," I said. "I'm going to be a dad."

I think it took a few seconds for what I said to register, because he closed his eyes and leaned his head against the back of the chair. Then he sat up, opened them, and said, "Are you shitting me?" I shook my head. He grinned. "Holy crap." He got up and did a few steps of the goofy Russian-ish dance he used to do when I was a kid, to make me laugh. "You're sure?" I nodded again. "Holy fucking crap." He poured us both more Scotch and sat down. Leaning forward, he knocked his glass against mine. "There's no love like the love a father has for his son, you know that, right? No love on Earth. Do you know that, kiddo?"

Of course, I didn't have the first clue. "We don't know if it's a boy, Pop. It's too soon to tell."

He didn't seem to have heard me. "Nothing like it on Earth, kiddo. Nothing like it on Earth."

9

SUNDAY EVENING, LO and behold, my fake river wish comes true. When we get home from the store, there's a message on the machine from Julie saying she's running late, and that she's sorry but we should probably go ahead and eat. I spend a minute or two being wounded — we have an unwritten pact to spend Sunday evenings together, all three of us, no matter what — but then I notice Owen watching me from the doorway, the solemn expression on his small face most likely a reflection of my own, and I square my shoulders, smile, and tell him we're going out, just the two of us, for some father-son Q.T.

"What's that?" he asks, suspicious, and I tell him he's about to find out. I ask him to feed Jerry (completing finite tasks gives kids confidence, according to Julie's books), and I watch the dog sniff at his kibble a few times before tentatively digging in. When he's through eating, I take him out in the yard and watch him work his way around the perimeter while the sun begins its descent. He takes his time, investigating the rosebushes and Gus's apparently immortal rhubarb patch before settling on a spot deep in the ivy by the back fence. By the time we head inside, the sky is a mosaic of pink, orange, and gold. I tell Owen to turn off the TV and put on his coat, and when the two of us are in the car, heading toward town, I say he's in for a serious treat.

I can feel his feet kicking against the back of my seat. "What kind of treat?"

"Meat," I say. "Good old, mass-produced American meat. With

a healthy dose of antibiotics and growth hormones to boot." In the rearview mirror I catch the expression on his face, which I place somewhere between apprehension and delight.

I park in front of Cattlemen's, a dive I used to frequent with Bill, back in the day, and watch a young woman in a napkin-size top, despite the season, and extreme low-rise jeans wrestling with the heavy metal door, and for a second I get a glimpse of the inside: the familiar fake-wood paneling on the walls, the antique jukebox in the corner and the ever-present cloud of smoke hanging above the patrons' heads, the strings of colored Christmas lights that decorate the place year-round.

Across the street, at Mo's, we claim two stools at the counter and I order milk shakes, chocolate for Owen and black-and-white for me, from a man who is not Mo and is not Mo's son, in fact he's barely a man at all. I'd guess he's about seventeen. "Do you know Mo?" I ask — predictably, I guess, because the kid, who's got tusk-shaped earrings through both of his earlobes, rolls his eyes. "My grandfather. I'm Moses the Third."

"That's great. You're carrying the torch," I say.

"He's not dead or anything," he says. "The Seahawks are playing, and he's too lazy to drag his ass off the couch."

I glance at Owen nervously, but he seems not to have heard the *d*-word. "My father used to bring me here when I was a kid," I offer, hoping to steer the conversation onto cheerier ground.

"You and everyone else in town," says Moses the Third. "You know what you want?"

"As a matter of fact, we do," I say. I order us each a cheeseburger, a double for me and a single for Owen, who grips the counter with both hands, spinning his stool back and forth while we wait. The milk shakes come out first; they're thick and wonderful, and I tell Owen how my father used to buy huckleberries on the side of the road every July, and then he'd bring them here in a baggie and they'd blend them into his shake. "It caught on, so they named the huckleberry shake Gus's Favorite. He was kind of a legend around here, you know," I say, calling Owen's attention to a row of signed, framed photos on the wall behind the counter. Gus is up there, along with twenty or thirty others, most of whom I recognize by sight, but only a few of whom I know by name. On Gus's left is Wilmer Rosebud, his fishing buddy and favorite judge. On his right is the current mayor, the former next to him, and Stan a few frames down. I point to Gus. "Recognize that guy?"

Owen shakes his head, the end of his red-striped straw stuck in his mouth.

"Sure you do. It's him," I tell him. "It's Gus. He used to come here all the time. He was the consummate regular." Which is an understatement. For nearly a decade, until Bennie entered the picture, he came here every single day at the exact same time and ordered the exact same thing. "That booth in the corner was unofficially his," I say, pointing. "I bet half the state's mining policy got hammered out right there, over hamburgers and huckleberry shakes."

He seems to consider this. "Are we regulars?"

"Not here," I say.

"Then where?"

"Nowhere, really."

"Why not?"

I'm pondering this when the doors open and a family of four walks in. The Zilinkases: Donna, her husband, Tom, and their two Aryan-Nation-looking twin boys. One of them is in Owen's class, but honestly they look like carbon copies of each other, and I have no idea which one's which. I raise my hand to wave. Tom either doesn't see me or pretends not to, and Donna makes the smallest nod possible in response.

They stand in the doorway a while, looking around as if they're in a five-star establishment, waiting for the maître d' to show them to their table, but eventually Tom leads them to the corner booth — Gus's booth, I can't help thinking. Donna's in fur, again, only this one's white, and full-length, even though it's practically spring outside, and Tom makes a big show of helping her out of it and hanging it on a hook.

"Isn't one of those boys in your class?" I ask Owen. He nods. "You want to go over and say hi?"

"No," he says.

"You sure?"

The vehemence with which he shakes his head surprises me.

"Why not?"

"Because," he says, like I have to him so many times.

"Because why?"

"I don't like them."

I look over: Tom is punching buttons on his cell phone, and the boys are emptying the salt and pepper shakers onto the table while Donna inspects her nails. "Fair enough," I say.

Our meals appear then, steaming in red plastic baskets, and I take a moment to bask in the truly divine scent of deeply unhealthy food. Owen watches, wide-eyed, while I unwrap my burger from its red-and-white-checked paper wrapper and empty the fries out of their cardboard cone onto my plate, then do the same for him. I pick up my burger, take a bite, and say, "Delicious," because it is. He follows my lead and picks his up, too, but doesn't eat. He's regarding it with what looks like dismay. I ask him what's wrong.

"Is it meat?" he asks.

"It is meat."

"Is meat — " He pauses. "Is meat made out of cow?"

I nod, hoping this isn't headed where I'm pretty certain it is.

"You mean, *dead* cow?"

And what can I say? I nod again. "Yes. It's dead cow, honey. You like it. It's delicious."

He's frowning, though, studying his plate. He glances up at Gus in the frame on the wall, then back down at his food. "Dead, like Gus is dead," he says, but this time it's not a question. It's a statement of fact.

"Hey, Gus would be lucky to taste this good," I joke, but it's not even remotely funny. He puts his burger down.

I eat mine anyway, more to make a point now than because I actually enjoy it, but Owen won't even try his. "One bite? For me?" I plead, but he just shakes his head and sits there looking unhappy. "You want something else? Chicken fingers?" I ask, but he makes a face, and I eat his food too, on principle I guess, though by the time I've polished off everything on both our plates I can't remember what principle it was. I ask Moses the Third for the bill. While we wait, I nudge Owen with my elbow. "Knock-knock," I say to cheer him up.

"Who's there?"

"Hoo."

"Hoo who?"

"Hey, you're supposed to be a little boy, not an owl," I say, punching his shoulder.

He rubs the spot and doesn't smile. I pay the bill and leave a couple of dollars' tip on the bar. Before we leave, I glance up at the photo of Gus, who looks for all the world like he's glaring down at me: like he disapproves. *For the record, Pop, you weren't always a master at this, either,* I tell him in my head.

Or apparently not in my head, because Owen says, "A master at what, Dad?"

"A master at nothing, champ," I say, and we step into the night.

10

LIKE I SAID, Julie's a world-class sleeper, she always has been, and she doesn't wake up or even stir Monday morning when I rise in the dark, dress, and throw my swimsuit and goggles into a miniature nylon duffel with "Adidas" and its logo emblazoned on one side. Before I leave, I stand by the bed a minute, watching her. She likes to sleep on her stomach with both arms over her head and her hands clasped together. Sometimes, like now, she clasps them so tightly her fingers turn white. "Jules," I say quietly. "Honey, your hands." She startles, makes a small moaning sound, and turns onto her side.

The pool is supposed to open at six, but it's dark inside and I'm the only car in the lot. I wait with the heater running until six twenty or so, when a blue Honda Civic pulls into the spot next to mine and a young woman in a hooded San Diego State sweatshirt gets out and hurries in the direction of the Aquatic Center's glass doors. I follow her and wait a few feet back while she flips a little frantically through a bunch of color-coded keys on a large metal ring. "I'm sorry I'm late," she says without looking up. "Our power went out and my alarm clock didn't go off. It must have been the wind."

"What wind?" I say.

She finds the key she's searching for and slips it into the lock, then opens the door. When she turns around and ushers me through, I see she's Owen's teacher — or rather, his "director," as they're dubbed in Montessori World.

"Miss Pietryzyck, hello," I say. "I'm Logan Pyle, Owen's dad."

"Sure. Of course. It's *Peet*-rick, by the way," she says. "The *y* is silent. And the *z*. How are you?"

I apologize as I pass through the door. "Do you swim? I haven't seen you here." She follows me, and it's only once she's walking around the lobby, turning on lights, that it dawns on me that today, she's in charge.

"Not anymore. I swam in college, but since then this is the closest I like to get to a pool," she says. Her glasses and sweats make her look younger than she has the other times we've met.

"What stroke?" I ask.

"Butterfly. And sometimes back." She looks around the room as if checking things off a mental list, and then she looks at me. "It's nice to see you, Mr. Pyle," she says politely. "Have a nice swim."

In the men's locker room, I change quickly and stretch like I always do. There's a tall mirror at one end, by the scale, and I'm smart enough to avoid the latter, but not the former, where I pause for a minute or so, inspecting my reflection as objectively as I can. I start at the top. So far, thank goodness, my hair is hanging on; it's a mess this morning and, as usual, in need of a trim, but it's still dark and I'm pleased to report there's as much of it as there was ten years ago. (Gus claimed I got the Calloway hair genes, not his.) I do look tired, though, and some lines I swear weren't there a few months ago have appeared around my eyes. I let my gaze drop down to my middle, where, like Gus, I tend to carry my weight. I can't pretend I'm not depressed by — and a little ashamed of — what I see: an abundance of pale, soft flesh, a hefty portion of which bulges over the elastic waistband of my trunks. By turning to the side, blocking my love handles with my hands, and sucking in my gut, I discover I can approximate my normal self (me minus the extra twenty or so pounds I've somehow collected these past few months), but holding my breath that way soon makes me dizzy, and I give up. I drape my towel around my neck and head for the pool.

The usual lifeguard is a middle-aged man named Dennis, and it's hard not to feel a little self-conscious, today, alone in the cavernous space with Miss Pietryzyck, who's perched cross-legged on a folding metal chair, snapping her flip-flop against the sole of her foot and watching me swim. The thing about swimming, though, the reason I do it — the reason I always have — is that once I'm in my groove, I don't feel self-conscious; I don't feel *any* way. It takes a few laps, usually, but once I get going, my arms and legs start moving on autopilot, every muscle in my body knows exactly what it's supposed to do, and then, as if aware it's not needed for a while, my mind just kind of shuts down, folds in on itself in the best possible way. On good days, after I've finished my mile, getting out of the pool feels more like emerging from a deep, dreamless sleep than from water.

Which is not what happens today. I can't stop *thinking* — about Owen, about Julie, about Gus — and I never come close to finding my groove. In fact, I feel worse climbing out of the pool than I did when I got in. This is disappointing. I spend a solid ten minutes under the hot shower, trying to clear my head. I'm coming out of the locker room when I see Miss Pietryzyck again, signing someone in.

When she's finished, I ask her if she has a minute to talk. Warily, she says yes. She's taken off her sweatshirt, and her pea-green T-shirt proclaims "Life Is Good" across the chest.

"I was hoping we could touch base," I say.

She seems nervous, fiddling with a gold *E* that hangs from a chain around her neck.

I say, "Owen really enjoys being in your class," to put her at ease.

She smiles. Her teeth are small and perfectly straight, like a child's. "That's always good to hear," she says. "He's a totally sweet kid."

"Actually, I was hoping to get your input," I say. "He's been acting a little, well, how shall I put this? He seems to be going through some, well, he strikes me as a little, I don't know, *erratic* is maybe the word, lately, and I was —"

She cuts me off. "Are you talking about the baby stuff?"

I nod. Now I'm the one feeling anxious. "My wife says it's common, she has all these books, but I don't know. I worry. But all parents worry, right? You're probably going to tell me I'm just being oversensitive, and I'm making something out of nothing. I'm sure you get this kind of thing all the time."

She lets go of the *E*. "Actually, Mr. Pyle, that's not quite true. To be perfectly honest, I'm concerned about Owen, myself. He's not making the kind of progress, socially speaking, that we like to see in kids his age."

My heart thumps, and my hands start to sweat. "Oh," I say.

"I don't want to alarm you, but it's not something to ignore, either."

I nod and swallow hard.

"It's just that right now is a critical time, developmentally. A huge part of normalization happens, or it's supposed to, between four and six. That's when their minds are most absorbent. After that, the window closes. And then you're looking at a chain reaction of social issues, kind of a domino effect. Plus the other kids can sense insecurity a mile away, it's like blood in the water, and the not-so-nice ones tend to exploit it, I'm sorry to say."

"I wasn't aware of any window," I say, confused.

She goes on. "I don't know how you feel about this, but if you'd like, I could arrange for Owen to spend some time with someone. A specialist." I notice, when she says it, that she has a slight lisp.

"Specializing in what?"

"Children. You know, like a psychologist, or a counselor. They're very skilled at finding out what, if anything, is going on."

"I'm sorry," I say, "but I don't think I understand."

She nods, as if my confusion is expected. "I hope you don't mind my asking, Mr. Pyle, but has anything changed at home?"

How can I possibly answer her? I look down, hoping to buy some time. I have no idea what to say. Am I really supposed to tell this virtual stranger how it felt, watching my father take leave of the world? Or should I talk about Julie, instead? Should I stand here and explain that Julie got a *haircut*? That she's practically disappearing before my eyes? Or, that lately, she seems to shrink from my touch? Shall I elucidate for the earnest and well-meaning Miss Pietryzyck how each day since Gus died, my marriage — and hell, my whole universe — seems a shade less recognizable to me?

"No," I say, "nothing's changed."

She presses her lips together, and I have the distinct feeling she doesn't believe me. "Well, if you think of anything," she says, glancing in the direction of the pool. She's getting ready to go.

I feel desperate, suddenly, for her to stay. "Wait," I say. "There is something. His grandfather — my dad — died over the summer, after a long illness. He had lung cancer, and his wife, Bennie, was a nurse, so she took care of him, I mean, we all did. He lived in the house until he — " I pause. She frowns. "It was difficult. Really hard, toward the end especially. And now Julie, Julie's been, well, she's been working a lot. Like really a ton. She's prosecuting the Holliman case, up in Tobey? You know, with the asbestos? You've probably seen it on TV."

"Those are big changes," she says, in a tone of voice I'm sure she learned in school expressly for dealing with unstrung parents. "Particularly for a young child. If you're opposed to counseling — which I take it you are — there's another option. We could move him into the Elm classroom, see how he does with the smaller kids. He is on the cusp, age-wise, anyway, and sometimes a change of environment is precisely — "

I cut her off. "You mean, hold him back?"

"We avoid that term here. It tends to be stigmatizing."

"Damn right it's stigmatizing," I hear myself say. Has she not heard a single word I've said? "I don't know if you've been doing you're job with your eyes closed, but getting stuck with a bunch of toddlers is the last thing in the world Owen needs."

She looks down and takes a step back, away from me. "Sorry," she says. "You asked for my opinion. I'm trying to help."

But I'm not finished yet. "And frankly, I take offense at the suggestion that he'd be better off talking to some stranger — some *specialist* — than to his own flesh and blood. What do you know about kids, anyway? You're practically one yourself. How long have you even had this job?"

"I apologize," she says, straightening up. "Apparently I've offended you. That wasn't what I intended." I'm not sure but I think there are tears in her eyes, which suddenly look very green. I've never seen eyes so green before. I look down. She's wearing rainbow-striped flip-flops, and a silver ring around one of her toes. "If you'll excuse me, Mr. Pyle," she says in a tight voice. "I'm not even supposed to be out here right now, talking to you. I'm supposed to be in there. It's my responsibility to make sure nobody drowns."

11

JULIE SQUATS IN front of the coat closet, burrowing around in the milk crate where we keep mittens, hats, and scarves. She doesn't say hello or even turn around when I come in. "Why can't I ever find anything in this house?" she moans.

"I'll get the maid right on it," I say, intending to sound lighthearted but I guess it doesn't come out that way, because Julie takes a second to turn around and frown up at me, over her shoulder.

"What's that supposed to mean?"

"Nothing." I drop my swim bag on the floor beside the radiator. "Is Owen ready to go?"

"Apparently not," she says. She sits back on her heels and blows her still-unfamiliar bangs out of her face. "I'm so late, and I can't find my hat."

"It's supposed to be fifty-eight today. You don't need a hat."

"My *hard* hat," she says.

"You have a hard hat?"

"We're touring the mine again, and it's regulations. Could you help me look, please, instead of just standing there? Hart will be here any minute."

"Hart," I repeat.

"Honey?"

I go over to her and start pushing coats around. "Why is Hart going?"

She rakes her fingers through her hair. "It was here, I swear, and now it's not. Are you sure you didn't move it?"

"Why would I move something I didn't even know you had?" She's not listening, though. I glance in the direction of the stairs, then say, "I just ran into Miss Pietryzyck, at the pool."

This gets her attention. She looks up. "*Peet*-rick, Logan," she says. "Two syllables."

"We talked about Owen." She stops what she's doing. Frowning, she listens while I do my best to summarize Miss Pietryzyck's concerns. I use the terms *absorbent* and *window*. She frowns harder. I tell her she suggested Owen see a counselor, or even switch into the younger class.

"And what did you say?" Julie says.

"I said no way." I omit the bit where I'm pretty sure I made Miss Pietryzyck cry.

"To which one?"

"Both."

"She's only trying to help." She starts digging again. "We're going to have to talk about this later. Right now I really, really need to find my hat."

"I was thinking, maybe what he needs is to get outside more. Play some sports. I was thinking baseball. I've been thinking I should teach him how to swing."

Without looking up, she says, "What about swimming? Isn't that a sport?"

"Hello, Julie — he sucks at swimming," I say, more vehemently than I intend.

"Lower your voice," she says, glancing up the stairs.

I lower my voice. "You know it and I know it. He can hardly make it across the pool. It's pathetic."

"You need to take it easy, honey. He's only been at it a couple of months. And he's getting better. Give him some time. He's not you."

That's when I spot a sliver of yellow plastic up on the top shelf, peeking out from behind one of Julie's handbags. "I'm going to talk to him," I say. "Man to man. I'll find out what's going on."

She looks up at me. "I wish you'd wait for me. I think we should talk to him together."

Out front, a car horn toots shave-and-a-haircut. "That's me, shit," she says, frowning in the direction of the street.

I stand on my toes and reach for her hat, which is marked "Property of US EPA" in orange letters along one side. "Abracadabra," I say.

"Thank goodness," she says. As she stands up, I notice she's wearing a skirt. She looks way too pretty to be slogging around in a mine. I get an uneasy feeling in my chest. I place the hat on her head and she smiles up at me. "My hero."

The car honks again. I look outside. A shit-brown Jeep Cherokee sits idling by the curb. The driver's-side window is down, and inside sits Hart, wearing mirrored sunglasses, the kind you'd wear to climb Mt. Everest. He grins and salutes. I don't salute back. "Why's he going, again?"

"His book, remember? And I told you, he's giving me a ride. See you tonight?"

"All the way to Tobey? That's a mighty long drive."

"I've got to go, babe." She starts to turns away, but I catch her wrist.

"Are you and Hart having an affair?"

Her mouth falls open. "Don't be nuts," she says.

"Would you tell me if you were?"

"I would never do that. I love you," she says earnestly. A small smile spreads across her face. "And besides, where would I ever find the time?"

"That's not funny," I say.

"And if I did have time, it wouldn't be with Hart." She picks up her bag, shoulders it, and stands on her toes to kiss me.

"Because he's an imbecile," I say.

"No, because he's gay."

I look out at the Jeep. "No."

"Sure. He talks about his partner, Seoul, all the time."

"Hart and Seoul? Come on," I say.

"I'll be back late," she says. "Thanks for finding my hat."

After they go, I toast some bread for me and Owen and butter it, and then I stand at the bottom of the stairs and call up to him. "Get your butt in gear, kid. We're going to be late."

In the kitchen I pour some milk and what's left of the coffee into a travel mug, pick up the phone, and dial Bill's cell. I need to talk to someone who isn't four years old, or my wife. Bill doesn't answer, though, and I leave him a message asking him to call me back. "It's not about the offer," I tell his machine, "so don't get all hopped up."

"*Owen*," I call again, after I hang up. "What *gives?*" He doesn't answer, so I climb the stairs.

I find him in his room, still in his rodeo pajamas, curled up fetally on his bed, sucking his thumb with his back to me.

"Oh, Christ. What's going on, buddy?" I ask, sitting down. "School starts in fifteen minutes."

"I don't want to go," he says.

"Why not?" I ask.

"I want to stay here with you."

"You can't do that," I say.

"Why can't I?"

"Because you're a kid, and kids go to school. It's what they do."

He doesn't move. "But I'm not a kid," he says. "I'm a baby."

My heart sinks. Miss Pietryzyck's words echo in my head. I reach for him and flip him over so I can see his face. "Is something the matter at school?"

He shrugs.

"Come on. I'm your dad. You can tell me. What's up?" I think again of what Miss Pietryzyck said — specifically, the "blood in the water" part. "Is someone bugging you?"

He shrugs again.

"Who is it?"

He doesn't answer.

"I know you don't want to rat anyone out, and I respect that. But if you tell me, I might be able to help. Do you want to tell me?"

He seems to consider this. Then he shakes his head.

I look at the clock on his nightstand: it's eight-eighteen. I look up at the ceiling, at the glow-in-the-dark stars, and I try, really try, to remember what it was like to be four. "Champ," I say, "I don't know what's going on, exactly, but what I do know is that if someone's giving you a hard time — I don't care who it is, or what they say — the important thing is that you stick up for yourself."

He frowns and says, "But they're bigger than me," in a small voice.

"Hey. It's not the size of the dog in the fight, it's the size of the fight in the dog. Gus used to tell me that."

He frowns harder.

"Listen. The point is, pound for pound, you're as tough as any kid out there."

"I'm not."

I feel something well up in me. I reach for his arm and hold it. "Yes, you are. You're as tough as any kid anywhere. You're a fighter and a half. You've been through stuff those other kids can't even dream of. And don't you ever, ever let anyone tell you otherwise." I realize I'm squeezing his arm too hard, and I loosen my grip. "Sorry about that," I say.

He takes his thumb out of his mouth and sits up. "What stuff?" he says.

I pause and think of Julie. I think of her in the passenger seat of Hart's Jeep, zooming away from us. I picture them making their way over the mountain pass that leads to Tobey. They're having a grand old time. She's laughing, and her hair is flying everywhere. Her hand is out the window, and her freckled fingers carve long Ss in the air as they climb.

I clear my throat. "You know your scar?" His fingers float to the approximate spot on his chest. I don't wait for him to say yes. "Well, the truth is, it doesn't just stand for *sweetness*." His face is serious. I clear my throat again. "The truth is you were born with a, a — " Again, I pause. I think of him in his incubator: his tiny hands, his tiny feet. The tubes and the wires and the jagged, blinking lines on the screen.

I take a deep breath. "There was a problem with your heart. A big one."

His eyes get very wide.

"No, it's okay," I say. "I mean it wasn't, then, or we didn't know if it would be, but you fought and you fought. You were this tiny little creature, with all the cards stacked against you, but you know what? You *won*. We all did." I clear my throat and touch his hand, the one resting on his chest. "So that scar stands for *strength*, too. Strength is something you've got in spades, kid."

There's that tiny line, still, bisecting his brow. "What cards?" he says.

"Not real cards. I just meant — It doesn't matter." I take hold of his knee. "You're stronger than you think, is the point. You've always got to remember that. Okay? Can you remember?"

He nods.

"Can you say it out loud?"

"I'm stronger than I think," he says, unconvincingly.

"Once more, this time with some oomph in it."

"I'm stronger than I *think*," he says. He smiles shyly.

"That's my boy," I say, giving his knee one final squeeze.

12

BILL HAWKS IS my closest friend, and my oldest friend, and he possesses many fine qualities, but patience, tact, and a gentle touch are not among them. When I get home from dropping Owen off, he's sitting on my front steps in running attire. He has his dog, Mulligan, with him on a leash, and they both stand up as I approach. "Get dressed. We're running the loop."

"I can't," I say. "I have to run some errands for Julie. Besides, I already swam."

He says, "Bullshit. Look how fat you're getting. Jesus."

I open the door to the house and Jerry comes bounding out, panting and wagging his tail, standing on his hind legs to lick Bill's hands and face. Jerry adores Bill — or whatever the dog equivalent of adoration might be. In fact, Bill is the only person, or living creature, really, for whom I've seen Jerry show any real affinity at all, since Gus. "Hey, mellow brother," Bill says, scratching behind the dog's ears. "Should we drag your master's fat ass up the big hill?"

"His fat master's going to leave you in the dust," I say.

"Hurry, would you?" he says. "I haven't got all day."

"The loop" we've been running since middle school is a grueling six and a half miles that starts at my house and follows Third Street south all the way to Basin Road. At Basin we turn left and weave our way along the base of the hills toward Harvey Canyon Road, which climbs gently at first but gets steep as the canyon narrows, and today I'm wheezing way before we're even halfway up. "When was the last time you did this?" I ask Bill, who doesn't appear to have broken a sweat.

"A month ago, with you," he says, turning around and jogging backward. "You look awful. You're not going to have a coronary on me, are you?"

"I'm okay," I say. "I told you, I already swam."

"Can I offer you a bowl of crybaby soup?" He leads Mulligan in a circle around me to drive home his point.

The road dead-ends in a dirt parking lot, where we always stop to stretch our legs against the same massive log. Today, instead of stretching, I sit down, hold my head in my hands, and breathe. Bill doesn't comment, stretching one calf and then the other.

He's lean and muscular and never gains a pound no matter what he eats. An ex-Marine, he claims he never felt more alive, or happy, than when he was shooting people and jumping out of helicopters. But he shattered his femur in Somalia in 1993, and he's been flailing around ever since, searching, I suppose, for something one-thousandth as exciting as war.

"I was surprised you called," he says, without looking at me.

"Yeah, me too," I say. I think about the last time we spoke. We got into it about the offer, and we both said some things we probably shouldn't have. I know I did.

"I mean, I'm glad you did," he says.

"Me too." I stand up and stretch out my shoulders, which always get tight when I run.

He asks how Owen's doing and I say okay. I ask about Sam, his daughter, and he says, "You should thank God Owen's not a girl. I'd lock her up until she was thirty-five if I could. Ready?" he asks, and I nod.

We unclip the dogs from their leashes and start up the Ridge Trail, which is exactly what it sounds like, and Bill takes the lead as we follow it up and up, catching glimpses of town, far below, through the pines. The dogs dart in and out of the woods, running ahead and then pausing at the forks and looking back, asking which path they're supposed to take. We're about halfway across when, finally, my endorphins kick in. My breath comes more easily, and I feel like I could run another fifteen miles. I catch up with Bill and pass him. "Oh, yeah?" he says, and picks up the pace.

At the summit, a bald spot a few hundred yards above the tree line, we both stop. It's our custom. I sit on a flat rock and catch my breath. The air's thinner up here, and I'm glad to see even Bill's breathing hard. "Hoo-wee," he says, leaning over to rest his hands on his thighs.

"I think I might need some advice. It has to do with Julie," I say, squinting down over the neat grid of maple-lined streets that makes up our town. From up here it all looks so orderly, so logical, so *contained.*

"Uh-oh. It must be pretty bad if you're coming to me." What he means is, he's not exactly a role model when it comes to romantic relationships. The women he's drawn to tend to be troubled souls, sometimes violent, often drinkers or worse, and his relationships with them tend to be volatile and short. Many involve the loss of small or large sums of money. Some involve the emergency room. One or two have involved the police.

"I don't know," I say. "That's the problem. I can't tell what's going on. She's so busy with this case, and when she's not working, she hardly seems to notice I'm there. When she does notice, it's to tell me I've screwed up in some way. It didn't used to be like this. We used to get along. We used to enjoy each other, you know? I'm worried that she's changing or something."

He nods and squints into the distance. "Okay. Sex?"

The dogs pant. Jerry gets down on his belly in the dirt.

"I'll take that as a no."

I feel a stab of guilt. Julie would hate me talking to Bill about our relationship — she's not exactly his biggest fan. It started when Julie and I were first together: Bill was newly single and, suffice it to say, not at his most genteel. Regularly he would turn up at the house, often late at night, always uninvited, and usually plowed. Inevitably he'd make the dog bark, which would inevitably wake the baby. I'd get up and let him in, and he'd sit in the living room while Julie or I rocked Owen back to sleep, and regale us with unsavory anecdotes about whichever woman he currently did or did not love. I've explained to Julie that he's really a wonderful guy with a sharp mind and moreover a huge heart, but she remains skeptical, and though I wish that weren't the case, I can't blame her. In her mind he's a womanizer, and selfish, and worse, he reminds her of her dad—a lifelong military man, a misogynist (her word), and most of all a nasty drunk.

"There's sex," I say now, and stretch my arms over my head.

"Just not as much as there used to be," he says.

I say, "Perhaps."

Hands on hips, he turns to face me. "You know what they say about that: If you're not fucking your woman, someone else is."

"That's disgusting," I say.

"So who are the suspects?"

I think of Hart in his sunglasses. "There are no suspects. That's not what's going on."

"I see," he says. His smug tone suggests otherwise.

"I changed my mind. I don't want to talk about this. You were right. I shouldn't have come to you. Forget I even brought it up. Let's talk about something else."

"Fine with me." He looks away again, at the slate-gray mountaintops on the other side of town. "How about we talk about you getting off your ass and selling the goddamn parcel? This offer won't be around forever."

"I told you, that's off the table." I start jogging again.

"Look, there it is, I just put it back on," he says, following.

"There's nothing to say," I say, heading toward the root- and rock-strewn trail, which drops down the western slope of the mountain and joins up with the river path. "You know where I stand."

"Sure. You think I'm a greedy asshole with no conscience who'd sell his firstborn for the right price. I heard you loud and clear last time."

"That's not what I said." I glance over my shoulder at him, trying to gauge whether he's serious or just giving me a hard time. In the process I stumble on a root and almost fall down.

"Careful," he says. There's an edge in his voice.

Regaining my stride, I say over my shoulder, "I haven't changed my mind, and I'm not going to."

"You know what? That's fine. I know you don't care about my rent, or the fact that I have a daughter who's talking about college, or Clarissa, who's bleeding me dry. I understand. But what if the offer got bigger? Would that change your mind?"

I stop, turn, and look at him. "How much bigger?"

"Aha," he says. "So size does matter."

"I didn't say that."

"Come on. What's your number?"

"Excuse me?"

"What's the magic number that's going to change your mind?"

"There is no number," I say, starting up again. "Gus left me that land, it's my inheritance, and that's not something you can put a price on. So no, I'm not going to sell. Jesus, between you and Julie, I'm starting to sound like a broken record." I pick up my pace.

He adjusts his effortlessly. "Well, you know what? Julie's smart as shit," he says. "You should listen to her."

Under other circumstances I'd appreciate him saying this, but today it feels like a betrayal. "Why does everyone seem bent on telling me what my own father would want? Why does everyone insist they knew him better than I did? He was *my* father, he left *me* the land, and it's *my* prerogative to decide what happens now," I say. "Why is that so impossible for everyone around me to comprehend?"

We run for a few minutes in silence and I think the subject is closed, but suddenly Bill stops running, so I stop too. "I'll say this once and only once," he says. "Living your life based on what a dead man might think — the operative words in that sentence being *dead* and *might* — is not going to make you, or anyone who has to live with you, happy."

I don't say anything.

"You say Julie's the problem. You say she's changed."

I wipe sweat from my eyes with my sleeve. "I said I don't want to talk about Julie anymore."

"But you know what? I'm wondering now if maybe it's you who's the problem. Maybe you're the one who's changed. Or maybe you haven't. Maybe that's why your marriage is in the shitter."

"Is that what you think? That everything's my fault?" His shirt is sleeveless, and his ropy arms are crossed over his chest, so the giant *Semper Fi* banner he has tattooed on his biceps is boldly displayed. I glance at the words. "Isn't that supposed to be about loyalty?" I ask.

His eyes narrow. "Watch yourself," he says.

"Well, how about showing me some?"

He shakes his head. "I'm trying to help you. You've just got your head too far up your ass to see that."

"Well, I guess I should be grateful then, Dr. Hawks. You're very insightful and wise. And you're very fucking condescending, especially for someone who's been divorced three times."

He holds his hands up, showing me his palms, and starts backing away. "And you, my brother, are one stubborn fuck," he says, and then he takes off.

"Hey, wait, come back. I shouldn't have said that," I say, lunging for him, but he's already out of my reach. He runs remarkably fast, with the dogs at his heels, and I realize how much he must have been holding back until now, to keep pace with me. His red shirt gets smaller, and he disappears around a bend. The trail is rocky and steep, and I do my best to follow but it's clear I'm not going to be able catch him. "Bill, wait *up*," I shout when he reappears, one ridge over, but he doesn't turn around. My knees are on fire, and after a quarter-mile or so I stop and walk. All the way home I curse him, going over the things he said in my head. He doesn't know what he's talking about, I tell myself. His parents are alive and well, living in Phoenix, and like I said, his failed marriages speak for themselves. The fact that his daughter is a half-decent human being is an astonishing piece of luck. I tell myself these things over and over, but I feel worse with every step.

When I finally make it home, I find Jerry, sitting panting on the front stoop, the end of his leash pinned under the terra cotta planter so he can't run away.

13

INSIDE, I CHECK the machine in case there's an apology from Bill
but there isn't, and instead, a message from Julie reminds me – yet
again – about the boxes I'm supposed to take to Owen's school.
There's great urgency in her voice, despite the fact that the auction's
not until Saturday. I erase the message. But a few minutes later,
standing at the sink eating an English muffin, I start thinking about
what Bill said earlier – not the part about Gus, the part about Julie,
with someone else – and the food goes dry in my mouth. Damn
Bill. I swallow the muffin with cold coffee, and without further ado I
shower and dress and load the boxes into my truck.

I park in front, in a fire lane, and let the hazards flash while I carry
one of the boxes into the front-hall lobby, where Harold Moss, the
school's surly security guard, sits behind a desk eating a burrito and
watching TV. He asks me to sign a guest register, and instructs me to
leave the boxes on the stage in the auditorium, but doesn't offer to
help.

I carry the first box down a carpeted hallway, which is lined with
paper tracings the kids made of themselves and then cut out. According to Owen, Miss Pietryzyck's instructions were that the kids
decorate their silhouettes to depict the person they aspire to be, and I
pass lots of firemen and doctors, and girls wearing jeweled tiaras and
pouffy pink skirts. One kid has painted a three-piece suit onto his and
taped on a briefcase; another is a soldier, another a policewoman. I
find Owen's at the very end, and I put down the box I'm carrying to
take a look. He's drawn a red sweatshirt with a hood and zipper and

colored the legs dark blue. The hair is brown and unruly. I start to get a warm feeling in my chest, which spreads when I notice the shoes: tan sneakers with the approximation of an orange Nike swoosh — *my* shoes. He's made his paper figure into me. The warmth travels all the way to my fingertips, and I feel an irrational desire to share this news. I look up and down the hall but there's no one around, which is probably for the best. Still, I'm proud. Who wouldn't be? I study the figure until a couple of administrative-looking types appear at the end of the hall, and I gather the box from the carpet and continue on my way.

I make six trips, pausing in the middle of each to admire my brown-paper self, and by the time I've deposited all of the boxes in the auditorium, I've decided that before I leave, I'll go downstairs and look in on Owen, see what actually goes on in Spruce for myself. Technically, I'm not supposed to. Parents are asked to schedule visits ahead of time. But I'm here, and I pay these people a lot of money, and I decide it's well within my prerogative to take a peek. To avoid Harold I go out through a different door from the one where I came in, descend a flight of stairs, and follow another carpeted hallway, this one dark gold, all the way to the end, to a door marked "Spruce," Owen's classroom. When I get there, I look up and down the hall. There's no one around, so I peer through the window in Spruce's door, searching for my son.

Here at Eden, they don't separate the kids into grades. Instead, they do what's called "multi-age grouping," so Owen's class has kids as old as six and as young as four. They don't sit at desks, either, and there's no chalkboard at the front. In fact there *is* no front. The room is divided, informally, into different areas among which the kids rotate, busying themselves with a variety of ordained tasks — setting a table, buttoning a shirt, identifying shapes, tying bows, separating tiles into color groups, pouring sand into different-size jars — intended, so I've been told, to let the children's natural "love of order" guide them to learn. Julie insists it's brilliant, and that the research backs her up. (We argued over this. Eden — and the whole Montessori concept — struck me as fussy and, frankly, bizarre. I wanted Owen to go to public school, same as 99.9 percent of people we know — including, I noted, Julie and myself. Plus — I couldn't help pointing out — what kind of masochist shells out a small fortune for something they're giving away for free? "You sound exactly like Gus," Julie said. Needless to say, she prevailed.)

I spot Owen now, in the far corner, with a few other kids. They're sitting on a yellow mat on the floor, arranging wood blocks. Miss Pietryzyck, now in gray pants, a pink top, and pearls, stands over them and nods. Every once in a while she touches one of them on the head. When she touches Owen's head, he looks up and smiles. After a while she leaves them and stands over another group, one that's doing something with blue liquid in bowls. I'm perplexed: he looks perfectly content, and no one's messing with him. So why would she imply that they were? Why would she say Owen's not *normal?* He looks like he's doing just fine to me. Better than fine. The truth is, he looks a lot more "normal" than some of the other kids around here, from what I can see. In the corner, a little girl sits by herself, banging a wooden doll against a clock.

Driving to the store, though, I have an uneasy feeling I can't seem to shake, and by the time I park behind the silo, I'm almost grateful for the day's worth of busywork that's waiting for me inside.

I spend what's left of the morning, and then the afternoon, wrapping up the inventory, which ends up being even more discouraging, if that's possible, than thinking about Owen's school. I spend a lot of energy trying *not* to think about how much money we're losing on a daily basis, which is a challenge, given that the merchandise I'm counting — and there is a great deal of it — is all the stuff we didn't sell. When I've finished counting, I turn on the computer and enter the grim collection of numbers into Excel.

Then I open my e-mail. There's nothing new to speak of in my inbox, and I'm about to close it down, but instead, as I've done every week or so for months, I click on a message from someone named Bartholomew Valentine, the professor who replaced Carlos Pearl when he moved to Brazil. It's from last spring, and this Valentine person is reminding me that I have only a year left to submit my dissertation, assuming I still want my degree. He asks me to call him at my earliest convenience so we can discuss. He seems like a nice enough guy, if a tad officious, and I meant to call him. But that was June, and so much was going on with Gus, I never managed to pick up the phone. I'm ashamed to admit I never even wrote him back.

Now I click "Reply" — as I have a handful of times since then — and start to compose a message. *Dear Professor Valentine*, I type. *First, let me apologize for my delay in responding to your note*. I sit back. It's a fine start — but now what? *It's been a busy few years* — but I stop again. I delete *busy* and change it to *very eventful*, but *eventful* is even worse; it sounds downright jolly. Then I delete *very* — because adverbs weaken prose. I start again. *This past July, my father passed away*, I type. But immediately I go back. Gus abhorred euphemism. *My father died in July*. My hands have begun to sweat. I press on. *He had cancer. He suffered a slow and painful death, relinquishing a small part of his personhood each day while we stood by, helpless to do anything but watch. Now, without him, it's like a bomb went off. It's like there's a crater the size of Jupiter at the center of all of our lives. Nothing's working, Professor Valentine. My family's a hair's-breadth from bankruptcy, thanks to me, and I'm starting to believe my wife doesn't love me anymore. My son wants to be a baby again, did I mention that? And I'll tell you a secret, Professor, I don't blame him. I'd be a baby again, too, if I could. Who wouldn't? Who doesn't dream of a blank slate? A mother's breast? Who among us doesn't covet youth? Don't you, Professor? Please call me at your earliest convenience, so we can discuss.* I sit back; my heart is racing. I take a deep breath, wipe my hands on my jeans, and click "Cancel." Then I close the program and push the keyboard away.

I look at my watch. It's past time to pick up Owen. I turn the computer off, and while it shuts down I swivel around and look outside once more. A couple of leather-jacketed teenagers are sitting on a wooden bench in the sunshine, kissing. The girl wears a short skirt and big black boots, and while they kiss, the boy moves his free hand higher on her thigh.

I'm looking for my keys on the desk when I see an envelope with the words *Lion's Head* and their pretentious black-and-gold logo, just sitting there: the offer. I pick it up, feeling a pang of curiosity — until I think of all the things Bill said, and the curiosity sours. I glance at the kids outside once more. They look like they might eat each other up. Good for *them*, I think, and instead of opening the envelope, I tear it and its contents in half. This isn't *about* money. Bill — and Julie — should understand that. It's about holding on to what we can, while we can, because so much of life is heartbreak. We want what we can't have. And sooner or later time steamrolls even the most careful plans, and death bears everything and everyone we love away.

I tear the halves in half, sweep the paper scraps into Bill's ashtray, find some matches in the drawer, and light the little pile on fire. I'm surprised at how gratifying it is, watching it burn. Soon the smoke alarm starts to sing. I stand on the desk to turn it off, then get down and open a window. When the smoke has cleared, I close the window and turn off the lights, but I leave the ashes there, for Bill.

14

THE DAY HAS turned overcast. In front of Eden, Owen stands alone, thumbs hooked under the straps of his backpack, waiting for me to arrive. When he sees me pull into the circle, he trots to the curb, opens the back door, and climbs in, buckling himself into his seat without asking for help. I ask him about his day and he describes for me, in great detail, a game they played with a ball and a parachute in the gym. He talks all the way across town, to Turtle Mountain, the natural-foods store Julie likes best. I park and open his door, take his hand, and together we cross the street and go in.

I take the list Julie made for our first-ever three-person Thanksgiving feast out of my pocket and look around. The place has a frenzied, pre-holiday feel that makes me tense, right off. In the produce section, earnest-looking men and women frown at vegetables and fruit, turning pieces over in their hands. We wade into the fray, gathering Granny Smiths, lemons, broccoli, onions, celery, porcini mushrooms, and potatoes, me ticking each item off Julie's list. Owen stays close by my side, holding on to the tail of my shirt. We venture into the interior and he asks if he can ride in the cart. I'm scanning the shelves for the particular brand of bread crumbs Julie prefers. I tell him no.

"Why?" he asks.

"Big kids walk."

"But I want to ride. Mom lets me," he says.

I locate the bread crumbs. "Mom's not here," I say, and add the package to the cart. We soldier on, seeking out the more esoteric supplies Julie has requested. In front of the meat case, I pause. There are frozen, free-range turkeys from a nearby organic farm. But Julie's list includes no meat, by design; she wants our Thanksgiving dinner to be "cruelty-free." I glance over at Owen, who's drifted into the bulk-foods aisle and is watching a woman fill a bag with beans. I peer back into the meat case; reluctantly, I move on. In a different section I find the particular absurd product Julie's list prescribes — something called Texturized Vegetable Protein, which looks like canned dog food, molded into a vaguely turkey-shaped loaf. As I'm depositing the offensive thing into the cart, it hits me anew: Gus is gone.

He loved all holidays, but Thanksgiving was his favorite. He loved everything about it. He always invited a slew of people, whomever he could get to come; the more, the merrier was his motto. He had a tradition of going to his friend Roy Harrington's ranch down the Bitterroot and picking out one of Roy's prizewinning birds himself. Roy would catch it, Gus would carry it from the field to the chopping block, and Roy would always let Gus drop the ax. He took me with him every year, sometimes letting me stroke the bird's wattle before it met its end.

Later, at the table, still wearing the frilly apron of Bennie's he would always borrow to carve the bird, he would go around and have everyone say something they were thankful for. I always dreaded being put on the spot, but no one else seemed to mind. Bennie usually talked about God and nature and love. Stan would talk about Marirose and make a dirty joke about Gus's carving job, and Marirose would say something sweet and trite about friends being the family you choose. The neighbors, or the mailman, or the guy Gus met the other week in a bar, would talk about their children, or their health, or all the people who helped after a fire almost burned down their church. When it came around to Gus, he would inevitably weep — which inevitably mortified me — and I spent many of his speeches staring down at my plate.

It's so strange though, now, to think all of that's in the past. I look into my cart with dismay. I don't have Roy Harrington's number, and even if I did, chances are I wouldn't call, but still: standing here, staring down a loaf of whatever in God's name Julie's making me buy, I feel more than a little lost.

The line at the checkout is fifteen or twenty deep, and when Owen asks if he can go look at the fish case, I tell him sure, just don't wander off. To pass the time I take a magazine off the rack and start flipping through the pages, when I feel a light tap on my shoulder and turn around.

"I thought it was you," says Bennie, grinning. "You look like you've seen a ghost. Come here!" she says, and holds out her arms. I let her hug me, breathing in her familiar sweet scent. "It's so good to see you," she says, into my ear. She steps back but holds on to my wrist. "Gosh, it's been a while. You look good," she says, squeezing, then letting go.

"You look great," I say, and it's true; what a difference four months can make. Her coal-colored hair is getting long again, and it's loose today, falling almost to her shoulders and framing her face, which since the summer has found some of its former, full shape. Her dark eyes are bright and clear. Gone are the shadows under them, and the hollows beneath her cheekbones, and the drawn, sorrowful expression I grew accustomed to these last few years.

"Bullshit," she says, looking down.

"No, it's true. You've put on some weight."

"So have you," she says, swatting at my middle.

Instinctively, I suck in my gut. "I meant it as a compliment. You look wonderful. Really."

She smiles. "This is so funny. I was thinking about you just this morning, and now here you are," she says. "What do you think it means?"

I don't say anything.

"Not like ha-ha funny," she says. "You know what I mean." She tucks some hair behind her ear and asks how I've been.

"Pretty well," I say, looking over at the fish case, where Owen's peering through the glass at some crabs.

Bennie nods, and when I ask her the same, she says she's doing pretty well, too. She says she's been getting some shifts at an urgent-care clinic in Tobey and still making her jewelry, selling it on the Internet when she can. I ask about the cabin, and she says it's doing fine, some small repairs here and there, but what do you expect from a place that's almost a hundred years old? She repeats the offer she's made before, about us using it whenever we want, and I tell her we'd love to, but it's hard to get away. (Only the second half of this statement is true: Julie's said she doesn't feel right going there anymore, now that it belongs to Bennie.) When I ask her what brings her to town, though, her face changes.

"You don't know." She uses one hand to sweep her hair off her neck, a nervous habit she's always had, then lets it go. "Of course you don't. How would you?" Next to her there's a box of bananas from Mexico on special. She picks up a bunch, frowns, and puts it down. "I'm seeing someone. He lives here, in town. He works for the U."

"Oh," I say, swallowing hard and trying not to look shocked. I shouldn't be: Bennie's a gorgeous woman, and smart, and still young (just five years older than me, I remind myself). On the other hand, it has only been a few months.

She nods, sending the silver hoops in her ears swinging. "His name's Vincent. He's a fisheries biologist. Trout stream integrity is his focus. He writes books — kind of freshwater ecology and toxicology for the masses." She glances down at her cart, which I notice is very full, and smiles at me a little sadly. "He's a really good guy. You'd like him."

"I'm sure I would," I say. I look down. She's not wearing her wedding band anymore.

"Hey," she says, slipping her hand into her pocket. "I have an idea. We're doing Thanksgiving. That's why I'm here. He's got a son, Doug, and the twins — Alison and Katie — plus his parents, and a couple of his – our – friends. And I was thinking just now, why don't you come? The three of you. Unless you have other plans."

"We don't," I say quickly, and then, thinking of Julie, wish I hadn't. "I mean, thank you, but I don't think we can."

"Come on, why not?"

I can't think of a reason to give her.

"It's Thanksgiving. You're supposed to be *with* people. I can't bear the thought of the three of you, alone in that house, without, without – " She pauses, peering into my cart. "Without *turkey*. What in God's name is that?"

I can't help smiling. "Julie wants our Thanksgiving to be cruelty-free."

She smiles too. "Come on, what's a family holiday without cruelty?" She touches my arm again. "'The more, the merrier,' right? I mean it. I won't take no for an answer."

"I'll have to check with Julie," I say. I glance around for Owen. He's not in front of the fish case anymore, and I start looking around.

"Hey." Her smile fades. "Is this because of July? I mean, you know. The funeral. Afterwards?"

Now I feel my face flush deeply. "Of course not."

"It is, isn't it?" She narrows her eyes. "I was hoping you'd forgotten all that. I have."

I keep looking for Owen. I spot him in front of the lobster tank.

She takes my wrist. "Look at me. Please? It was a hard time, okay? None of us were at our best. We had a lot to drink that night. I don't blame you for what happened – if anything, I blame myself. I wasn't exactly a paramour of propriety and grace." I don't tell her she's used the wrong word. She tugs on my wrist. "Can't we just put that behind us and move on?"

For a moment I'm back in July, in the dark hallway at the Holiday Inn: the green-and-gold carpet, the smell of old smoke and the expensive Scotch we'd both been drinking, the feeling of Bennie's body pressed up against mine. "Forget what?" I say, because I know it's what she wants to hear.

Now, finally, she smiles. "Much better. Does this mean you'll come?"

"I guess it does," I say, against my better judgment.

"*Great*," she says. "You know what? I think we were fated to run into each other. I'm so glad I came here instead of Whole Foods."

"Me too," I say, but I'm thinking of Julie and wondering how I'm ever going to explain.

Owen appears then and pitches himself against my legs.

"Oh, my goodness," Bennie says, dropping my wrist. "Look at this strapping young man. Hi there, O."

"Look who it is," I say, palming the top of his head. "Can you say hi?"

He hides his face in my pants. I try prying him off, with little success.

"I think you've grown six inches since the summer. And gotten twice as handsome."

He shakes his head, burrowing his face into my crotch.

I try to push him away. "Owen. Please look at Bennie and say 'Thank you,' like a regular kid." He clings to me even tighter. "You're being rude," I tell him, but he won't budge. "You know better." I tell Bennie I'm sorry, and not to take it personally. "He's going through some kind of phase."

She looks down at him, then back up at me. Her face is somber. "Don't apologize," she says. "We're family. The regular rules don't apply."

15

ONE CAUSE JULIE doesn't feel passionate about, evidently, is our electric bill; it's barely dusk when we pull into the driveway but every light in the house is on.

I cut the ignition, turn around in my seat, and take hold of Owen's ankle. "I need a favor," I say. "Can you do one for me?"

He nods.

"You should ask what, before you agree."

"Okay. What?"

"Don't tell your mom we saw Bennie."

He frowns. "Why not?"

"Because."

"Because why?"

"I want to tell her myself."

"Why?"

"Because I do."

"Why?"

"*Owen,*" I say. "Enough. Can you do me the favor or not?"

He nods his head, and I tell him to go ahead in.

Inside, the smell of onions and garlic and something more exotic, maybe turmeric, fills the house. I find Julie in the kitchen, standing in front of the stove, stirring something in a pot. There's a glass of wine on the counter, the open bottle nearby. She's still in her work clothes, a black skirt and white top, but the shirt is untucked and she's kicked off her shoes.

I put down the grocery bags I'm carrying and come up behind her, kissing the back of her neck. She whirls around, a stunned expression on her face. "Jesus," she says, laying her hand on her chest. "You scared me."

I step back and ask her who she thought I would be, but she ignores the question, takes a drink of her wine, and goes back to stirring. "It's your dad's recipe for vindaloo," she says. "With lamb from the Gardiners' farm."

I can't remember the last time she was home this early, much less cooking, much *less* cooking actual food. A cookbook sits open on a stand and she's got music playing, Loretta Lynn, one of her favorites, and she checks the cookbook, then starts singing along: *"I'm proud to be a coal miner's daughter. I remember well the well where I drew water."* Like I said, she has a wonderful voice. She did spots for an ice-cream shop on her local radio station when she was a kid, and supposedly she brought the house down as Adelaide in *Guys and Dolls* her senior year in high school, but she gave it up after that.

"What's the occasion?" I ask, opening the refrigerator and helping myself to a beer.

"The occasion," she says, picking up a cutting board covered with something green and chopped, parsley or maybe cilantro, and scraping it into the pot with a knife, "is that I had a very good day. A great day, I might even call it."

"Cheers to that," I say, lifting my beer.

She nods, lifting the spoon to her lips. When she tastes the sauce, her eyes get big. "Oh, boy," she says. "I hope you're in the mood for hot."

It's so nice — and rare, these days — to see her in this kind of mood, I decide that telling her about seeing Bennie, and about Thanksgiving, can wait. I stow the groceries I bought while she puts on rice and calls into the living room for Owen to turn off the TV.

"Just give me a sec," he calls back.

"I can't imagine where he got that," I say, and she smiles a little sheepishly, scooping his macaroni and cheese into a bowl and carrying it to him on a tray. I turn the music off and switch on the news, which is all about Afghanistan. When she reappears, twenty minutes later, she's carrying him on her hip. First she motions for me to turn the TV off (she doesn't like him hearing about war), and then she tells me they're going up for a bath. I stand a moment in the sudden quiet, listening to her footsteps on the stairs.

I gather Owen's tray from the living room, get myself a second beer, and turn the kitchen TV back on. Now a group of journalists from other countries are sitting around a table with Charlie Rose, bashing the United States. I half listen, washing Owen's dishes and scooping Jerry's food into his bowl. Once he's eaten, I let him out back. He pokes around the now-defunct flower beds for a while, pees at the base of a rosebush, and comes inside.

Julie comes down half an hour later with her hair wet and combed straight back. She's in jeans and a T-shirt and her feet are bare. She looks great, and I tell her so. Bill's declaration from earlier echoes in my head. Before heading up to read to Owen, I kiss her on the neck.

"Mm," she says, leaning against me. "We started *The Velveteen Rabbit*. And don't forget to have him brush." She's paranoid about Owen getting cavities.

"I *did* brush, Mom," Owen shouts down from upstairs.

"Double-check," Julie says. "Make sure."

"Don't worry so much," I say, and I tell her, as I have many times before, that Pyle men are blessed with good, hard teeth.

The vindaloo *is* hot.

Julie and I sit in the dining room, which we haven't done since who knows when. She's set the table with Gus's mother's china and the good silverware, and she's even dimmed the lights and lit candles, the whole nine yards. I pour us each a glass of Cabernet Sauvignon and raise mine to my lips, which are already burning from the food. Julie's talking about the Eden auction, and how she finally convinced Tom Zilinkas to donate a week at his lake house to the cause.

"That's good," I say, and she looks incredulous.

"Good? It's spectacular. The place is unbelievable. Do you know how much a week there is worth?" I shake my head. "Me neither. I guess we'll find out," she says. Taking a drink, she starts describing the place. "It has eight bedrooms, a pool table, one of those chef's kitchens, a hot tub, a private dock with canoes and kayaks and this amazing speedboat, a vintage something-or-other, perfectly restored — it's *gorgeous*. I can't even imagine how much a place like that costs." While she talks, I eat, and while I eat, I think about Gus: it's so strange to be sitting in here without him — and Bennie. Come to think of it, I'm not sure we've ever eaten in here alone, just the two of us. Julie keeps talking. I glance up at Gus's portrait, which hangs over Julie's head. She's still talking animatedly, gesturing with her hands. I scoop some more stew onto my plate. "Are you even listening? What did I just say?"

"Tom Zilinkas took you to lunch at his golf club last week, and he wouldn't let you pay."

She takes another drink and says, "Sorry. I thought you were somewhere else." She takes her napkin out of her lap and sets it on the table. She's hardly touched her food. I point that out and ask her if she's feeling okay. She nods and drinks more. Her teeth are dark from the wine. "Lunch was kind of late," she says, and pushes her plate away.

Whoever cooks doesn't have to clean, that's the rule, so I start on the dishes while she sits down at the breakfast table, crossing her legs under her and drinking yet another glass of wine. She picks up *Time* magazine, and over the running water I ask her what's going on in the world. "Nothing good," she says, putting it down. I can tell from the way she's talking, slowly and with a different rhythm than usual, that she's had a lot to drink. "I want ice cream," she says, confirming my suspicion. "Ice cream and cigarettes. I'm going to the store." When she stands up, she teeters a little and reaches for one of the chairs.

I dry my hands off and go over to her. "You're going nowhere," I say.

She makes a pouting face. "On what grounds?"

"You're loaded, sweetheart," I tell her. When she sits down she almost misses the chair. I say, "I rest my case."

Next thing I know she's behind me. She takes the sponge out of my hand, leans against me, slips her hands inside my front pockets, and starts moving her fingers around. I turn and face her.

She tilts her face up to mine. "Are you done down here?"

Upstairs, I undress us, slipping her T-shirt over her head and her jeans down over her hips, then wriggling out of my own clothes as quickly as I can and kicking everything onto the floor. It's been too long, and we are greedy, both of us. We don't say much, but I'm enjoying myself and I'm pretty sure Julie is too. I whisper her name into her ear and she makes sweet indistinct noises, sighs and grunts, in reply. She finishes before I do, and afterwards she falls asleep instantaneously with her head on my chest.

But I can't sleep. I guess I'm feeling guilty, because every time I close my eyes, Bennie's face appears, and after half an hour or so I give up. I take my book off the nightstand and carry it down the hall to the sewing room, where I sleep when Julie and I fight, and though we haven't fought tonight, I turn on the lamp and sit down on the single bed. Bennie's old foot-pedal Singer still sits in the corner, next to her dressmaker's dummy, and her Shaker cabinet is still stocked with patterns and pincushions and every imaginable color of thread.

There's a row of pictures in frames on the windowsill — a selection of Gus's favorites, left over from when he was alive — and I put my book down and get up and go over to look. The first one is of Bennie at the cabin, painting. It's taken from behind (by Gus, surely) so that you see her back, then the painting of the cabin she's making, and the real cabin beyond that. Next there's one of her and Gus up there, together, standing in shallow water, holding hands. Gus is in waders and no shirt, and Bennie wears a billowy blouse and huge floppy hat and holds her skirt up so it won't get wet. The next is of Owen astride a Harley-Davidson at the state fair. The next is of Owen, too, as a baby, sitting in Julie's lap holding a picture book, pointing to something on the page. Beside that there's one of me as a teenager. I'm in my baseball uniform, looking awkward and unhappy, scowling at the camera with a mouthful of braces and a mop of brown hair.

The last one is of me and Julie, right after we got married, and I pick that one up, carry it back to the bed, and sit down. It was a gorgeous Indian-summer day in October, five years ago, and the two of us stand in front of City Hall under a maple, whose fallen leaves create a canary-colored carpet around our feet. Julie wears a suit of rough ivory silk that her sister sent her from New York, and in the bright sun it looks luminous, like spun gold. She couldn't close the jacket over her belly by then, but she didn't mind. Her smile is confident, almost defiant. She has one arm around me, and with the other she holds the bouquet of tiger lilies I bought her against her chest. I look closer. She doesn't know it, then, but the flowers have left pollen on her jacket, two saffron-colored streaks that won't come out no matter how hard she scrubs, or what she uses: detergent, baking soda, vinegar, bleach. I study her face. She looks so hopeful, so happy, so proud, my heart breaks a little for her — and maybe for me.

It's almost two by the time I turn out the lamp and head back down the hall, to our bedroom. When I open our door, I discover Owen has come in and usurped my place in the bed, and I start to cross the threshold to get in, too, but something stops me.

I don't know what. I stand there, seemingly paralyzed, looking down. Julie's on her side, one bare shoulder uncovered, and Owen's back is pressed against her front, her arm wrapped around him and her hand tucked under his chin, and he clasps the hand with both of his, as if in prayer. Outside it's begun to rain, hard, and raindrops slide down the windows, changing the light to liquid as it passes through the panes and collects on the bed, where the two of them lie curled together in such a way that it's hard to tell where mother ends and child begins. Is this hell or is it heaven? I have no idea. I reach for the doorjamb and hold on for support.

Something's not right inside of me. Something's gone missing;

some essential element of my humanity has been lost. Or maybe, just maybe, it wasn't there in the first place.

After what feels like a lifetime, standing there, I step into the hall, and at the far end, in the sewing room, I pull back the covers on the single bed, where I spend what's left of the night.

Part II

16

"WHAT IS THE matter with you?" Julie whispers into my ear. "How could you not tell me?"

It's Thanksgiving Day, and we're high in the South Hills, having just entered Bennie's new boyfriend's house. Our host, Vincent—a gaunt, bespectacled figure, fifty-five or perhaps even sixty years old—has just disappeared down a brown-carpeted hallway with our coats.

"I already said I was sorry," I whisper back. "But we're here, now. I'm not sure what else you want me to do."

"No, not that," she says. "I meant how could you not tell me that it's *him*. Vincent Vargas."

I tell her I don't know what she means.

"Bennie's boyfriend. Vincent Vargas? He's only like the most important eco-toxicologist in the state—maybe in the country. Maybe in the world."

"I didn't know," I say. "Is that bad?"

"Bad? I've only been trying to get a meeting with him for the past six months. Bad—what planet have you been on? It's fantastic."

"So you're glad we're here."

"No, I'm not glad. I'm totally unprepared. If I'd known, I would've read his most recent article in *Orion*, and I would have gotten some case summaries together, and I definitely would have brought my deposition notes."

"Jules, no. You would not have. It's a holiday. We're here as *guests*."

She doesn't seem to hear me. The look on her face is determined. She turns and looks at her reflection in an oval-shaped mirror decorated with what appear to be egrets that hangs on the wall, and fusses with the ruffled collar of her blouse. "I would've put on some eyeliner, at least."

"You look fine."

"Right," she says. With the white shirt, she's wearing a short plaid skirt, black stockings, and high heels.

"You look great. Doesn't she, O?"

Owen nods. He's standing very close to her and gripping my Louisville Slugger — the morning's bribe to get him dressed and out of the house — with both hands.

"Welcome, *Pyles*," Bennie says, appearing at the top of the stairs and throwing open her arms. She looks positively regal, in a maroon velvet dress with a low V at the neck, and a skirt so long she has to hold it up a few inches to come down the stairs.

She kisses Owen first, then Julie, and finally me. I hand over the two bottles of red wine we brought, and we follow her into the living room, a large open space with shag carpeting, a stone fireplace and chimney, and mirrors along one wall. A wide picture window overlooks the valley and town. Seated on a large, black leather sectional are ten or twelve people I don't know. Plates of cheese and crackers, vegetables, and shrimp decorate a glass coffee table in the middle, and everyone is holding a drink.

"Hey, everybody?" Bennie says, and they stop their conversations to look. "I'll just go around clockwise," she says after she introduces us, and she points and ticks off names and epithets — "June, Vince's niece," "Harold, Cathy's boyfriend," "Lydia, Joanna's mother-in-law" — while the individuals in question smile and nod or raise a hand. "And that's that. The quiz is before dessert," she says. "Please, make yourselves at home." She asks what we'd like to drink, and I start to answer but Julie jumps in.

"Where's Vincent?"

"Cooking. He has a top-secret Vargas-family turkey-basting technique — but don't ask. He might tell you, but then he'd have to kill you." She grins at Julie, whose face is stone.

"Excuse me," Julie says, moving toward the kitchen as if pulled by some unseen force, which I suppose in a way she is. I'm embarrassed, but Bennie doesn't seem to notice or pretends she doesn't. She turns to me and Owen and smiles. She's wearing dark, plum-colored lipstick that makes her mouth look particularly full.

We follow her to the wet bar at the far end of the room, where she pours a drink, hands it to me, and then squats down to Owen's level. "How about a soda?" she says.

"I can't have soda," he says. He's turned shy again. With one hand he grips my pants.

Bennie glances at me curiously but doesn't comment. "How about juice?"

He shakes his head. "Too much sugar."

"You're one tough customer," she says, and silently I agree. "There's a whole gaggle of kids just about your age downstairs," she tells him. "We've got a jungle gym and a pinball machine and Nintendo, and lots of yummy snacks. I could take you down and introduce you. How does that sound?"

He shakes his head, turning away from her and diving onto my leg, grabbing at my thigh so vigorously it actually hurts. I try to peel him off gently, to no avail, and he rearranges himself so he's standing entirely on one of my feet. "Easy, champ," I say. "What gives?" He won't look up. "Come on. You're among friends," I say, but he won't let go. Finally I concede and take him downstairs myself.

In the basement, a handful of kids are playing pinball or Twister, others are watching TV, and some others are outside on the grass, where there's a wooden climbing apparatus and a set of swings. "This doesn't look so terrible," I say. "What do you think?"

It takes a lot of coaxing, and I've almost finished my Scotch, but I manage to convince him to approach the youngest-looking group of kids, the ones playing outside. A boy with red hair who looks a little older approaches and asks Owen why he's carrying a bat. Owen looks up at me. So does the redhead. I say, "It's not just any bat. This is a very special bat. Lou Gehrig hit a home run with it against the St. Louis Cardinals in 1928. Do you know who Lou Gehrig is?"

The redhead shakes his head.

"Bud, want to tell him?" Now Owen shakes his head. I clear my throat. "Lou Gehrig was one of the greatest baseball players of all time, and a stellar human being at that. He started off as a poor kid whose immigrant parents could hardly afford to send him to school, but he went anyway, and he became this legend. He was one of the greatest baseball players of all time."

"You already said that," Owen says.

"It's worth a lot of money, this old piece of wood," I say, in conclusion.

"How much money?" the redhead asks.

"A lot," I say. (This isn't exactly true. When I had it appraised, I learned it would indeed be worth a few thousand, maybe more, if Gus hadn't had it inscribed. The presence of my name, the appraiser told me, effectively renders the thing worthless.)

"Cool," he says, and asks Owen his name. Again, Owen looks up at me, but this time I shake my head.

"Owen," he says. The kid glances at me for confirmation, and I nod yes. The boy says his name is Walter, and he invites Owen to come play on the swings. Owen accepts. He hands me the bat. Before I go I squat down and take hold of his collar. "Who's the champ?" I ask, and he says, "I am."

"You good?" I say, and he says he is. I hang around for a few more minutes anyway, watching to make sure.

When I am, I walk up the hill and around to the front, where I stow the bat in the truck. Back inside, I find Julie in the kitchen, leaning against the granite center island, a glass of white wine in her hand. She's all light chatter and wide smiles. "Babe," she says to me. "There you are. We were just talking about you. Actually, not you exactly, Gus. Were you aware that Vincent and your dad worked together?"

110

"I was not," I say.

"Vincent testified for him before the state legislature about the Leland-Kelly project in, what was it, 1985?"

"Please, it's Vince. Vincent's my dad," Vincent says. "And you're close, it was 1989."

"Is that how you and Bennie met? Through Gus?" I ask. Nobody answers.

"I'm so sorry, eighty-nine, of course. My brain is turning to mush," Julie says.

"I highly doubt that," he says, smiling at her. "In 1989, you were probably in diapers, anyway. Am I right?"

She blushes adorably and says, "Not quite."

He's got oven mitts on both hands, and he leans over, opens the oven door, and pulls out the bottom rack, on which sits an enormous, expertly trussed, half-browned bird.

"Gorgeous," Julie says. She turns to me and raises her glass. "Isn't this fun?" I say nothing. "I was just telling Vince about the wonderful Thanksgivings Gus used to have." She turns back to him. "He used to call them his 'roundups,' and he'd invite everyone he could find, especially people who didn't have family around, or who were going to be alone." She's firing on all cylinders now. Perhaps she doesn't realize she's talking about this man's new girlfriend's deceased husband? I try to catch her eye but she's oblivious. "One year he even had the guy who fixed the water heater over. It was so great. The guy turned out to be a complete riot. I mean, he actually was a part-time stand-up comedian. Remember, babe?"

"I remember," I say.

Vince asks Julie to pass him the baster.

"It looks delicious," Julie says. I've had about enough.

Now Vince looks at me. "I was sorry to hear about Gus," he says. "Everyone was."

"Well, not everyone," I say. They both look at me curiously. "I just mean he was a polarizing figure. He had as many enemies as he had friends, and they felt just as passionately about him."

111

There's a long, awkward silence. Vince fills the baster with liquid from the pan, which he squirts over the bird, and we all watch the golden juice trickle down.

"I've always loved Thanksgiving," Julie says. Now this is a blatant lie. But she's just getting started. She starts talking about the glorious Thanksgiving dinners her family used to have when she was a kid, in Maryland. She leaves out the part where her dad would drink a bottle of Old Crow and light the neighbors' boxwoods on fire — or whatever.

"Excuse me," I say finally. "I'm going to investigate the shrimp."

In the living room, I take a seat next to a woman whose name I've already forgotten and hover on the outskirts of a conversation she and some others are having about the reintroduction of wolves. She seems to object to it, on principle, but I don't listen closely to why. I want to talk to Bennie. But she's in constant motion, darting in and out of the room, bustling around, replenishing the hors d'oeuvres, re-filling drinks. I keep trying to catch her eye but I can't even manage that.

I sip and nod my way through a couple more stories about wolves, and then grizzly bears, but when the conversation turns to politics, I stand up. No one seems to notice me exiting. I pass the kitchen, where Julie is stirring a bowl of what looks like peas and nodding earnestly while Vincent talks. I hear the words *asbestos, tremolite,* and *Holliman,* and I continue on my way. At the end of the hall, I find a powder room with pink plaid curtains and matching toilet-paper cozy sitting on the tank. I dry my hands on a pink towel with a ruffle around the edge and wonder what's become of Vincent Vargas's wife.

Across the hall from the powder room, another door is halfway open, and beyond it I can see the unmistakable blue glow of TV. I push the door open the rest of the way and find myself in a den-type room. There is indeed a TV; it's large and showing football. All along one wall are fish tanks, with fish in them. In the center of the room, in a reclining chair, sits a young, thin man with greasy hair. He's wearing a dingy white undershirt and drinking beer from a can, and a cardboard box of Busch Light sits on the floor to the right of his chair. I clear my throat.

Without turning around, he says, "Speak, ye who enter."

"Hello," I say. "Sorry. I don't want to disturb you."

"Too late, you already have."

I pause where I am, unsure of whether he's serious or not. "I was hoping to find the game," I say. It's not true. I know next to nothing about football and care even less.

"Who's your team?" he says.

I look at the screen and say, "Green Bay," for no reason except I can't tell who else is playing.

"You are correct, sir," he says, and reaches into the box with his right hand. "You've earned yourself one barley-flavored libation." He stashes one can between his knees and hands a second to me. "I'm Doug," he says. "Resident black sheep of the Vargas herd."

"Nice to meet you," I say. I crack open my beer and take a sip. It's sour and not close to cold, but I drink it anyway. We watch the game. Wherever it is, it's freezing; the cheerleaders wear earmuffs, and the people in the stands are bundled to within an inch of their lives, standing and cheering while snow falls through the lights. When a commercial comes on, I ask Doug about the fish.

"I don't know anything about them," he says. "It's a philosophical choice."

"Interesting," I say, even though it isn't.

"All my life, I've played second fiddle to those slimy little fuckers," he continues.

"That's tough," I say. "What do you do?"

"Ah, an existentialist in our midst."

"No. I meant for work."

"I write computer script."

"That must be fascinating."

"If you're like ninety-nine percent of Americans, you don't even know what computer script is."

I don't answer him. The game comes back on. The field is turning

113

slowly white. "Winter," I say to change the subject. "What's that?"

"You ever play?" Doug asks. Finishing his beer, he tosses the can in the direction of the wastebasket and gets two fresh ones out of the box. I set mine on the floor. I'm still only halfway through the one in my hand.

"Football? No. I swam."

"I was a thespian. I played Mercutio once, in high school. You might say that was the zenith of my acting career. After the opening-night show, Vincent sat me down and told me I was wasting my time. Egomaniacal motherfucker couldn't stand watching me do well up there. Had to take me down a couple of notches. Told me acting was a fine hobby, but I needed to think about my career."

There's a long silence, which is fine with me. He watches the game, and I go over to check out the fish. I notice most of them are covered with black spots, lesions, or some kind of sores. "What's wrong with them?" I ask. My voice sounds loud and unmodulated in my ears, which generally means I'm getting drunk.

"They have no defense," he says. "Two of their starting linemen are injured. And special teams is a disgrace."

"No, the fish," I say. "Is he running some kind of experiment on them? I mean, your dad. They don't look too good."

Doug laughs. It's a bitter laugh. "Yeah, right — Vincent Vargas, the mad scientist in his lab." I wait. He takes another long drink, then says, "He rescues them. That's what he does. It's his passion. He finds the sickest fish, and then he brings them home and tries to save them." He snorts. "Same with women."

"Pardon?" I say, interested.

"Since Mother died, it's been one after another. I call it 'The Parade.' You've met the most recent?"

"Bennie?"

"It's hard to keep their names straight, they march through so fast."

"She seems nice enough," I say, warily.

"She's not," he says. "It's my understanding she's a pro at this."

"At what?"

"Her last husband was some old fart who croaked and left her everything — a pile of cash, and some fishing cabin grandfathered into the National Forest, the kind of pad guys like you and me couldn't afford if we worked for a hundred years. I told Dad, but of course he doesn't believe me."

I let this sink in. "Is it serious?" I ask after a few moments.

"Them? I give it a few weeks more, maybe a month." I'm ashamed at the burst of relief I feel, hearing him say this. "She'll see what a conceited dick he is and pack her things, or vice versa."

"She lives here?"

At that moment, one of the teenage girls pokes her head in the door. "Dinner," she says. "Dad said to let you know."

"Tell Dad thanks," he says. "Tell Dad he's a real swell guy."

She rolls her eyes, says, "Get a life, Doug," and then disappears.

The next couple of hours are a blur involving food, Wagner on the stereo, and a woman named Penny or Jenny who talks my ear off about her kids. One's autistic, and she can't stop telling me about amazing things he can do: name the members of British Parliament, speak Mandarin, count the grains of rice in a bowl. I drink more — wine, now — and become restless. When I can't stand another minute, I excuse myself, mumbling something about checking on Owen.

I do check on Owen. He's in the basement with the other kids, watching *The Empire Strikes Back*, the scene where Luke Skywalker and Darth Vader are doing battle on the bridge. He sits on a bean-bag chair by one wall, sucking his thumb. From the doorway I try to get his attention. When I do, I hold up my thumb and shake my head, but he ignores me. I watch a minute, while Darth Vader tries to convince Luke to come over to the dark side. Luke refuses. In the corner of my eye, a shape moves outside, crossing the yard. It's very dark but I can just make out a figure in a parka and long, sweeping skirt.

17

GUS MET BENNIE by chance. She was working at her grandfather's tourist-trap jewelry shop outside Ronan, and Gus was on his way home from visiting clients up north, when he stopped in to buy a present for his girlfriend at the time, a realtor named Louise. Bennie sold him a silver squash-blossom bracelet set with green and orange stones, which in the course of the sale she confessed she'd coveted for years but couldn't afford. He left, but he couldn't stop thinking about her. He broke it off with Louise, drove back to Ronan, and presented Bennie with the bracelet.

That was in August. I didn't hear about it until October, when he sat me down one Sunday morning to tell me he had met a magnificent woman, and that they were very much in love, and that she was moving in.

This was my senior year in high school. I'd just turned seventeen. The first time *I* met her was on a Friday evening soon after, when I got home from swim practice and saw Gus's car in the driveway. He'd been on the road for a few days, working with clients in the eastern part of the state. I let myself into the house and heard the shower running, so I went upstairs to welcome him home and ask what he wanted to do about dinner. I opened the bathroom door and saw her through the glass. She was naked – of course – and she had her eyes closed, rinsing shampoo from her hair. I'd never seen a naked woman before in real life, and the ones I'd seen elsewhere were utterly forgettable, compared to Bennie. She was magnificent indeed. Stunning. I couldn't move. "Bear? That you?" she said. When

I didn't answer, she opened her eyes. "Oh, my God," she said, trying in vain to cover her nakedness with her hands.

I found Gus downstairs. He was in an apron, cutting up an eggplant for his signature spaghetti sauce. He was in an excellent mood, listening to the World Series on the radio and humming while he worked.

"How old is she?" I asked.

He kept cutting. "I didn't hear you come in."

"How old? Tell me."

"You mean Benedicta, I take it."

"How could you do this? Why didn't you tell me she was my age?" I said. "It's disgusting. How could you?"

"She's not your age, kiddo. She's twenty-two," he said. "And I promise you, she's incredibly mature. She's had a hard life. Her father died in a car accident when she was twelve, and she raised her two younger brothers practically by herself. She had to grow up fast. You look flushed, kiddo. Are you feeling okay?"

"You can't be serious about this. What about Louise?"

"Louise is a great lady," he said, sliding the eggplant cubes into the pot. "But Bennie is my salvation."

Fully clothed (and only marginally less magnificent), his salvation joined us for dinner. I kept my eyes down the whole time, too mortified to look at her, and over Key lime pie, Gus announced they were engaged.

"Are you going to congratulate us or what, kiddo?" he said. He reached over and caught her hand. He'd bought her a gargantuan diamond ring at an estate sale in Billings, and she blushed when he held it up to display.

"You're officially embarrassing me, Augustus," she said, and leaned over to kiss him on the lips.

She moved in just a few days later, and all that winter nobody could stop talking about how transformed Gus seemed. "He's half the cranky bastard he used to be, a shadow of his former nasty self," Stan would joke, a statement I could neither confirm nor deny, since

I did everything in my power to avoid them both. I spent all my time with Bill, or swimming, or at school, or at the movie theater where I worked, or driving around the neighborhood after dark, waiting to go home until I saw their bedroom light go off. "Why are you so bent out of shape?" Bill would say. "She's hot. And besides, you're out of here in less than a year. Maybe you should count your blessings. Enjoy the show while you can."

But he had no idea. I couldn't even look at her without turning red. At night, when I closed my eyes, it was her face I saw: her almond skin, her full lips, her wide-set, bark-brown eyes. I hated her for making such an idiot of me. And I hated Gus even more. It didn't help that the whole town was in on it: the guys at school had a field day with the news.

That spring, when my college acceptance letter arrived from Massachusetts, I actually got down on my knees and thanked God for giving me a reprieve. Bennie may have been Gus's salvation, but for a few weeks at least, I believed I too had been saved.

I was wrong. The second week of June, Bill and I were landscaping and I slipped on a wet branch and cut my thigh open with a pruning saw. I came home late that night with a line of stitches stretching from my groin to my knee. The worse news was that for two full weeks, I wasn't supposed to leave the house.

That summer Gus was working a water-rights case on the Rocky Mountain Front, so it was just Bennie and me at home. The very first day of my convalescence, she knocked on my door. Without inviting her in, I asked what she wanted.

"I thought I would bring you some lunch."

"No, thank you," I said.

"Come on. I made chicken salad." I didn't answer. "Okay, I admit it, I already fixed you a tray." Nudging the door open with her foot, she came in and set the tray on my desk, then started to go but stopped. Leaning against the doorjamb, she said, "Did I do something wrong?" I said no. "Have I offended you in some way?" I said no again. She looked thoughtful. "Then why are you such a dick?"

I felt my face warming.

"It's okay," she said. "Realistically speaking, if I were you, I'd probably hate me too." She was wearing khaki shorts and a lacy white top, and she looked about as lovely as anything I'd ever seen.

I glared at her. "I don't hate you," I said.

"What? I couldn't hear you. Could you speak up?"

"I don't hate you," I said, louder.

"Good. Now that that's out of the way, would you mind if I kept you company?" She sat at my desk. "I'm starved." She started eating my sandwich. "And honestly, I'm kind of glad you got hurt. I've been lonely as hell."

The next day, she knocked again, and the day after that, and before I knew it she was spending most of the day with me, playing board games, watching bad TV, reading books out loud. She was wonderful company (Gus wasn't mistaken), and when her session of night classes ended that week, we started spending evenings together, too. I got so used to talking to her, I'd miss her the moment she wasn't there. One morning, she knocked on my door early, leaned into my room, and said, "Prison break?"

She knew of a spot in the Paradise Valley called the Boiling River, she told me while she drove, which was supposed to have the power to heal.

"Says who," I said.

She grinned. "My people." (She's seven-eighths Salish Indian and one-eighth French colonialist bastard, she likes to say.)

"For real?" I asked.

"Just wait."

She drove right up to the edge of the river, where previous visitors had cordoned off pools with rocks, took off her clothes, everything but her sky-blue underwear and simple, skin-colored bra, and started down the bank. I hobbled after her in my shorts. It had been a rainy spring, so the current was strong. The bottom was rocky and uneven, and the water was either scalding hot or freezing cold, depending on where you stood — either way, it hurt. A few yards in, she took hold of my arm. It was the first time she'd ever touched me, and I thought my heart might explode, right there. But it didn't. It kept beating. We waded in together, holding on.

When we were out in the middle, she said, "How do you *feel?*" shouting to be heard over the water and the wind.

If I were a more reckless person, or perhaps a braver one, maybe I would have told her. Maybe I would have said that I had never felt so good and so terrible in my entire life. Maybe I would have said that I had never wanted anything the way I wanted her. And maybe I would have said I hated her for that. Maybe I would've told her I wasn't sure I'd ever be able to forgive my father for bringing her into our house. Instead, I shouted, "It hurts. It hurts a *lot.*"

She grinned and squeezed my arm. "That means it's working. It means it's real."

Afterwards, we sat on the hood of her car, drying off. She pointed to the red scar on my thigh. "See? It's looking better already. Maybe you'll think twice next time, before you doubt ancient wisdom." She traced it with her index finger. Then, looking up at me, she drew her finger away.

We didn't say much, riding home. Gus was sitting on the stoop when we got there. He jumped up and threw open his arms. "Where the hell have you two been?" he said. He kissed Bennie and thumped me on the back. "Turn that frown upside down, kiddo. I have great news. They want to settle. The bastards know they don't have a case. Tonight, we drink Champagne."

And we did drink Champagne — or they did. After dinner Bennie got two glasses down from the cabinet in the dining room and Gus popped the cork. "To us three," he said, lifting his glass to make one of his all-time favorite toasts. "May we get everything we want in this life, and may we want everything we get."

18

THE SLIDING-GLASS DOORS open onto a small patio with a glass-top table and four chairs. I cross the patio and walk out onto the grass. It's turned into evening; the sky is a dark electric blue, perforated with stars, and the scent of wood smoke and something else, something sweeter, hangs in the air. I pass the swing set and the jungle gym, both of which look like they've seen better days.

Bennie stands on a low stone wall, facing the lake of white lights that is town. I say her name and she turns around, hiding the pipe she's holding behind her back.

"Hi," I say.

"It's you, thank goodness," she says, and takes down her hood. "I thought you were one of the kids. Hang on." Raising the pipe to her lips, she holds the flame of a lighter she's taken out of her pocket up to the bowl and inhales. She holds in the smoke for a few seconds, then exhales a plume of sweet-smelling white. "Want some?" she asks. I nod and join her on the wall.

I take the pipe, and she steps close to light it for me. I haven't done this in ages, and the smoke burns going down.

"Good?" she says.

"Very," I say. She smiles. We stand shoulder to shoulder, looking out. The yard abuts a golf course, I see; a few feet in front of us are a sand trap and a mottled, unkempt-looking green. In its center there's a hole, marked by a frayed yellow flag that flaps in the breeze.

"Happy Thanksgiving, right?" she says, nudging me with her arm.

"Happier now," I say.

She sits on the wall, so I do too. "I'm really glad you came," she says.

"I am too." We sit for a while, watching the lights. She takes another hit, holds in the smoke, and exhales.

"Want to know a secret?" she asks, handing me the pipe. "I didn't think you'd show. I really didn't. I bet Vince, actually, that you'd come up with an excuse." After some time, she draws up her legs and crosses them, but she can't seem to get comfortable. Eventually she lies down on her back with her head on the stones. A silver half-moon gleams in her ear. I know the pot's working, because I have to remind myself why I can't touch it.

"How is Julie?" she says, as if it's clear that's who we've been talking about.

Part of me wants to tell her the truth: that I hardly know, these days, how Julie is, and that with each one that passes, it seems more difficult to find out. That's the part of me that wants to touch her earring. A more appropriate part prevails. "Julie's okay," I say. "Busy, you know. How's Vince?"

"You know what?" she says. "He's good. He's really, really good." As she talks, an old, familiar ache blooms near my heart. "I'm actually *happy*, Logan. Can you believe that?" She giggles — a strange sound, coming from her. "I mean, I wouldn't have believed it, if you'd told me six months ago. Things were so miserable there, for a while. A long while. But I don't have to tell you that." She reaches for my hand. "You were right there with me in the valley of the shadow of death."

The ache has spread through my entire chest cavity. I feel hollowed out inside. I take my hand away. "It would be okay if you weren't happy yet, you know. It has only been a few months."

She sits up and faces me, her expression one of surprise. In the moonlight, her lips look very dark, her skin very white. "Why would you say that?"

"I didn't mean anything by it. I'm just making the point."

"What point?"

"That it's soon. It's fast."

"Pardon me?"

"He's been gone four months. That's fast."

"Your father was dying for four *years*, Logan, and as you may recall, I was there every day. Every single day — and night — for four years."

"I know that. Julie and I were there too — and Owen."

"Exactly. You had them and they had you."

"You had me, too," I say.

"It's not the same," she says. She won't look at me. "Please don't pretend it is."

I don't say anything. My head feels like its own entity, independent of my body. I squeeze my hands into fists, then release. I look up. The stars are sliding around in the sky.

After a few moments, she says, "Shit. I'm sorry. I think I'm a little fucked up. I don't know where all that came from. Jeez."

I don't know what's happening to me, either. Maybe it is the pot. I say, "If I tell you something, will you promise not to get mad?"

She nods. "Okay."

"You're going to get hurt."

"What?"

"He's not right for you. Vincent. I'm only telling you because I care."

"What are you talking about?"

"It's true."

"What is?"

"He doesn't love you."

"Says who?"

"Says his son."

She laughs, then, and covers her mouth with her hand. "Doug? I'm sorry, but Doug's a train wreck." Her smile fades fast, though. "What were you doing, talking about me with Doug?"

"You don't have to listen to me. You'd be in excellent company if you ignored every single thing I said." I stand up abruptly — too abruptly, I guess; the ground is uneven, and I stumble a couple of yards down the hill toward the green, struggling to stay upright. When I get my balance, I'm standing on the lip of the sand trap.

"I don't like you like this," she says, and stands up too. "I think we should go in."

When I speak, my tongue feels thick in my mouth. "I want to stay here," I say.

"Logan, it's cold. You don't look so good. Here," she says, extending a hand. "I want you to come inside."

And then, suddenly, there are tears in my eyes. "I don't care what you want. You got his money. You got the cabin," I say. "You even got his watch. Nobody gets everything they want, not even you, Bennie. So go inside. I don't care. I'm staying here."

"No, honey," she says, almost pleading. "You're not making any sense. He gave you the house and the land. And you have his watch."

"Don't bullshit me," I say. I feel dizzy again. "I know what I have — a house full of bad memories, and piece of land that I can't afford to keep and I can't bear to sell. Some gift, Gus. Some legacy. Thanks a hell of a lot."

She studies me a moment, then says, "I'm going to get you a cup of coffee."

"Fuck coffee," I say. "And fuck him. Fuck Gus and his gifts. And fuck you, too, Bennie. Doug was right, you're a gold digger. And a whore. You're a gold-digging whore, okay? So good night, Bennie. Sleep tight. And don't forget to give Vince a kiss." I can't stay up anymore so I sit down. I mean to sit on the grass but I miss and end up on my ass in the sand trap.

Bennie hugs herself, watching while I brush sand off my clothes. Without saying anything, she turns and starts up the hill.

"Wait, come back," I say. I lie down to make my head stop spinning. "Bennie, come back, please," I beg the stars.

Who knows how much later, she does come back, only she's not Bennie anymore, she's Julie, and she's mad as hell. "Logan? My God,

I've been looking for you everywhere. What are you doing on the ground?"

I sit up. She's standing by the swing set holding Owen, who appears to be asleep. The two of them make a single, odd-shaped silhouette against the glass doors.

"I asked you a question," she says.

I stand up slowly. "I was getting some air."

She looks around. "With whom?"

"Nobody."

She takes a couple of steps toward me, then stops. "You're stoned, aren't you? You've been out here all this time, with her, getting stoned. I should have guessed."

"Stoned?" I say. "Nobody says *stoned* anymore. You sound like someone's parent."

"I am someone's parent," she snaps. "And in case you've forgotten, so are you."

19

FRIDAY JULIE WORKS. Between sunup and sundown, she speaks to me exactly twice. The first time she calls, it's to say good morning to Owen. "Please put Owen on the phone," she says. The second time, she reminds me to pick up her dress from the dry cleaner. "It's the long black one," she says. "You know, with the beads."

We hang up and I go into the living room, where Owen's watching cartoons. "Take your thumb out of your mouth," I say. "And turn that off. You're going to melt your brain."

"But it's *Tom and Jerry*," he whines.

"I don't care. I said, turn it off." He doesn't move. My head pounds. "Owen."

"You're mean today," he says.

I march over to the sofa, snatch the remote off the arm, and turn it off myself.

Julie gets home late, long after I've put Owen to bed. I've heated up some frozen lasagna, and I ask her if she's hungry but she shakes her head. She pours herself a glass of red wine and carries it upstairs, where she spreads Tobey depositions out all over the bed.

I'm exhausted. Down the hall, in the sewing room, I undress and lie down. I'm sure I won't be able to sleep, but I close my eyes anyway and when I wake up it's morning. It's early, only six thirty according to the clock radio, but when I go to the window I see that Julie's car is already gone. Her note in front of the coffeemaker says, *Back before the auction. Please don't forget my dress.*

There's no swimming this morning, on account of the holiday

126

weekend, so I take Owen with me to the store, where I pitch an ultra-light, ultra-pricey tent next to my desk and set him up inside with a bag of organic, air-puffed something or other and a DVD. Then I get to work. First I file all the paid invoices, and then I start writing checks, recording each in our ledger book. I'm about to tally up the total, a terrifying prospect, when the phone rings.

"Kiddo," says Stan Mayfield. "It's Saturday — "

"I know, I know: What am I doing in the mines? Somebody has to run this place," I tell him. "And it's not looking like it's going to be Bill."

"That kid's a bad investment," he says. "I've been telling you that for years."

"Stan, I'm really busy," I say. I don't want to be talking to Stan about Bill. In fact, I don't want to be talking to Stan at all. I tell him I'm in the middle of something important, and that it's not a good time.

"Well, when is? This is important, too."

I listen for his TV in the background, but all I hear is quiet. "I don't know when. Not now."

"Kiddo."

"I told you, I need time to think."

"You were supposed to have thought," he says.

I rest my head in my hand. "Look, I just can't say yes. I know it's what you want, but I can't."

Owen chooses this moment to stand up in the tent. He points to his crotch and says, "I need to go potty."

I tell Stan to hang on and say, "Go ahead. You know where it is."

He shakes his head. "I want you to take me."

"I can't. You go."

"I want *you*," he says.

"I need to get off," I tell Stan.

"Listen," he says. "There's a cold front on its way. They're saying three feet of snow in Tobey by next week. Time is a fuse here, kiddo."

"I don't think you heard what I said," I say.

"Kiddo, you've got to stop thinking about yourself and think about Gus."

So I do. I close my eyes, and I conjure Gus up in my head. He's not in his grave this time; he's very much alive, standing on a windswept ridge high above the Bluebird-Rothman gold mine, the first one he designed. He took me there when I was seven or eight, and I remember standing in front of him, peering down into a pit so vast the giant earthmovers below looked like ants. I remember him holding me by the back of my pants. The gold was in tiny particles, he explained, mixed in with the dirt, and they used a special solution of chemicals to leach it out. "Your pop turns dirt into gold," he said. "How many kids do you know who can say that?"

"*Dad*," Owen says now.

I open my eyes. "This conversation's over," I tell Stan, and we hang up. "Okay, champ, I'm all yours," I say. But it's too late. He's smiling a weird, familiar smile I haven't seen in years. I look down. His blue jeans and sneakers are wet, and around his feet a small puddle is taking shape, beading up on the tent's water-resistant, formerly white floor.

The evidence — Owen's pants and shoes — has been destroyed, or at least washed, and is banging around in the dryer by the time Julie gets home. I meet her in the front hall, take her messenger bag, and lean down for a kiss. She presents me with her cheek. "Have you been drinking?" I ask, catching a faint whiff of alcohol on her breath.

"At the office," she says, going through the mail. "We had a toast."

"To what?"

She takes off her jacket and drops it on the stairs.

"Was Hart there?"

"Don't, okay?" She kicks off her clogs. "Who's the sitter?"

"Sam," I tell her. "She's in the kitchen, making Owen's food."

She drops the mail, mostly catalogs and solicitations, in the trash, which is technically an umbrella stand. "We can't be late," she says wearily. "I'm supposed to be hosting this thing." She starts unbuttoning her blouse as she heads up the stairs.

I'm dressed already, so I go into the kitchen to join Owen and the babysitter, Bill's daughter, Samantha. A sweet and formerly sweet-looking girl I've known since her birth, Sam has, over the past year, dyed her hair black, installed a silver spike in her right eyebrow, and had a multicolor, winged dragon-thing tattooed over the majority of her back. I know this last bit because despite the fact that it's November, she's wearing a tank top with tiny straps and standing in front of the stove with her back to me, stirring a pot of noodles, which causes the dragon-thing's spread wings to flap up and down. For a moment, I remember her as an infant. She was the first baby I ever held. I can still remember the wonder I felt, holding an entire human being, a whole *life*, in my hands. She's smart as a whip, anyway, and great with Owen, which is good; on looks alone, no way Julie would let this person within fifty feet of our son.

"What does your old man think of that?" I ask.

"Of what?"

"The graven image on your back," I say. "The tattoo."

"He thinks it's gross. But he thinks everything's gross on girls. He has like fifteen tattoos, but he didn't even want me to pierce my ears. He's a total hypocrite." She cuts the flame and carries the pot to the sink, where she dumps the pasta into a strainer and turns her face away from the sudden cloud of steam.

"I think it's cool," Owen pipes in. He's sitting at the table holding a crayon in each hand, one blue, one green. There's a pad of paper in front of him, on which Sam has drawn the letters of his name for him to color in.

"Why, thank you, Owen," she says. "That means a lot."

She puts the pasta back in the pot and pours in some sauce. I'm having trouble taking my eyes off her back. "Didn't you have to get his permission?" I say. "I mean, they wouldn't just go ahead and do — *that* — to a teenager without a parent's okay. Would they?"

She shrugs. "My mom came with me so it wasn't an issue." Sam's mother is Cassandra, whom Bill met in 1993, just a few months after he got back from Africa. She was a dancer at The Landing Strip, this beguiling waif figure with lots of black eye makeup, a cocaine habit, and a tenuous relationship with reality, and (not surprisingly) Bill fell head over heels. She was pregnant with Sam when Bill kicked her out for the last time, but he didn't even know Sam existed until he ran into the two of them at Walmart and he saw this miniature version of himself, minus the tattoos and hair, sitting in the stroller, and Cassandra confessed. "It was my sixteenth birthday present," Sam says. "My Grandma Bea gave me a check and said I could spend it however I want."

"I'm sure your Grandma Bea will be thrilled," I say, and she smiles over her shoulder.

"I'm almost five," Owen says. "I'll be five January fifteenth." He's quite the little chatterbox, tonight.

"Five is a very distinguished age," Sam says.

I can tell he's about to ask what *distinguished* means, but he changes his mind.

"Will you have a big birthday bash?" Sam asks.

Owen looks at me for guidance.

"Sure we will," I say. "You only turn five once, after all."

"Honey?" Julie's voice calls from upstairs.

"The Zilinkas twins' party is tomorrow," Owen tells Sam. "They're having a moon bounce and a magician and pony rides."

"Isn't Zilinkas the guy who wants to buy your land?"

I tell her she's confused. "What is it?" I call up to Julie.

Sam puts a plate down in front of Owen and goes back to the stove to make one for herself.

"*Logan,*" Julie shouts.

"I said, '*What,*'" I shout back. "If you'll excuse me," I say to Owen and Sam.

Upstairs, Julie is standing in a black bra, black underwear, and high-heeled shoes. "Wow," I say — less because she looks sexy, though she does, than because of how thin she looks. I can see her whole rib cage, and I fear her collarbones might come right through her skin.

"Where is it?" she asks. When I don't respond immediately, she says, "My dress. You did pick it up, right?" Again, I say nothing. "Oh, no," she says. "Don't tell me you forgot."

"I'm sorry, honey. The day got away from me. I'm really sorry. Can't you wear something else? That closet's full of dresses."

Her hands go to her head. "God, here I am killing myself, trying to keep us afloat, and I ask you to do one thing, one simple task, and you can't do it. Shit," she says, heading for her closet and throwing open the door. "Shit, shit." She takes a different dress out, looks it up and down, makes a face, and puts it back. She does the same with another, and another after that. "Shit," she says one more time, then looks up at me. "Are you just going to stand there and watch?"

Stung, and a little stunned, I start to leave. But then, in the doorway, I turn around. "I'm sorry about your dress, Jules. I am."

She's standing in front of the mirror, holding up a dark green dress with complicated straps. "Whatever. It's not the end of the world," she says, shoving the green dress back into the closet. She pulls out a black one. This one's velvet, and short, with a low neck, long sleeves, and a thin gold ruffle around the hem.

"No, I let you down," I say. I clear my throat. "Not just the dress. Thanksgiving. I shouldn't have accepted without talking to you. And I know I acted like a total shithead. I don't know what's the matter with me."

She doesn't look at me. "I do. You're sad. I get it. We're all sad. I just wish you'd let me help you — that you'd let us help each other — instead of pushing me away." She holds the dress up. "What do you think?" she asks, eyes on her reflection.

I go closer, so she can see me in the mirror. "I think you'd look great in all of them. You'd be the prettiest one there if you wore a burlap sack."

She doesn't smile. "That doesn't help me decide," she says. She takes the dress off the hanger, steps into it, and slips her arms into the sleeves, then reaches behind her back for the zipper. "Would you mind?"

I'm glad to be asked. I stand behind her, looking at the two of us in the mirror. The zipper is tiny, too delicate for my fingers, and I fumble some, getting it closed.

"Please be careful," she says.

When I finish, I put my hands on her shoulders, which feel like twin knobs in my hands. "Gorgeous," I say.

She won't look at me, though. She looks down at her wedding ring, the gold band with three blue stones Gus had made for my mother in 1973. Turning it around her finger, she says, "I thought it would be better by now." Her voice sounds unsteady.

"What would?"

"Everything. I thought we'd be happier. I really did."

"Honey?"

"I'm sorry," she says. "But I can't help it."

"Help what?" I say.

Still looking down, she says, "I loved him, you know I did, but part of me just wanted him to hurry up and die. I had that thought, sometimes."

"Because he was in pain?"

"Yes — because we all were." She looks up for a moment. "Sometimes, at night, you'd be with him, and Owen would be sleeping, and I would be lying there all alone, thinking about how it would be when it was over, when it was just us — me, you, and Owen — with nobody sick, nobody in the hospital, nobody dying. Because we never had that. We never got to be normal. I'm sure it sounds selfish, and ridiculously naive." When she looks up this time, her eyes are bright with tears.

"No. It isn't naive — or selfish. I'm really sorry, honey, I am," I say, and I mean it, even though I'm not sure, anymore, what I'm apologizing for. She sniffles and nods, and I squeeze her shoulders again.

"Things will get better. I promise. Hey. You look beautiful. You really do."

She looks up, sniffling, and touches one of my hands. "Thank you, babe," she says, and manages a smile. Her reflection's eyes meet mine, and for a second or two, I swear, we look exactly like ourselves.

20

EDEN'S AUDITORIUM IS decorated to look like Hawaii, with paper palm fronds lining the walls, pineapple centerpieces on the tables, and tiki bars doling out drinks with umbrellas in fake coconut-shell cups. Ukulele music spills from two big speakers flanking the podium, up on stage. At the door, perky parent-volunteers distribute grass skirts to the women, shirts printed with surfers and flowers to the men, and everyone gets a plastic lei.

"Put it on," Julie whispers into my ear, as we enter.

"Not a chance," I say.

"Please, just put it on?" she says again, and in the interest of peace and harmony, I slip the thing over my head. "Violet, Mary, Carol," she says, smiling and kissing the other auction-committee mothers on the cheek. I take our coats to get checked, and when I come back she's migrated in the direction of the bar. She's in a conversation with Donna Zilinkas, who's wearing an astonishingly short dress and a necklace involving more diamonds than I've seen in all my life, cumulatively, and what appears to be a matching tiara on her head. Julie speaks animatedly while Donna nods. Julie touches her chest, then her forehead, then her hair. Donna leans in and says something, and they both laugh.

"Hiya, Logan. You hanging ten?" asks a voice on my left. I turn around. It's Jennifer Huber-Green. Predictably, she's embraced the occasion with gusto. She's got a grass skirt over her dress, which involves a plunging neckline and more-than-ample cleavage. Next to her stands her husband, Mike, a skinny guy with long hair and a beard, who I know from experience wouldn't stop talking about bike racing if the auditorium caught on fire.

"Hey, Jennifer. Hey, Mike," I say.

"What table are you at?" I tell them twelve, and my heart falls when Jennifer says, "Hey, us too! Goody."

"Fantastic." I duck away, heading for the bar.

There's a line. While I wait, I half watch the slide show of items that are set to be auctioned off, which plays on a large screen above the stage. Prizes flash by: gift baskets, guided fishing trips, kids' parties, dog training, a Mexico vacation, massages, mountain bikes, iPods, rides in a hot-air balloon. When an immense stone house on a lake comes up, I figure it must be the Zilinkases', and I scan the auditorium for Julie, so she'll get to see the fruits of her labor on the big screen. I spot her up front by the podium, talking to a woman I don't recognize, and I try to catch her eye, but she doesn't look up. The line moves forward. Images of the Zilinkases' place appear, one after another. Julie wasn't kidding: room upon room, each decorated to the hilt according to different themes, all directly overlooking Flathead Lake. The place must be worth a few million dollars, at least: cathedral ceilings, antler chandeliers, a guest cottage twice the size of our house, two huge kitchens, a hot tub, a wide, sloping lawn, a tennis court, and of course a private dock, to which is moored the infamous speedboat Julie told me about. And she was right, it is something to behold — all mahogany, beautifully restored, with white leather upholstery and chrome trim, its bottom painted bright green. I couldn't even begin to guess how much a thing like that costs.

Luckily for me, I don't have to. Tom Zilinkas is standing beside me, suddenly, and he says, "That gorgeous girl set me back a quarter of a million bucks. And that was before I had her shipped across the pond."

I assume he means Flathead Lake. "You bought that in Bigfork?"

"No, Mr. Pyle, I did not. I was referring to the Atlantic Ocean. A Saudi prince owned her last. She's a 1959, twenty-six-foot, Carlo

Riva runabout. Only a couple like her in the world." He watches the slides. "This global warming business is terrific. We had her out all afternoon, Thanksgiving Day. If the weather holds, we'll be out there Christmas, too."

I say, "You must know a lot about boats."

He nods again and takes a sip of his beer, admiring the boat's image on the screen. He's wearing a tuxedo, the only guy here who is, and on his feet are shiny black cowboy boots with silver-tipped, pointed toes. He's taller than me, and clean-shaven, with beady black eyes and a head of thinning blond hair, underneath which his scalp is so shiny and robust-looking, I imagine him massaging it with oil. The slide changes to one of a sunset over the lake and the Swan Mountains taken, presumably, from his dock. He turns to me. "Do you?"

"Only the ones I sell," I say, and step up in line.

"Right. Canoes and such. At your camping shop," he says, and follows. He seems to have joined me, which means he's cut in front of perhaps ten or twelve people. I don't look back.

"Right. It's called The Gold Mine. We sell whitewater kayaks and some inflatables, and a couple models of canoes. Plus all kinds of outdoor gear."

"A little bird tells me you haven't been selling much of anything, these days." He knocks my elbow. I move up in line. We're almost at the bar, thank goodness.

He finishes his beer and deposits the bottle on a table nearby. Nodding at the screen, he says, "Whoever said money can't buy happiness obviously didn't have enough. Am I wrong?"

The question appears to be rhetorical, because before I answer he steps in front of me and orders vodka on the rocks, then rejects it because there's too much ice in the glass. He gets a new one and, curiously, waits while I order a beer for myself and a pink coconut concoction for Julie, wherever she is. Drinks in hand, I turn to Tom. "I better go deliver this," I say. "Have a nice night."

But he blocks my way. "So how long are you and your partner going to tease my cock?"

"Excuse me?" I say.

The smug smile is gone. "You strike me as a reasonable man, so how about you listen to this story — you listen, and you tell me if this story sounds reasonable. My investment group puts seven figures on the table, seven *figures*, for a patch of land that's hardly even being used, and the fellows who own this patch sit on my offer for almost four weeks. How does that sound, Mr. Pyle? Does that sound reasonable to you?"

It takes me a few seconds to get my head around what's being said. Apparently Sam wasn't confused. "I didn't know the offer was yours," I say. "I didn't know you had anything to do with this." More urgently, I look around for Julie. Why does it feel like I spend half my time these days wondering where she is?

"I thought talking to you might help move things along. Call me old-fashioned, but I like to do business face-to-face."

At the front of the room, I spot her. She's up at the podium, talking to a big man in a suit and bolo tie whom I presume to be the caller. I turn to face Zilinkas. That he's behind the offer only makes me more sure I meant what I said to Bill. "I'm afraid there's been a lapse in communication. The land isn't for sale. If you'll excuse me, I'd like to deliver this to my wife."

My heart thumps as I make my way through the maze of tables and palm trees and parents to the front of the room, toward the podium, where Julie is — or was; by the time I get there, she's disappeared, and who's standing by the podium, in her spot, but Miss Pietryzyck. She's holding a clipboard and a pen, checking things off a list. She looks uncomfortable and out of place, in a summery yellow dress and scuffed shoes with thick heels.

Holding the two drinks, I approach and say hello.

"Peet-rick," she says. "Two syllables."

I apologize. "You must be getting pretty tired of that."

She smiles briefly, feigning politeness, then goes back to her list.

"My wife says I have some kind of mental block when it comes to names," I tell her. "How about a peace offering?" I hold out Julie's drink.

"I don't really drink," she says. "Especially not at this kind of thing."

"You mean stuffy, lame events with a bunch of boring old people?"

"No," she says unsmilingly. "Work functions I'm required to go to and pretend I'm having a good time."

"I see," I say. I stand next to her for a few awkward minutes, scanning the room for Julie, who's nowhere, and finally I say, "I'm really sorry about the other day, at the pool. I'm afraid I took some of my frustrations – or, concerns – out on you."

"Thank you. I appreciate that," she says. I see her face relax a little. She smiles, and I smile back.

"Are you sure you won't have this? It's going to go to waste."

"Maybe just a sip." I hand it over. Her smile fades. "He's a really sweet kid, Owen," she says seriously.

"I'll drink to that."

She puts the green straw between her lips and takes a tiny taste. "I'll be sorry to lose him, but I think you're making the right choice."

"What do you mean?" I say.

"I was worried you were going to be one of those parents who punishes their child for being different. Who holds them to some preordained standard that even they can't explain. The new arrangement may take some adjustment, but I truly believe he'll be better off."

A pit opens up in my stomach. "What new arrangement?"

Her eyes get very big. "Oh, dear," she says, setting the drink down on the stage. I set mine down too. She doesn't say anything. Red splotches appear on her neck and threaten her face.

"Is it a done deal? I mean, with Owen. Is it decided?"

She nods unhappily. "I'm so sorry. I assumed you knew. I assumed – "

"It's not your fault." I scan the room for Julie. She starts to apologize again but I cut her off. "Please. You've said enough," I say.

I cross the room, heading for our table, where I'm hoping Julie will be, but when I get there the Huber-Greens are the only ones sitting down, so I keep walking, pretending I don't see Jennifer waving at me, pointing to the seat on her right. Stopping by a surfboard display, I look around the auditorium again but I don't see Julie anywhere, and I'm about to give up when all the way on the other side of the room, at the tiki bar, I spot her. The bartender is handing her a glass of wine.

She leaves the bar, heading in the opposite direction from table twelve, stops under the Exit sign over the double doors that lead to the courtyard, and looks around once before opening one a few inches and ducking out. I follow.

Outside, I find her in the courtyard, standing under some lights by the heated koi pond with a man. The man is Tom Zilinkas. He's smoking a cigarette and so is she. A cloud of smoke hangs cozily over their heads.

"Hi, honey," says Julie. "Having fun?" It's cold out. She's got one arm crossed over her body.

"Not as much as you," I say.

"I'd second that," says Tom Zilinkas, winking.

"I spotted Tom smoking, earlier, and I pounced," she says. "Poor Tom." She brings the cigarette to her lips and inhales. "You two know each other, right?"

"Oh, yeah," Tom says. "We go way back." He grins and flicks some ashes into the pond. The fish go crazy; in two seconds, the flat black surface turns into a writhing gold-and-orange swarm.

"They think it's food," I point out.

"Stupid fish," Tom says.

"I need to talk to you, Jules," I say. "It's important."

"Jules," Tom repeats. "I like that. What kind of jewel are you, Jules? A sapphire? An emerald? A diamond in the rough?"

I glare at him, but she smiles, blowing out a thick stream of smoke. "An aquamarine, I think."

"Julie," I say, "this is important." I turn to Tom. "Do you mind?"

He looks at Julie. "Thanks for the cigarette," she says, and gestures toward the auditorium, "and for all your support. You guys have been amazingly generous."

"The pleasure is all mine," he says, and takes her hand. "Until tomorrow, then."

"We're looking forward to it," she says.

He kisses Julie's hand and winks at me – again. "And remember, no gifts," he says. "That's the only rule." He flicks his cigarette butt into the fishpond and goes inside.

Julie watches until he's gone, and then she turns to me. "What's so urgent?" She's shivering now. I offer her my jacket, but she shakes her head.

"I spoke with Miss Pietryzyck," I say.

"Peet-rick," she says, glancing at the glass doors. "They're starting the auction. I have to go in." She's hugging herself against the cold, moving her weight from one high-heeled shoe to the other.

"She told me about Owen."

She stands still now and looks at me. "It's true. I had coffee with her and Francine this morning, and we all agreed."

"Who's Francine? And what about me? What about what I think?"

"Erica made a really strong case for the switch. We can always undo it, if it doesn't work out. And this isn't about you, it's about Owen – what's best for him."

"Who's Erica? And it is about me. I'm his father. You and I are supposed to be a team. We're not supposed to go behind each other's backs. We're supposed to make decisions together."

"Is that so?" She looks at me, hard.

I say, "Yes, it is."

"So you can probably imagine how I felt when Tom said he'd made an offer on the land."

"You know?"

"Yes," she says. Her voice is nearly as chilly as the air. Glancing once more at the doors, she says, "I have to go in."

"Wait. We need to talk about this," I say.

"Okay, talk," she says. I have no idea what to say. She looks at me for another long moment, and then she goes inside.

I follow. We're just sitting down at the table when she stands back up. I ask where she's going. "I see Erica," she says. "I want to make sure she's okay."

"Erica? Who's *Erica?*"

"Miss Pietryzyck. Erica. That's her name."

Erica, I think, watching Julie go. It's so simple: Erica. Why haven't I ever thought of calling her that?

We ride home in silence. When we get there, Julie goes straight upstairs to check on Owen and doesn't come back down. I find Sam in the living room, under Gus's old Pendleton blanket, watching *Law and Order* on TV. I sit at the opposite end of the sofa from her, on the arm, and watch too. The redheaded D.A. is questioning a guy in a jail cell. The guy tries to lunge at her but he can't, he's shackled to his chair, so he makes a lewd gesture with his tongue instead.

"He's a pedophile," Sam explains. "He molested like seventeen kids."

"Lovely," I say. "How'd you two do?"

"Good," she says. Eyes on the screen, she says, "He really wanted to sleep in your bed. He said Julie lets him, and that you wouldn't be mad. I hope it's okay." At the commercial, she stretches her arms over her head, yawns, and says, "Did you have fun?"

"No," I say. "Actually, no fun was had by me, whatsoever."

"That blows," she says.

"Well put." I fish my wallet out of my pants, count out a hundred and fifty dollars, and hand it to her.

"That's way too much. Here," she says, and tries to hand it back, but I refuse.

"Happy Birthday," I say. "Just don't tell your old man. And don't use it to get anything else pierced, or tattooed. Nothing that won't come off with soap and water. Deal?"

She looks at the money, then up at me. "Sure, I guess. Thanks."

I walk her to the door and watch her get in her car, watch until her taillights disappear around the corner, onto Third.

In the living room the TV is still on. I go back in and watch the rest of the show. After that, I watch one where college kids sit around drinking and saying inane things, and after that I go upstairs.

In our bedroom the blinds are down. It's very dark. As my eyes adjust, I make out the shape of Julie wrapped around Owen, their chests rising and falling in rhythm. I'm tired. I stand there only a minute or two before stepping into the hall and closing the door.

21

"Tell me once more now, who thinks it's acceptable to throw a birthday party on a Sunday, before noon?"

We're in the kitchen. Owen's eating the eggs I made him and I'm fixing Julie's tea. Pen in hand, she's poring over some documents she says she has to get through before we can leave.

"What exactly do you have against Tom, anyway?" she says, without looking up. It's the first time she's spoken to me since last night, at the school.

"He's arrogant, for starters," I say. "Give a guy like that a few dollars, and he thinks he owns the world. He thinks everyone else is just waiting to do his bidding." The kettle has begun whistling. I take it off the stove and pour boiling water into her waiting mug, this one bearing a photo of Owen dressed as a lion on his first Halloween. I drop in a tea bag, Earl Grey, and leave it on the counter to steep.

She looks up at me. "Maybe he's willing to compromise — donate a piece of the land to a trust, something like that. Have you even talked with him? He's not a bad person. And money is money, last time I checked. Gus would say you're cutting off your nose to spite your face."

"This is why I didn't tell you in the first place — because I knew what you'd say. And for the record, Gus would tell that baboon exactly where he could stick his offer. You know he would. And you're right, he's not bad — he's awful. What kind of prick spends half a million dollars on a boat?"

Owen looks up.

"Language," Julie says.

"Or woos his wife by buying her new breasts? And what kind of ass-wipe wears a tuxedo to an auction at an elementary school?"

"Okay," Julie says. "That's enough." She picks up her pen again and goes back to her work.

"He's not getting one inch of that land. He's not getting anything of mine, ever."

"My tea," she says, without looking up.

"What about it?"

"Could you take out the bag? If you leave it in too long, it gets bitter."

A couple of hours later, we arrive at the Zilinkas home. It's on University Avenue, a stone's throw from campus, on the most expensive block in town, just a few doors down from the house Owen and I admired last weekend.

Julie says, "Wow."

"Wow," Owen says, too.

On the curb a man in a black uniform stands waiting. He opens Julie's door, then mine, calls me "sir," and offers to park the car. I say, "No, thank you," closing my door and waiting for Julie to close hers, which she does, and I park us in an empty space a few blocks up.

We walk back toward the house with Owen between us, holding our hands.

"Supposedly this place was built way back in 1893," Julie is telling him. She looks particularly pretty today — especially for a kids' birthday party — in an old-fashioned-looking dress printed with apples, a cardigan, and her black motorcycle boots. "For the university's first president. There used to be a tunnel under the river that went from the billiards room to the basement of the Hilda Hotel."

"What for?" Owen asks, swinging our arms.

"So his friends could visit," she says.

"Special lady friends," I say.

She gives me a look. "But during Prohibition, the FBI found out about it and they had it sealed up. Isn't that romantic?"

"What's Prohibition?" Owen asks.

"How do you know all this?" I ask. We're right in front, now. I eye the uncannily green lawn with suspicion. "Jules?" I turn around to look at her. She's bent over, checking her hair in the passenger-side mirror of somebody's car. "Is it even true?"

"Does it matter? It's a great story." Straightening up, she smoothes down her skirt. "*Okay*," she says. Owen lets go of my hand, and the three of us head up the walk.

A person in black pants and a white collared shirt answers the door. This person takes our jackets and Julie's purse, informs us that the guests are in the backyard, climbs the round staircase, and disappears, leaving the three of us in the ridiculously grand, marble-floored front hall.

"Shit," Julie says.

I follow her gaze to the corner, to a table underneath an elaborate crystal chandelier. It's covered with gifts. There must be fifty or sixty of them there, boxes of all sizes and shapes wrapped in all manner of ribbons and bows.

"He said no gifts. Didn't you hear him?"

I say, "I heard him. He did."

"This is not good," Julie says, frowning. "How about if you stay here, and I run into town and get something? Two somethings. Okay?"

"No. Nobody's running anywhere. The guy said no gifts. In plain English."

She looks half frantic. "Then what do you call those?"

"Bribes," says a man's voice. We turn around and see Tom standing in the doorway, holding a voluminous glass of red wine in his hand. He's wearing a pressed pink oxford, new-looking jeans, a belt with a shiny buckle, and a different pair of pointy-toed boots. "People kissing our asses, that's all. These boys need more toys like they need a hole in the head. Come on, ladies and gentlemen. The circus is out back." Behind him is a large, open kitchen, around which maybe a dozen black-and-white-clad people bustle. "Cecelia," he says over his shoulder. A middle-aged woman in a maid's uniform appears. He puts a hand on her back. "Please go upstairs and ask Mrs. Zilinkas when she'll be gracing us with her presence." He smiles at us and winks. Cecelia disappears.

He leads us through the busy kitchen and a gargantuan dining room, with all kinds of food laid out on a vast table, and outside, onto a large, half-moon-shaped patio, where adults stand in groups, talking and holding drinks. Plunging his hand into a huge aluminum tub, he produces a beer, pops off the cap, and hands it to me, dripping. He turns to Julie. "You prefer vino, yes? How about some rosé?"

"It's a little early for me, but thank you anyway," she says.

From a passing tray he snatches a glass of Champagne with raspberries floating in it and holds that out to her. "Hair of the dog, my darling. Trust me on that," he says. Blushing to match the berries, she accepts. He makes a little bow and excuses himself.

"See, he's charming. You can't say he's not," she says once he's gone.

"I can't?" I say, and turn to face the yard.

Charming or not, he wasn't kidding when he said "circus." On the lawn (which is enormous and slopes gently toward a distant row of hemlocks) there is, quite literally, a circus under way. There's a moon bounce shaped like a big-top tent, and three red rings have been set up on the grass. In one, kids are being led around on horseback. In the second, clowns juggle, ride unicycles, and knock each other down. In the third, acrobats in bright-colored suits climb on a jungle-gym apparatus, dangling from one another's wrists and contorting themselves into implausible shapes. There's a face-painting station, a balloon man, a cotton-candy truck, and a man leading what appears to be an actual black bear around on a leash.

Owen is holding on to my pants. "What do you think, baby?" Julie asks him.

"I think it's shameful. These kids are what, seven?" I whisper in response, but she doesn't hear or pretends not to. I palm the top of Owen's head.

Julie's phone begins to ring. She looks at it and frowns. "It's Stan. I have to take this." Looking at Owen, she says, "Maybe your father will take you for a pony ride."

He shakes his head.

"Cotton candy?"

He shakes his head again, and reluctantly she pockets the phone. "I know. How about we get our faces painted?"

He lets go of my pants, then, and follows her over to the face-painting booth. I take a seat at one of the tables and watch from afar as a woman dressed like a little girl slathers Owen's face with white.

When they return, he has a pink nose and whiskers, like a cat. "What kind of cat are you?" I ask.

"I'm not a cat. I'm a mouse," he says, and Julie smiles at him and smoothes back his hair. She's got a red heart on her cheek and a fresh glass of Champagne in her hand. She glances down at her watch. "I have to call Stan back," she says. Owen looks distressed anew. She squeezes his shoulder. "I'll just be two minutes, baby, I swear." Taking out her phone, she heads back into the house.

Owen looks at me and announces he wants to go on the moon bounce.

I look over at it. From where we are, I can see some of the boys and girls from Owen's class bouncing behind a clear plastic wall. "I don't know. Those look like pretty big kids in there," I tell him.

He frowns. "I'm a big kid," he says.

"That's what I keep telling everyone. Why don't you get in there and kick some butt?"

He takes my hand and we step onto the grass. We don't make it fifteen feet, though, before a woman dressed in a Gypsy costume stops us in our tracks. She puts down a painted stool she's carrying. "Sit, please, friends. The Mysterious Madame Olga will now read your palm," she says, in an absurd, Dracula-like accent.

I look down at Owen, who's lingering behind my legs. I reach back and grab at his hand, so he's in front of me, and squat down. "Come on," I tell him. "I thought you said you were a big kid."

"I did," he says unhappily.

"Then let the lady read your palm. It's fun."

"I want to go on the moon bounce," he says.

"Okay," I say. "Then go ahead."

And amazingly, he does; he puts his hands in the pockets of his pants and walks away from me. Just like that. Pride fills me. He doesn't even look back before he climbs the red-and-white-striped steps and tumbles in.

"That's my son," I tell Madame Olga.

"I figured," she says.

I go back up to the patio to get my beer and find Julie, and my beer's there, where I left it, but Julie hasn't come back. Of course she hasn't. Tom Zilinkas emerges from the house carrying a tray of raw meat, and I consider asking him if he's seen her but decide not to, and instead I pull a chair off to the side and sit. It's another beautiful day; the sun warms my shoulders and my hands and the top of my head, and I have a good view of the moon bounce, where every now and then I glimpse Owen's striped shirt, airborne, through the plastic wall. A pretty, extremely pregnant mother approaches, holds out her camera, and asks if I can take a photo of her and her son. I say yes, and I'm holding the camera, instructing them to say "Cheese" when I hear someone calling my name — or rather, screaming my name.

Scanning the crowd, I spot Jennifer Huber-Green standing by the moon bounce, shouting and waving her arms, a look of panic contorting her face. Without thinking I'm in motion, sprinting across the lawn to where she stands.

"It's Owen, he's fighting," she says breathlessly, pushing me toward the moon bounce. I leap up the inflated stairs, push through the plastic curtains, and step inside, where I see a handful of terrified-looking kids pressed up against the four walls. In the middle of the floor, two boys I recognize as the Zilinkas twins are holding Owen down. Or rather, one tries to hold him down while the other slaps at him with his palm. "Stop that, now," I shout, making my way across the undulating floor. The twins look up, and Owen takes the opportunity to roll over and kick one of them, hard, in the groin. The kid crumples. "Stop, Christ, *stop*," I shout, but as I watch, Owen takes the second twin's wrist in his mouth and bites down. The twin screams. "That's *enough*," I say. I grab Owen by the pants, pick him up, and football-carry him toward the door.

On the way out we almost knock down Donna Zilinkas, who's rushing in. She doesn't acknowledge me, and I watch her stumble across the red and white tubes, toward her boys. She's wearing very high heels, and one of them punctures the floor. A loud whistling noise ensues, over which I hear her shout, "What did you two do? What did you *do?*"

Clutching Owen to me, I hurry up the hill and into the house, into the kitchen, which is empty except for staff. I sit him on the counter and ask where it hurts. He says it doesn't, but I inspect him anyway, while a cadre of black-and-white-clad caterers pretend not to watch. Incredibly, he seems okay. In fact there's no damage I can detect at all, except for some red marks on his arm, where he got smacked. "Want to tell me what in Christ's good name happened out there?" I say, lifting him onto the floor.

He looks down. "I hate them."

"And?"

"They hit me. You saw." His eyes gleam; I can tell he's trying very hard not to cry.

"Those little fuckers," I say. "It's okay. You don't have to say anything else." I check him for injuries once more but find none. I put my hand on his shoulder. "Hey, kiddo, you sure held your own out there." Checking to make sure we're alone, I put two fingers under his chin and make him look me in the eye. "I'm not kidding. You did great. I'm proud as hell of you." He smiles through his tears. "Don't tell your mom I said that, okay?"

He nods. He looks a fright. Thinking of Julie's alarm when she sees him, I try to smooth down his hair. Then I tell him to hang on, and I get a dishtowel, wet it at the sink, and try unsuccessfully to wash the smeared paint off his face.

"You'll need real, old-fashioned cold cream for that," says a voice behind me. "It's nasty stuff." I turn and look. It's one of the caterers. He shrugs. "I'm an actor, by trade."

I toss the towel on the counter. To Owen I say, "What do you say we find Mom and blow this pop-stand?" I take his hand and we move quickly through the rooms, looking for Julie. We don't find her downstairs, so we follow the spiral staircase to the top, where hallways lead right and left. We try left first and make our way down the hall, saying her name but getting no response. I open a couple of doors and look inside: the boys' rooms, apparently, one blue, the other green. They have matching queen-size beds, computer terminals, and flat-screen TVs. I pull their doors closed. There's a guest room and an office, but Julie's nowhere to be found.

We backtrack and head down another hall, at the very end of which is a closed door. Through the door I can hear Julie's voice. She's laughing.

I open the door, and we find ourselves in another, shorter, hallway.

"You're so bad," I hear Julie say. Her voice sounds bizarre. I can't imagine she's talking to Stan Mayfield, or anyone at Mayfield and Pyle, that way.

But I don't have to imagine. "And you're so beautiful," says a second voice: a man's.

My skin prickles. I let go of Owen's hand and tell him not to move a muscle. "I mean it, *stay*," I whisper, and he nods. I proceed down the corridor, to the end, and I find myself standing in one of the grandest bedrooms I've ever seen. There's a cathedral ceiling, two enormous windows, and a Jacuzzi in front of a fireplace. But the feature that attracts my attention is the bed.

Or rather, my wife, on the bed. Julie. And she's not alone. She's with Tom Zilinkas, and they're lying down, facing each other. Each is propped up on one elbow, and one of Julie's feet is up, so her shin and knee and the better part of one thigh are exposed. Their heads are close together. Julie's dress is open at the neck, and Tom Zilinkas has his hand on her breast.

"What the hell?" I say. I take a step toward the bed. "Get your hands off her, you fucking prick."

"Oh, my God," Julie says. She sits up. She starts tugging at her dress, trying to cover up. "This isn't what it looks like, Logan. Nothing happened, I swear."

"It doesn't look like nothing happened," I say.

"No. Yes. It was nothing. Please, listen. You have to believe me." She's trying to button her dress. Her hands shake. "Please. I can explain if you give me a chance. Please."

"We're leaving," I say.

"I was making a phone call. I had too much Champagne," she says, fumbling with the buttons. "I hadn't eaten. I got lightheaded. Tom said I could lie down."

"We're leaving. *Now*," I say.

"Amigo," he says. "Take it easy. She's telling the truth. Nothing happened."

I say, "Go fuck yourself, Tom."

"Honey," Julie says.

"You can fuck yourself, too," I say. "I've had it." I start to go.

"*Wait*," she says. "I'm coming with you. Just *wait*." She's still struggling to do up her dress. Her fingers search frantically for the buttons, which I notice, for the first time, are red and shaped like tiny pieces of fruit: apples. "You can't just leave me here. Wait, please," she sobs.

I turn away from the bed and find Owen, standing behind me. His eyes are wide. I pick him up roughly under the arms and hug him to me, jogging back down the hall, down the stairs, and out of the house. All the way home, I see Julie's buttons. *Apple-shaped buttons*, I keep thinking, throwing clothes for me and Owen into a duffel. I add our toothbrushes, and a razor for me. *Apple-shaped buttons*, I think, feeding the dog. I pull the door closed. I carry Owen and the duffel to the truck and load them in. I back down the driveway. *Apple-shaped buttons*, I'm still thinking. Whatever gave someone the idea for *that?*

Part III

22

OWEN WON'T TALK.

It's afternoon now and we're in the truck, the two of us, barreling north on U.S. 93.

"Please, say something, champ," I say, trying to catch his eye in the rearview mirror. "Just let me know you're alive back there." He frowns. His face is still unnaturally white; the rushed, rough washing I gave him before we left succeeded in reducing him to tears but not in removing the paint.

"You know," I say, forcing cheer, "lots of little boys would be thrilled, right about now. They'd think going on a road trip with their dad was fun."

He doesn't respond. His thumb is in his mouth, and he's looking out the window. We pass one ranch, and then another.

"Owen."

He looks at me briefly, then away.

"Owen. I need you to work with me here. I need you to be on my team. This is very important. We're undertaking a mission, here, you and I are, and I need to know I can count on you, come what may." I'm not sure where this is coming from, or where I'm going with it, but at least he's looking at me now. "Because if you're not with me, if you want off this mission, now's the time to say so. Just say the word, and I'll turn this car around right now and take you home. I'll take you right home to Mom, if that's what you want. Is that what you want?"

"No," he says, very quietly.

"What do you want?"

"I want to be on your team," he says.

"Good. Because that's what I want, too." I catch his eye. "We'll be great, I promise. Do you believe me, champ? Do you believe your old man?"

He looks unsure.

"Honey," I say, in a gentler tone, "everything's going to be okay. I promise."

Still, nothing.

"*Okay?* Owen."

Finally, he nods.

I say, "Okay, then," and he goes back to looking out the window. We pass an airfield and a falling-down barn. Every once in a while, there's a house. Most are small and sorry-looking. Some are trailers. Some look like they've been burned. The sky is a bruised gray-blue. I point out what looks like a cluster of bison in the distance, off to the left, but Owen, whose eyes are better, says they're just cows. After half an hour or so, his head falls against the side of the car seat, and he sleeps.

I turn the radio on to the classical station and drive north, trying not to think about anything except the road. I keep both hands on the wheel and obey the speed limit. In a small town on the edge of the bison range, I pull off for gas. When the car comes to a stop, Owen wakes up and asks where we are.

"We'll be back on the road in no time," I say.

"But where are we going?" he asks sleepily.

I decide to tell him the truth. "Flathead Lake."

"Why?" he says.

"When we get there, I'll explain," I say, and get out to pump the gas.

It's colder up here than at home, and clouds are blowing across the sky, west to east. I switch the frigid pump from one hand to the other, scanning my surroundings, wishing the tank would hurry up and fill. Thankfully, there's not a soul in sight. To the right of the gas station is an empty lot, littered with bottles and cans and sun-bleached cardboard boxes that once held beer. To the left is a diner with a Closed sign hanging in the window. Same with the beauty shop across the street. Next to that, the marquee over a Christian bookstore reads "One Million Good Books!" I shove my free hand deep into my pocket and make a fist to warm my fingers, and I remember something from the headlines a few years ago about a triple murder here, in a flower shop. When the tank is full and we can get moving again, I'm relieved.

We've gone another twenty-five miles when Owen says, "Dad?"

"That's me."

"What does 'Fuck yourself' mean?"

I tighten my grip on the steering wheel. "It's something you say when you're very angry at someone."

"You said it to Mom."

"Yes. I did. I was upset."

"Why?"

"Because I was."

"Why?"

"Because she did something that made me mad."

"What did she do?"

Here I pause, considering what to tell him for a long moment. He says, "Dad?"

"She kissed Tom Zilinkas," I say.

"Why?"

"I don't know."

"Why were you so mad?"

I pause again. "Well, she's my wife. I'm her husband. She's only supposed to kiss me." I glance at the speedometer, which says I'm doing eighty-five. My knuckles are white. I take a deep breath and ease off the gas.

"Why?"

"Because. That's the promise you make when you marry someone, that you'll only kiss them." I check the rearview. He looks perplexed. "I know it sounds strange, but that's the way it is. It's the rules."

"Did you ever?"

"What?" I say, knowing exactly what he means.

"Kiss somebody besides Mom."

I lie and say, "Of course not."

"Why?"

"Because I love your mom very much." This, at least, is true. Or I'm fairly certain it is.

It seems to comfort him, anyway. He puts his thumb in his mouth and leans his head against the seat. I hope he'll nod off again, but a few minutes later he says, "Is that why we're going to Flathead Lake? Because of what Mom did?"

I can't think of how to answer truthfully. I say, "You should rest."

"I'm not tired."

"Well, I am. I need to focus on driving. I'm going to turn the radio on."

All I can find is country now, though, not the old, good kind about heartbreak but the new, bad kind — about NASCAR and Walmart and America kicking ass. I turn it off. In silence we careen across the bison range. It's late afternoon now, and sunlight slants through the clouds in thick and thin gold bars. In the distance, the Mission Mountains loom. I think of all the times I've been here before: with Julie, with Gus, with Bennie and Gus. Once, the four of us drove up here together to watch Bennie's new niece get baptized. We were in the church, halfway through the service, when Bennie saw Gus hand one of her uncles his business card. She was furious. All day she wouldn't speak to him. On the way home, she insisted Julie sit up front in the old Buick, which Julie was happy to do. While she and Gus talked shop, Bennie slipped off her shoes and put her feet up. "Tell your wife she's welcome to him," she said, not quite quietly enough for them not to hear. She curled up on the seat, using her sweater as a pillow and pressing the hot, stockinged soles of her feet against my thigh.

In the rearview mirror, I check on Owen. His eyes are closed. I try not to think about the lie I told him. I try hard not to think about that. I check the rearview again, to make sure no one is following us. There's not a soul in sight. I look at the speedometer and slow down some more, just in case.

I hope Owen will sleep for the duration, but after just a few more miles, he says, "Dad, I have to pee."

We're not near anything. "I'll see what I can do," I say.

We're both quiet for a while. Then Owen says, "Dad?"

"That's me."

I brace myself for another round of questions, but all he says is "I really have to pee."

At the exit for St. Ignatius, I pull off, hoping something's open even though it's Sunday, and after five now. On the way into town we pass two graveyards, one old, the other new. The sun is setting, and the sky is aflame.

But all the windows in town are dark. Everything we pass on the two-block-long main drag is closed. "Hang in there, bud," I say. "I'm going to figure something out." I do another loop through town as the last light drains from the sky. Weather is moving in; the stoplights swing in the wind.

I drive a few more blocks and pull over by an empty lot, where I park, unbuckle Owen's seat belt, and help him out of the truck. I lead him around the remains of a chain-link fence and a pile of old, charred wood. Behind some ancient oil drums, I say, "Have at it."

He looks up at me. The wind pushes his hair straight back.

"Come on," I say, "or we'll freeze our nuts off."

"I can't go here," he says.

"Why not?"

"It's too cold."

"For God's sake," I say. "It's winter in Montana. You can do it."

"I can't," he says, again. So I relent, scooping him up onto my hip and carrying him back to the truck.

We've just gotten back on the highway when I have another idea, and I swing us around so we're heading south instead of north, then I drive back into town. Instead of passing by the church this time,

I pull into the parking lot, which is empty, thank goodness, and I choose a spot in the far corner, away from the lights. Then I jump out of the car, zipping my coat against the wind. I open Owen's door, lift him out, and hold his hand, tugging him across the lot and up the old church's well-worn stone steps. "Won't it be closed?" he shouts over the wind.

"Churches don't close," I say, hoping it's true. At the top step I let go of his hand and try the big wooden door. It opens. We step inside.

Out of the wind, it's suddenly quiet and warm. The church air smells like incense, with a hint of something floral, and a pungent, pine-scented cleaner underneath. We're in a small entryway with a drab brown doormat covering the floor. Owen has his hand wedged between his legs, and he's standing with bent knees. I look around, desperate, and spot a sign that says Restrooms, with an arrow pointing down a hall. I hurry down the hall and Owen follows. We come to two doors, one with a silhouette of a boy angel, the other with a girl. I push on the men's room door, and it opens, thank God. Owen's still standing in the hallway with a hesitant look on his face. "Do you have to pee or not?" I ask, and he shuffles in.

When we're finished, I tell him I want to show him something cool, and I lead him back down the hall and through another set of doors, and the sanctuary opens before us, in all its glory.

"Wow," he says, and it occurs to me that he's never been inside a church before.

"What do you think?" I ask.

"It's huge," he says, gazing up at the soaring, whitewashed ceiling, which, like the walls, is decorated with frescoes of vermilion and gold and cerulean blue.

"See those windows? That's called stained glass," I tell him. "And these are called pews, and this is the nave, and — here, come on. This is called the altar. It's where the priest stands."

"How do you know?"

"Gus was Catholic. He used to take me to church, now and then.

160

Plus, I've been here before. I came to a baptism with Bennie and him."

"What's a baptism?"

"A ceremony that Christians perform when babies are born. They believe if a baby's baptized, it will go to heaven."

"Where's heaven?"

"Nowhere. It's a made-up place, but some people believe it's real." I look down at him. "It's called a ritual. That means it's a tradition that's been around for hundreds of years, so people keep doing it, even if they don't believe in the stuff it's supposed to mean." As I say this, though, I think about how it's not true. I think of Bennie, closing her eyes and crossing herself at Gus's graveside, her lips moving in prayer, her fingers traveling over the rosary beads as if of their own accord. I add, "It's comforting. Sometimes there's nothing you can do to change a situation, and doing something familiar, even if it's pointless, feels better than doing nothing at all. We should go."

He doesn't move. "Did I get baptized?"

"No. We're not really Christian. Your mom's definitely not. Come on."

"What are we, then?"

"We're just us." To distract him, I point in front of us, at the altar, where two winged marble angels stand watch. A huge gold cross rests on the altar's white cloth, flanked by ornate candlesticks made from the same gold. Behind the altar, a triptych of frescoes with scenes from Jesus's life covers the wall. The grandest is a depiction of the Crucifixion. Christ's head is wrapped in a crown of thorns, and blood drips down his forehead, into his eyes. Blood seeps also from the places where nails have impaled his hands and feet.

"What's wrong with him?" Owen asks.

It all seems like a lot to explain. "See that cross?" I say, instead. "And the candlesticks? And all the gold on the walls? It's *real* gold. And not just that, it's real *Montana* gold."

"Really?"

"Yup. Gus told me, and Gus knew."

"Gus worked in a gold mine," he informs me. "He dug up gold."

"That's partly true," I say. "He designed gold mines, but other people did the actual digging."

"When I grow up, I want to dig up gold, like him," he says.

"He didn't dig up any gold," I say again, suddenly impatient. "He was an engineer. He drew plans and did math. He never came near any gold, okay? And besides, he quit. He got worried about all the chemicals they were using, and he tried to make them stop. That made a lot of people really, really mad." Bennie's face appears in my mind. I think of her at the Holiday Inn. I think of the names I called her on the golf course. I think of her standing over me, looking down. "He had a knack for that, for doing things that upset people."

"But I want to be like him," he says.

"Selfish, you mean?"

Now he looks up at me, confused. His face is still ghostly white from the paint.

"Look, I'm sorry. Forget it, okay? Your granddad loved you very much. That's what matters. Come here," I say. We're heading back up the nave when I have an idea. At the baptismal font, I stop and lift the stone lid. It's heavy, way heavier than I expected, and I have to put it down quickly and with less control than I intend. It crashes mightily against the marble floor. Incredibly, nobody comes.

I peer into the font. The holy water is clear and perhaps six inches deep, with an accumulation of what looks like sand or silt — *holy* sand or silt, I suppose — at the bottom. I take a last look around before removing my jacket and unbuttoning my flannel shirt, which I slip off. I put my jacket back on over my T-shirt and, using the flannel as a facecloth, wash Owen's face. He struggles and makes noise. "I thought you wanted to be baptized," I say.

"It *hurts*," he wails.

"It's supposed to. It's holy water," I say. "It's cleansing you of your sins."

He stops struggling long enough to ask, "I have sins?"

"Of course not. It's a joke. Now please, stand still. I'm almost done."

"*Ow,*" he insists, yanking his arm away.

I make a few more passes, still holding his arm but trying to be gentler, before I let go. "All right. You're good as new. It's a miracle, bless the Lord." He pouts and rubs his arm, glowering at me.

"I want to go home," he says quietly, looking at the floor.

"Don't say that," I say.

He doesn't look up. "But I do."

"Please," I say. "I'm sorry I hurt you. Just don't say that, okay?" I squat down and start to pick up the lid, but then I change my mind. I dip my hands into the water.

"Why are you doing that? Do you have sins?" Owen asks.

I don't look at him. I splash my own face once, then again. He repeats the question. Drying my face on my shirt, I say, "You think you're the only one who gets to be new?"

Outside, we stand at the top of the stone stairs. It's night, officially, and the stars are suddenly showing themselves, emerging from the darkness too quickly to count. I cup my hand around the back of Owen's neck. "I'm sorry if I was a little rough on you in there. I really am."

He doesn't say he forgives me, but he doesn't move away.

23

SOUTH OF THE lake, where the road forks, I stop at a Circle K. "Dinner is anything you want tonight," I tell Owen. "Anything in the whole store. Go nuts."

"Even chocolate milk?"

I nod, unbuckling his seat belt and lifting him out of the truck. It's even colder, now, and a thin blanket of clouds obscures the stars. "Smell that? It's going to snow," I say. Crossing the parking lot, I hold on to his hand.

Inside, he follows me to the hot-dog station, where desiccated-looking tubes of meat turn on greasy metal wheels that probably haven't been cleaned since Nixon was president. Nonetheless, I help myself to a bun and a dog while Owen watches, eyes wide. He's not the only one watching: twin surveillance cameras peer down on us from opposite ends of the store. And up front, behind the cash register, a woman with a cherry-red beehive does her best to pretend to read.

"Let's make it quick," I say.

"Hot dogs have nitrates," he says, concerned.

"A few nitrates never hurt anyone, I promise."

"But they're preservatives," he informs me.

"Hey, I'm just hoping they work," I say. I smile, but he doesn't. I heap on some sorry-looking relish, yellow mustard, and chopped onion and plunge a plastic spoon into a stainless-steel vat of sauerkraut long past its prime. I glance at the cashier. "Clock's ticking, kiddo. You want a hot dog or not?"

He watches the meat roll for a few more seconds, then shakes his head. "You're missing out," I say. From the refrigerator case I get a carton of chocolate milk for Owen and one for myself. When I return he's holding a bag of pretzels. "Is that the best you can do?" I ask. "Can't we at least spring for some Doritos? Or Combos? Something with real fake cheese?"

He holds his ground. I take the bag from him, plus two dips, one cheese, one ranch, off the shelf, and deposit everything on the counter at the front, beside a plastic vase full of chocolate roses wrapped in foil.

"What about dessert?" he asks.

"That's more like it," I say. I add some burned peanuts, a couple of summer sausages, some neon-orange cheese-and-peanut-butter crackers, plus a couple of candy bars and two Cokes, for the road. I tell her I'm ready to pay.

The cashier looks over her glasses at the pile. "You are from here?" she asks, punching numbers into the cash register.

"Sort of," I say. From the thickness of her *H*, I gather she's not.

"I come from Bulgaria," she says.

"That's nice," I say.

"What is your little boy's name?"

I don't answer her. I watch her flip the shrink-wrapped summer sausages over a few times in her hand, looking for a price. She takes out a notebook and slides her finger down a very long list.

I say, "Skip the sausages."

"You sure?"

My pulse has picked up. I keep thinking about the cameras. I want very much to leave.

She says, "They are fine sausages."

"We're in something of a hurry. Please."

This is when I hear the crash. I turn around and see Owen. He's by the hot dogs again, only now the sauerkraut vat is on the floor, upside down, its contents spread out around his feet.

I march over and grab him by the arm.

He looks up at me. "I changed my mind," he says meekly. "I wanted a hot dog, too." His chin quivers. "That hurts," he says.

I loosen my grip. "Okay. Let's get you cleaned up," I say, and I try to pick him up, but he struggles against me, squatting on the floor, so I end up holding him under the arms, aloft, while he kind of runs in space. Quite a show for the poor soul tasked with watching those surveillance tapes.

I carry him, still kicking, into a vile restroom, where I sit him on the sink and do my best to clean him off. "You smell like a giant fart, congratulations," I tell him, scraping sauerkraut from his shoes.

Back at the register, the woman has tallied up our supplies. Her gaze travels from me to Owen and back to me again. "I'll pay for the sauerkraut, too, of course," I say. She nods while I hand her my credit card, and she puts our food in a bag.

The register spits out a receipt. She reads it, frowns, and looks up. "Denied," she says.

I tell her that's impossible and ask her to try again.

She does, and again I'm denied.

My heart thumps. "It must be your machine," I say. "Could you try once more?" She tries a third time, after which she says, "I am sorry. Over there is ATM."

I don't want to use the ATM, though; it's Julie's account, too, and I'm sure she's watching it — I certainly would be.

I read the cashier's nametag. "Anastasiya," I say. "That's a pretty name."

"Ana*sta*siya," she corrects me. "Like the famous dead princess."

"Is there any chance I could write you a check?" I ask.

She shakes her head.

I open my wallet. There's a twenty and two tens. Recalling with dismay the cash I doled out to Sam so readily last night, I pay for our food. Anastasiya doesn't meet my eyes, handing over the change.

In the parking lot, we eat, idling under some floodlights with the heater on. Owen picks and chooses daintily, sampling each item as if it's an exotic and strange delicacy, which I guess to him it is. Across the road is a Chinese restaurant called Double Yum, and while we eat I watch the Sunday-evening supper eaters come and go. It makes me think of Gus. He always loved going out for Chinese.

"Stuff taste okay?" I ask, handing a napkin back to Owen, who nods energetically. He has cheese dip on his chin. I reach back and wipe it off with my thumb, and he smiles. "See? I told you we'd have fun." I help myself to more chips and open one of the milks.

Across the street, a couple walks out of the restaurant. The man carries a doggy bag in one hand and car keys in the other, and the woman, who looks nothing whatsoever like Julie, has a little girl balanced on her hip. The girl's hair is blond, separated into pigtails tied with white bows. Outside the double doors the mother pauses to put up the girl's hood.

The tight feeling is starting in my chest. I'm thinking about Julie, wondering what she's doing. I imagine her sitting at the kitchen table, sipping something nervously, maybe wine but probably water, waiting for the phone to ring. Maybe she'll try working, to distract herself, or maybe she'll turn on the TV. Or maybe she'll just sit. I bet she's angry. I can only imagine how angry.

"*Dad,*" Owen says, "can I have my *milk?*"

"One milk, coming up," I say. Pushing the image of Julie from my mind, I dig through the bag, and then look on the seat, where I see two empty cartons, and I realize that I've somehow polished off his milk as well as my own. "I don't know where it went, kiddo," I tell him. "I'm sorry."

"It's okay," he says.

"No, it's not. That was your milk."

"It's okay."

"How about I go back in?" I glance at the store, but he shakes his head and I'm silently relieved. I start the engine and pull out onto the road. For a few miles I try to assuage my guilt. "We'll stop again later, I promise," I keep telling him. "How does that sound?"

But I don't hear his answer. On the lake side of the road, my high beams land on a giant ponderosa pine, decorated with ten or fifteen hand-carved, painted wood signs. It looks exactly like it did in last night's slides. I pull over and scan the names until I find the one I'm looking for: "Zilinkas," it declares in jaunty white script. "If You're Here, You're Home."

24

THE HOUSE IS even more obnoxious than it looked on film. When we enter the clearing, Owen gawks up at it from the back seat while I turn us around so we're facing the road again. I park on the far edge of a wide, oval-shaped gravel lot, under a stand of bare-branched alder and birch.

"Who lives here?" Owen asks, while I unbuckle his seat belt.

"No one. Can you believe that? Stay put; I'm going to get you some dry shoes," I say, going around to the back, where I open the door and dig through the duffel, but I guess in my haste to leave I forgot to pack any, so I grab the pair of thick wool socks I brought for myself instead, walk back around, and put them on Owen's bare feet. They come up almost to his knees, like boots. I lift him out of his seat and set him down on the gravel, tell him not to move, and return to the back, where I zip the duffel closed. Wedged between it and the wall, where I left it on Thanksgiving, is my Louisville Slugger. I take that in one hand and close the door.

Owen doesn't notice I'm carrying the bat, so entranced is he by the Zilinkases' house — if *house* is even the proper term. It's more of a mansion, really, with three floors, two separate wings, more windows than I can count, and two thick chimneys, one at each end.

No lights are on. I tell Owen again to stay where he is and not to make any noise, and in the dark I jog up the stone front steps to peer in the window alongside the enormous front door, which I recognize from the slides because of its knocker, a giant brass trout. I glance back at Owen and then try to see inside, but all I can see are a stone floor and what appears to be a carousel pony, standing on its hind legs and whinnying for no one in the dark. I leave the front door and head over to the garage, where through the window I see one car, a brand-new-looking Hummer, which I figure they probably leave here year-round. Satisfied no one's home, I jog back down the steps and grab Owen's hand.

A path leads us along the side of the house, past a tennis court, a small half-pipe, and some wickets set up for croquet. We keep going until the path dead-ends on a wide, flagstone patio with a table and chairs, all draped in something thick and white. I stand by the stainless-steel grill, which is built into a river-rock wall, and look out. Through the trees, the surface of Flathead Lake is the color of pencil lead. And at the end of a long dock, bobbing in the dark water, is Tom's boat.

Owen tugs on my hand and asks why we're here. I sit on the stone wall and pull him up so he's next to me. "What, you don't like it here? I think it's kind of neat."

He says, "I'm scared."

I pull him onto my lap. "Did you know there are elephants at the bottom of this lake?"

He shakes his head.

"It's true," I tell him. "A long time ago, in the old days, a businessman brought them all the way from India, so they could haul his logs to the train. He put the elephants on a steamer to get them to the mill, but a storm came, and the steamer sank."

"They died?" he says.

"Yes," I say.

"Did the businessman die?"

"I don't know. But here's the cool part. The water's so cold down there, they're perfectly preserved. They're one-hundred-percent intact. A hundred elephants underwater, hundreds of feet down. Like a whole underwater elephant world. Isn't that cool?"

He frowns in the direction of the lake. "But they're dead."

The moon, almost full, peeks intermittently from behind a veil of clouds. "I have an idea," I say. "How about we go check out that boat?"

He holds up his arms, the signal that he wants to be carried, so I pick him up and carry him down yet another set of wooden steps, and then one more, until finally we're level with the lake. I can hear the water lapping against the dock and the sides of Tom's boat. My pulse quickens. I put Owen down on the bottom step, and he sits and hugs his knees. I tell him I'm going to take a closer look, and I walk out on the dock.

The boat is tied to metal cleats with thick rope. I touch the gunwale with the toe of my shoe. I know next to nothing about boats — the last boat I was on was a friend's father's sailboat, and that was on the bay in Boston in 1998 — but I don't need to be an expert to understand that this one is quite the prize. It's gorgeous — just as gorgeous as it looked in the slides, if not more so. The body is polished mahogany, and the leather upholstery is bright white. In the moonlight, the chrome dials and instruments set into the dashboard gleam. The words *Tommy's Toy* are stenciled in gold letters on the stern, and a metal mermaid with an arched back and flowing hair decorates the bow, which points out into the lake.

I squat down and take hold of the mermaid. She's very cold. An indecent thrill rips through me, thumbing her tiny molded breasts. I close my fist around her and pull, and she snaps off; I'm surprised at how easily she gives way. "Cheap piece of crap," I say, standing up. "Make a wish," I tell Owen, but he shakes his head. "Okay, I will." I close my eyes but I can't seem to think. My mind is blank. This comes as a great relief. I open my eyes, wind up, and pitch the mermaid into the lake.

I'm not finished. I take the bat in both hands and adjust my grip, just like Gus taught me all those years ago. "Tension is the enemy," he always said. I close my eyes again and, like he taught me, try to visualize the tension leaving my body, "like water flowing from a pitcher," he would say. Then I open them. With one foot braced against the gunwale, I raise the bat over my shoulder and swing as

171

hard as I can, as hard as I ever have, and land a blow smack on the boat's lacquered mahogany nose. The impact sends pain shooting through my wrists and up through my arms, but when I lean down to assess the damage, there's barely a dent.

I'm disappointed. I wind up again and take another swing, this time hitting the glass — the windshield — straight on, and there's an enormous crack as the entire plate explodes, sending glass shards sailing in every direction. Instinctively I duck and cover my face, screaming for Owen to do the same. Then I jump up, shake off my jacket, and sprint back to the steps to make sure he's okay.

I kneel down in front of him and slowly peel his fingers back from his face, one by one. Holding on to his head, I inspect his eyes, cheeks, nose, forehead, scalp, and neck. "Thank God," I say, when I don't find a single cut. I hug him to me, hard. He's crying. "I'm so sorry," I say. "I don't know what got into me. I'm an idiot. A complete moron. Thank God you're okay." He cries harder. I take him by the shoulders and hold him a few inches away. "You're okay," I say. "That was very, very stupid of me, and very scary, but you're okay."

"But you're not," he sobs. "You're bleeding."

Slowly, I raise my hands to my own cheeks, which are wet, and when I take them away I see he's right, it is blood. Lots of it. I start to feel lightheaded, but I stand up anyway and touch my neck, which is also slick. "It's okay, champ, it looks worse than it is," I say in the calmest, most normal voice I can muster. I go back to the boat, step down into it, and squat in front of the mirror. It's dark, but there's enough moonlight coming off the lake to see three, four, five shards of glass stuck in my face: one over my eyebrow, two in my cheek, one just above my upper lip, one in my neck, below my ear. With unsteady fingers I remove each one, then move my fingers over my face until I'm convinced there aren't any more. When I'm finished, I lean over the side of the boat and do my best to wash off the blood. I dry my face on my sleeve and look around.

The boat is a mess of broken glass and bloody footprints. I glance up at the house, then out into the lake: I need to think. Stepping back onto the dock, I kneel and go to work on the knots. They're expertly tied, and my hands are clumsy, nearly numb from the cold, so the untying takes time. The water sucks at the sides of the boat while the temperature falls. Owen sniffles, and I pause to look up. He's a couple of yards away, shivering from cold or fear, probably both, biting down on his bottom lip in the way I know means he's fighting tears. My heart swells. I feel a lot like crying myself.

But I have work to do. I turn away from him and get back to it. By the time I get the last knot out, my fingers burn from the cold. I stand up, kick the lines into the water, place my foot on the stern of *Tommy's Toy*, and push off as hard as I can. Then I lean over, palms on knees, to catch my breath while the boat floats slowly away. A few yards out the current catches it, and it spins in a slow circle, then glides, swanlike, farther and farther out. When it's half a football field away, I stand up and silently hold out my hand. Owen comes.

"It looks so tiny," he says.

"If you were out there on the boat, we'd look tiny, too. It's called perspective."

"You mean when big things get small?"

"No," I say, scooping him up. "How things look different, depending on where you stand."

I carry him back up the steps, around the house, and across the gravel. He doesn't say anything as I buckle him into his seat, and neither do I. Leaving the Zilinkases', I turn left, north, instead of right, toward home. He doesn't ask where we're going, and I don't offer. I turn on the radio. It's a big-band station out of Polson, a show called *Songs That Got Us Through the War*, and Count Basie and Benny Goodman wail away while we pass through Bigfork and Kalispell and then veer west, onto State Route 2, following the winding road where it leads: through the trees, through the mountains, through the night. Somewhere along the way it starts to snow.

"See, champ? Your old man isn't *always* wrong," I say, but he doesn't answer. I check the mirror. He's staring out at the black world, a look of intense concentration on his face. We crest a hill and the lights of a town come into view. Now we're only a few miles away. I think about how good it will feel to lie down and close my eyes. Soon my high beams fall on the sign; "Welcome to Tobey," it says, "Gem of the Treasure State." I read the words out loud, just like I did four months ago, the last time I was here. It was for Gus's funeral. Once more Bennie's face appears in my mind; this time it's behind her grandmother's black veil, her cheeks shiny with tears.

"The treasure state. That means Montana," Owen declares.

"Good memory," I say.

"It's called that because of what's buried in the ground."

"Yes it is, champ," I say.

"Like Gus," he says. "He's in the ground."

I glance back at him. He's looking out the window. "Yes, he is," I say.

"Dad," he says, "when I die, will I get buried in the ground?"

"You won't die."

"But you said everything dies."

I catch his eye. There's a lump in my throat. I say, "No, honey, you misunderstood. When I said everything, I didn't mean you."

25

THE CABIN SITS seven and a half miles outside Tobey, at a sharp bend in a shallow and slow-moving tributary of the Kootenai River known colloquially as Fish Creek. Gus's father, Paul, built it with his own hands, from a single Montana white pine right after the war, and Gus used to tell me about coming here with his dad and his Uncle Ellis and a cousin, Dale, who was close to Gus's age. They'd fish and hunt and drink from flasks, pure Hemingway, a men's paradise, to hear Gus tell it, and like any paradise worth its salt, theirs was destined to be lost. In 1973, when Dale came back to Tobey from Vietnam and learned his fiancée had married another man, he drove himself to the cabin, drank a quantity of Paul's cherry brandy, and shot himself in the head. After that, Paul and Ellis shut down the cabin, boarding up the windows and nailing closed the doors, forbidding anyone to go inside.

Ellis died just six years later, though, and Paul two after that, and he left the cabin to Gus in his will. Gus, encumbered by neither superstition nor sentiment, drove up there the very same week, eager to reopen the place. He brought me with him. I was eight. It was a sunny day in April or May, and in his Buick we bounced along over the rutted dirt road, I remember, under the increasingly tight pine canopy, until the trees gave way and we came to the clearing, where we found the old A-frame, looking weather-beaten and perhaps forlorn but very much intact, crouched solidly in the shadow of the redrock canyon wall. We got out and I followed Gus around the perimeter, watching him inspect the windows and doors, leaning close to frown at the stellar job his forebears had done, sealing it up. From the trunk of his car he produced a crowbar, and I wanted to help but he had me stand back and watch and listen while he instructed me on the physics of prying nails out of wood.

When we stepped inside, I remember, there were drop cloths over all the furniture, and there was a terrible smell. Sweet and rancid, it was the smell of death, and I covered my face with my shirt and breathed through my mouth while Gus poked around and quickly found a family of raccoons nested in the wood stove. "Look at this," he said, beckoning me to come. As soon as I did I wished I hadn't. The mother was dead, hence the stench, but the babies were alive, or a few of them were, if barely, curled into the C of their mother's carcass, suckling futilely at her teats.

We stood there for a few moments, staring into the belly of the stove. Then Gus closed his eyes, crossed himself, and went out the door. When he came back, he was carrying a shovel and some of the wood he'd pulled from the windows. "Jesus Lord, have mercy on me, a sinner" was what he said. Leaning the wood against the stove, he took the shovel in both hands and severed the head of each baby raccoon quickly and methodically with the shovel's blade. Then he loaded in the wood, took some long matches from a nearby shelf, lit a fire, and latched the iron door. After that, he went into the kitchen, where he removed a panel from the wall that faced south, revealing a cubbyhole just big enough to hold a bottle. "Dad kept this here for emergencies," he said. He took down the bottle and opened it, dusted the mouth off with his sleeve, and drank. When he was finished, he held it out and said, "He never shared with me." I took it and drank too, fighting my gag reflex and swallowing it down.

This evening, all the lights are off, and in the clearing at the end of the driveway there are no cars. I'm not surprised, but I am relieved—and the slightest bit disappointed. I park close to the door and, leaving the motor running and the heat on, instruct Owen to stay put.

I try the front door but it's locked, so I head for the back door, which we always leave open.

Or apparently, always used to; it's locked. I lean against it and peer inside, through the glass. I can see an assortment of Bennie's things: paints, an easel, a boom box, a tin of steel-cut oatmeal, wine bottles, a hand-crocheted throw. She's certainly made herself at home. The window clouds up quickly from my breath. I step back and wipe the steam off with my hand, then put my hand back into my pocket.

We've always kept a spare key under the eave on the west side of the house, but when I go to get it, moving my fingers around the cold damp space in the dark, I find it's gone. I check the whole length of the eave, then the east side, and then the west again, but there's no key. I think of all the times Bennie said we're welcome here, any time. I think of Julie. I think of Gus. I try all the windows but none will budge. I step away from the cabin, dig my freezing fingers into the pockets of my coat, and look up. Clouds block most of the stars. Because I can't think of what else to do, I put up my hood and head back around front, to the truck.

We follow the winding road back down the canyon, this time following Fish Creek all the way into town, into Tobey. We pass by Galaxy, the vermiculite mine at the center of all the fuss. It's been closed almost twenty years, but tonight a police cruiser idles outside its gates, and I slow down to forty-five, the speed limit, driving past. Soon the canyon opens up and the land gets more level. We come to the elementary school where Gus went, then the fairgrounds, then the old mill and the dam, and the trestle bridge Gus said he used to jump off of as a kid. I look in the mirror to check on Owen. "You sleepy, champ?" I say.

"No" is his response.

We pass a couple of churches and a couple of cemeteries, including the one where Gus's body lies. I don't slow down.

We leave the side of town where things are old and enter the one where they're new: fast-food restaurants and car dealerships, Western-themed motels.

I decide on the Hot Springs Lodge, whose sign boasts not only "Free Cable" and "Hot Pool Open, Year-Round" but alarmingly low rates. I pull off the road and park near the office, under bright lights, and I'm about to tell Owen I'll be right back when all of a sudden I start to think. I hardly have any cash: What if there's some kind of flag on my credit card? I glance into the office, where a big man sits under a bright yellow light bulb, watching TV. I tell myself I'm being paranoid, and to calm down, but it doesn't help. I take a couple of deep breaths and loosen the neck of my coat, which is constricting my throat. And, of course, there's the matter of whether my credit card even works. I take out my wallet and recount the cash: just the lone twenty, now in the paltry company of a couple of ones.

"I have to go again, Dad," Owen says.

"Just give me a minute," I tell him. "I'm trying to think."

Because I can't come up with anything better, I put the truck back in gear and move us to the far corner of the parking lot, away from the lights. "Okay, kiddo," I say. "Here's where we're spending the night."

I lead a very circumspect Owen into the woods and stand beside him until he pees. When we're finished, I carry him back to the truck, sit him in the passenger seat, and go around to the back, where I keep some wool blankets, just in case, and while Owen waits, I fold the back seats down and build us a crude bed.

By the time I'm finished, his eyes droop. As gently as I can, I lift him out, close the door, and arrange him under the blankets, using my sweater as a pillow to prop up his head. Quietly I close the back door, and for a moment I stand there in the cold, hearing the sounds of water, somewhere close by. I'm remembering a night, years ago, that June when Julie and I met. I was taking her camping, to one of my favorite spots, but we were late getting to the trailhead so I pulled into a turnout and parked by a wide, shallow stream. We unrolled our sleeping bags right there, in the truck, and curled together to combat the cold. In the middle of the night she reached for me, and we made love urgently, no talking, no distractions, no lights except the moon and stars, no sounds but the river. Just the two of us pressed together, hip to hip. Julie says we can't know for sure, but I believe that was the night Owen was conceived.

In the bed I've made I lie on my side with my knees bent, one arm around Owen, listening to him breathe. I close my eyes but I don't sleep. At some point a tapping on the window startles me, but when I sit up and look outside there's nothing to see.

Owen whimpers and turns onto his back, and I prop myself up on my elbow, my face a few inches from his. There's just enough light from outside for me to make out the steadily haphazard motion of his eyeballs, moving under the lids. I watch his face twitch, wondering what he dreams. After a while I lie back down and close my eyes, too.

It was after we buried him. From the cemetery, we all drove to the VFW in town: me, Julie, Bennie, Stan, Marirose, and a long line of cars filled with people eager to raise a glass to Gus Pyle. Inside, we ordered Champagne. Julie nursed a glass, but Owen was back at the Holiday Inn with a sitter she didn't trust and soon she left, but I didn't; I stayed, letting whoever wanted to catch my arm, tell me what a great man my father was, and buy me a drink. Afternoon turned into evening turned into night. The crowd dwindled until only Bennie and I and Stan and Marirose remained. The four of us sat in a booth and Stan ordered a bottle of the best Scotch they had and insisted we drink it to the bottom in Gus's name. We were all sloppy by last call. Marirose (the least sloppy, it was decided) drove us back to the hotel.

I never told Julie — or anybody — what happened next. We said good night to the Mayfields in the lobby, and I walked Bennie to her room. She was holding on to my arm, and when we got to her room, she let go. She put her key in the lock, then turned to face me. I didn't even think about it, I just kissed her. I was kissing her, and then I was pressing my body against hers, one hand on the wall and the other making its way up under her dress. She was so warm, and I kept kissing her, and she was kissing me back, really kissing me, until suddenly she wasn't anymore, she was pushing me away. "No," she said, shaking her head and holding on to both of my arms. "It's not right, no."

I wanted her so badly. It was as if eighteen years' worth of submerged wanting had come to the surface, and I was powerless to push it back down. I kissed her again. At some point she'd started to cry. I tasted her tears, kissed them off her cheeks. She kissed me again and then she pushed me away again, harder this time. She opened her door and went inside. From where I stood in the hallway, I heard her fasten the chain.

I turn over. I look at Owen once more; he's still fast asleep. I'm as awake as I've ever been. I close my eyes again and try to force myself to relax. If we were at home, I'd go downstairs and swing my bat until I couldn't — My bat. My heart clutches. I sit bolt upright and move my hands over the truck's floor, hoping against hope that my fingers encounter what I know they will not. After a couple of futile minutes I abandon the search. There's no point in torturing myself. The bat's not here.

At first light I wake Owen, who is groggy and confused. The air in the truck is surprisingly warm and close and smells sour. "It's okay," I tell him, clearing a circle on the thickly fogged window with my sleeve. Outside, snow falls slowly from a brown-tinted sky. "I'm right here."

That this seems not to reassure him shouldn't come as a surprise, I guess.

"Come on, let's go see a man about a horse," I say. He looks up at me. I reach for the blanket but he resists. I give it a strong tug and see that his jeans are wet. "It's okay," I say.

He says, "When do we get to go home?"

"Take off your clothes," I tell him. "I'll get some dry ones from the bag." I don't. Instead I climb into the front seat, unlock the doors, and let myself out. I'm stiff and everything aches. I go around to the back, open the door, and unload Owen without discussion. In the growing light, I walk as quickly as I can without running and carry him, naked and bucking, across the parking lot and around the back of the motel, which is shaped like a horseshoe. I glance around to make sure no one's watching, then hurry past an ice machine and down a dark concrete passageway, which opens up in a half-enclosed concrete yard. Here, inside a circle of chain-link fence, steam rises from a small, rectangular pool.

When Owen sees the pool, he tightens his grip. His fingers dig into my shoulders, and his thigh muscles clutch at my hips. With some effort I shift him to my left side and open the latch. Inside the fence I set him down on the synthetic grass deck and put a finger to my lips. A sign in the corner lists the rules, the first of which, "Swim at Your Own Risk," is writ larger than the rest. A life ring and a hook on a pole hang from the fence. I look at Owen. He is shivering, standing on the turf in just his T-shirt. I motion for him to take it off, then, looking around once more, undress myself. I take his hand and step into the pool. As promised, the water is warm, almost hot.

He stands on the edge, though, hesitating. "Get *in* here," I whisper. "It's nice. We don't have a lot of time." His teeth are chattering, and his lips are turning blue. He's shifting his weight nervously from one foot to the other, curling his toes. He has his arms crossed over his chest, and below them the bottom portion of his scar bisects his belly.

I don't have it in me to argue. Before he knows what's happening, I have him in my arms, in the water. He fights me at first but then stops and goes limp. I hug him to me, walking us toward the deep end. "See, it's not so bad," I say.

"It's over my head," he says in a small voice, his mouth very close to my ear.

"That's okay," I assure him, pressing him to my chest. I don't know whose heart I feel beating, his or mine. Fat snowflakes drift earthward and disappear in the steam. Soon the water is up to my armpits. He clings to me, burying his face in my neck. "I've got you. Your pop's got you," I say. And for this moment, at least, I do.

26

IN A STRIP MALL a couple of miles away, I find a bakery called Edelweiss, tucked between a JC Penney and an AutoZone. I park and take a quick look at myself in the mirror. My eyes are puffy and bloodshot, and there are short, angry-looking cuts where the glass from the boat's windshield broke my skin. My hair is wet and disheveled, as is Owen's. I can't do anything about the cuts, or my tired eyes, but I run my fingers through my hair a few times in an attempt to tame it. Then I get out, open Owen's door, and do the same with his while he struggles and squirms.

His sneakers are still wet from the sauerkraut, so I carry him, barefoot, into the store, which is quiet. A man in big headphones sits by a ficus plant, typing on a laptop. In the opposite corner a dark-haired woman drinks coffee and feeds a child grapes.

I set Owen down on a ladder-back chair by the front windows, where right away he stands up on the seat, grips the knobs on the chair's back like a captain at the helm of a ship, and looks out. It's not even seven. The sky is a dull shade of pink, low and thick with clouds. Here and there an oversize snowflake floats on the air like cotton. The horizon is dark. I tell him to stay put, and I head up to the front.

There's only one woman in front of me in line, but she takes her time. She has to inspect a dozen different elephant ears, evidently, before settling on two she likes, chatting all the while with the proprietress, a heavyset woman with bleached-blond hair, wearing denim overalls and dog tags around her neck. First they talk about the weather (a storm on the way), then the hunting season (bears, apparently), and finally the NFL. When they're finished, and it's my turn, I get as large a cup of coffee as they have, plus a small hot cocoa with marshmallows, a chocolate croissant, and a cherry Danish. While she's ringing me up, I check on Owen. He's still manning the bridge, keeping us all on course.

"Sir?" says the woman. She wants twelve dollars and eighty-six cents.

"You're kidding, right?" I say, and ask if she's sure she added it up right. She makes a show of punching the numbers into a calculator, then showing me the screen. I hand her my sole twenty and she hands me my change, shaking her head when I pocket it instead of adding to the glass jar marked "Tips."

At a station in the corner, I doctor my coffee. When I turn back around, Owen is gone.

I mean he's *not here.* I look around the whole place but it's tiny — there's nowhere for him to be. Even so, I look under all the tables, then outside at the truck, but it's locked, the keys are in my pocket, and besides, he's not anywhere near it. I dash into the men's room, but he's not in there, or in the women's. With my heart thumping I hurry back to the front. I'm about to tell the blond lady to call the police when the woman with the child and the grapes says, "Hey, mister, isn't that your kid?"

She's pointing outside, and with my eyes I follow the line her finger makes. I don't even thank her before dashing outside.

A couple of doors down, in front of a place called Wok and Roll Two, there's a phone booth, the old-fashioned chrome-and-glass kind I thought was extinct but apparently is not, and inside this one, Owen stands on the triangle-shaped seat in his bare feet, holding a cartoonishly large, black receiver against his cheek. I put both my hands on the accordion door and push. "What the hell are you *thinking?* You can't just wander off. Give me that."

His eyes are huge, but he doesn't hand me the phone. In a tiny voice he says, "I wanted Mama."

"You need money for these," I say, still holding out my hand. I'm waiting for my heart to slow down.

"Not if you press O, like in Owen. Mama showed me how," he says.

"No," I say. "You didn't."

He nods. I hear the faint, tinny sound of a voice floating up from the earpiece. "It's Mama," he says, taking the phone away from his ear. "She wants to talk to you."

My heart hasn't slowed; if anything, it's beating faster. I step into the tiny booth with him and close the door. Inhaling deeply, I accept the phone. Before I put it to my ear, I cover the mouthpiece and say, "I thought we were a team, the two of us. You let me down."

His gaze falls to his feet, which are smudged with dirt and ruddy from the cold. I take my hand off the mouthpiece, hold the thing to my ear, and say hello.

"Give me one good reason why I shouldn't call the police" is the first thing Julie says. I try to answer, but she cuts me off. "What the hell is the matter with you? What are you thinking? Is he all right? Where have you taken him? How could you do this to me?" Her voice is high and frantic as the questions tumble forth.

"Honey," I say, "if you'll just let me explain."

"I don't want an explanation," she snaps, her voice unsteady with rage. "I want Owen home. I want him safe and at home, with me."

"Just calm down," I say.

"Don't tell me to calm down," she spits. "I'll calm down when I have my child back. How could you do this to me?" she asks again. "Have you completely lost your mind?"

"I didn't do anything to you, Jules. If you'll just listen, you'd — "

But she cuts me off again. "Do you know what I've been through these past twenty-four hours? Can you even imagine? Have you even tried? Do you know how close I've been to calling the police?"

"Julie, please. Don't be crazy. It's me. I'm his dad."

"Then bring him home. Right this minute."

I glance outside. It's snowing in earnest now — not the fat, pretty flakes from before, but small, seedlike pellets spinning purposefully from the sky. Just a few feet away, in front of Edelweiss, a woman state trooper sits idling in her cruiser, drinking coffee from a cardboard cup. I imagine my Louisville Slugger, washed up on the Zilinkases' beach. Silently, I curse Gus for having had it engraved. "I can't," I tell her.

She doesn't say anything for a long moment. I hear her take a deep breath. "You can, Logan. You can, and you will."

"It's going to be okay. I promise. I just need a little time. If you'd just give me — "

"No," she says. Her voice still trembles, but now she sounds more scared than angry. "Nothing happened with Tom, Logan, if that's what this is about. You have to believe me. Nothing *happened*. I got a little tipsy, and I acted like an idiot, a total idiot. But that's all. There's nothing else. If I ever in a million years thought you would — "

I'm remembering the buttons on her dress. Her bare knee. The smug smile on Tom Zilinkas's face. I say, "You broke my heart, Jules."

"That's ridiculous," she says. "It was nothing. I promise you. I was drunk. I told you. I was — "

"Stop, okay? Just stop."

There's a long silence. She sniffles, and I hear her blow her nose. She says, "Please, honey, just bring him home."

I watch the woman from the bakery load her daughter into a white sedan. The old phone line crackles. I think of the miles and miles of cables, the tenuous connection between the two of us right now. I imagine my voice traveling those miles, navigating the lonely, windswept landscape between her and me. "I told you, I can't. Not yet," I say.

"Logan," she says.

I don't answer.

"God help me, Logan, if anything happens to him, I mean *anything*," she says slowly, then stops. "I'll never forgive you, Logan. Never. Not as long as I live."

"Nothing's going to happen to him," I say.

"Did you hear me? Never," she says.

"I have to go now," I say. I look out at the parking lot. In the distance, the mountains are already dusted in white. As convincingly as I can, I say, "I know it doesn't seem like it now, but it's going to be okay."

"What is?"

"Everything," I tell her. But I'm not even sure I believe myself. After a few more seconds of crackling silence, I hang up the phone.

Part IV

27

AT FIRST I don't see Bennie, just her car, a black 1987 Chrysler LeBaron with flames painted on the sides. (I don't know how many times Gus offered to buy her a new car, one better suited for mountain life, but the LeBaron belonged to her late brother, Lawrence, who died in Iraq, and she always refused.) I pull up behind it and turn my motor off. A fading sticker on her bumper says, "Mess with the Best, Die Like the Rest," and underneath that, "Property of the USMC."

She's not supposed to be here. After checking my reflection in the rearview, I turn and look at Owen and see anew how ragtag he looks, with his mismatched outfit and his hair uncombed, my dirty socks on his feet again in lieu of shoes. A smear of red from our car-picnic breakfast stains his chin. I touch my thumb to my tongue and reach for his face.

"No," he says, and pulls away.

Only when I get out do I notice Bennie. She's on the roof, about halfway up, striking an uncomfortable-looking, straddle-legged pose, talking on her phone. A twelve-foot ladder leans against the house. When I look up at her, she frowns and raises her hand. The look on her face is severe, and her index finger is extended. I stop where I am and wait.

"I just got through telling your wife I have no clue where you are," she shouts down, a minute or two later, having pocketed the phone.

"Thank you," I say, going closer. "I didn't expect you to lie for us."

"I didn't lie. When I said it, it was true." She goes back to what

189

she was doing, which appears to be putting duct tape on a cracked skylight.

"I didn't think you would be here," I say.

She glances down at me, then back at the glass, and says, "Well, you thought wrong."

I shouldn't be surprised she's still angry. I clear my throat and ask if I can help.

"Nope, I'm good," she says. I'm not sure what to do or say. For a few minutes we watch her. She works intently, ripping the tape from the roll with her teeth. When she's covered about half the glass, she sits up and runs her hand over the patch. "That should hold," she says. "At least until spring."

"What happened?"

"A woodpecker flew into it. Broke his neck. Poor thing."

I shift Owen to my other hip. My back aches from all the driving, and my neck is stiff from sleeping in the car. Snow has accumulated on Owen's shoulders and in his hair. I brush it off.

Bennie shimmies over to the ladder and starts to climb down. Feet on the ground, she turns to us. "Are you going to tell me what's going on?"

I don't say anything, but I give her a look that's supposed to say, *Not now.*

I don't know if she gets my meaning or not. "I'm going in," she says, and heads toward the house. At the top of the steps, though, she turns around. "You can come. Unless you'd rather stand out in the cold."

Inside, I have to say, it's not so warm either. Bennie takes off her coat and boots without looking at me. Everything she says is addressed to Owen. For him, her face is soft and her voice, sweet. In her socks she crosses the cabin, sets a kettle on the stove, and asks him if he'd like something hot to drink. He looks at me. When I give my approval, he turns back to her and nods. From somewhere a cell phone rings: "The Toreador Song" from *Carmen.* She reaches into her pocket, checks the screen, and replaces it, blank-faced. The kettle whines. She doesn't move.

"The water," I say.

"Thank you." She goes to the stove and with an oven mitt that looks like a chicken picks up the kettle and pours hot water into Owen's waiting mug. "You like marshmallows, I seem to recall. Yeah? One, or two?" she asks. "Take off your shoes," she says to me, less an offer than a command, which I obey. I hang my coat on a hook in the mudroom, Owen's too, next to her blue parka and the ancient plaid hunting jacket Gus used to wear to walk in the woods. "Sit," Bennie says. We do, and she places a steaming mug in front of each of us. She doesn't sit down herself. From the refrigerator she takes a block of yellow cheese and cuts slices with an enormous, gleaming knife. Gus believed in buying the very best knives you could afford, and in keeping them sharp.

She puts a plate of cheese and crackers in front of Owen, and this time he doesn't look at me for permission before digging in. Back at the sink, she rinses the cutting board and opens the door to a dishwasher. This is new. Gus did *not* believe in dishwashers, or at least not here.

"You made some upgrades," I say.

"It was high time." When she leans over, her long hair falls forward, hiding her face.

Julie's "bandit" comment pops up, unwelcome, in my head. I push it down. "Good for you," I say.

She straightens up and looks at me, really looks, for the first time since we arrived. Her dark eyes are wary. She seems to be looking for something on my face. She tucks her hair behind her ears. "Do you mean that, or are you being ironic?"

I feel my face redden. "Of course I mean it. You know I never saw the 'rustic' appeal of this place. Self-inflicted discomfort." She frowns. "Hardship doesn't build character if it's hardship you create. Or that's what I always told Gus."

She bites her lip. "Right," she says. But I think I see the shadow of a smile.

I don't want to let this window of opportunity close. "I need to ask you a favor," I say.

"How long?"

"What?"

"How long do you want to stay?"

"Just one night, I promise. Maybe two."

The smile disappears, but she doesn't say no. Her gaze travels from me to Owen, then back to me. Her phone rings again, and she ignores it. Her dark eyes are locked on mine. She still doesn't say yes. "It's freezing in here," she says, finally. "Could you put a couple more logs in the stove?" I stand up. To Owen she says, "How would you like a nice, warm bath?"

All afternoon, snow falls. As the light fades from the sky, Bennie cooks us dinner: spaghetti with meatballs, garlic bread, a green salad on the side. I can't stop telling her how wonderful everything tastes. "Isn't it great, O?" I ask. He's taken only a couple of bites, but he nods his head, which is propped up on one hand. "Take your elbow off the table to eat, and sit up," I tell him.

"It's okay," Bennie says.

"Owen," I say, "please sit up straight."

He does as he's told, but before long he's slumped down again in his seat. "*Owen*," I say again, but Bennie stops me.

"It's okay, really," she says. "I don't know why everybody's always forcing kids to eat. No child ever starved with food in front of them, that's what *my* father used to say."

"Can I watch TV?" he asks. His eyes look glassy, and his face is still flushed from the bath.

She smiles sadly and shakes her head. "No TV here," she says. "But it's on my list. Maybe next time you come."

He looks at me and says, "I don't want to come back here. I want to go home."

I turn to Bennie and say, "I'm sorry. He's not usually like this."

"Like what?"

"Rude."

"He's not rude, he's a kid, and he's wiped *out*, anyone can see that," she says, standing up and smoothing down her jeans. "I'll make up the bed."

Leaving her plate at the table, she goes into the sunroom, unfolds the futon, and takes a stack of blankets and quilts from the steamer trunk that supposedly came over from Ireland with Gus's great-great-aunt. While she spreads the blankets on the bed, I get Owen undressed. His limbs are limp, like a rag doll's, which makes the process far more difficult than it needs to be. I tell him to stop playing around but he just looks at me, confused. "You can be one stubborn kiddo," I say, sitting on the edge of the futon, once he's in his PJs. I pull the covers up around his shoulders and ask what story he wants to hear.

"No stories," he says.

"Really?" I say. "I can think of one you might like. It has to do with a certain Dr. Root."

But he shakes his head. "No *stories*," he says, and turns onto his side.

28

BENNIE SITS AT the table waiting for her licorice tea to cool while I do the dishes, her big brown eyes on my back. I don't try to make conversation and neither does she. When I'm finished I turn the dishwasher on, wait until I hear it start filling, and wipe my hands off on the thighs of my pants. I thank her for the meal and tell her I'm exhausted and that I think I'll call it a day.

"Not so fast," she says. "Have a seat." A package of store-bought lemon cookies sits in the middle of the table, opened and untouched.

I do as I'm told, knowing what's coming next. I'm correct.

"You said you would explain," she says.

"Did I?"

She nods. Her hands rest on the table, fingers woven together. Her hands are lovely; I've always thought so. Long, pale fingers with nails she keeps very short.

"I can barely keep my eyes open," I tell her. "Tomorrow, I promise."

"That's not good enough," she says. "You're sleeping under my roof. I'm harboring you. I need to know what this is about."

"It's better if you don't."

"Try again," she says, putting her hands around her mug and looking up at me. "Have you hurt someone?"

"Not exactly." My fingers move over the sore spots on my face as if of their own accord. "Not counting myself." I think about the lake, and then about Zilinkas's boat, floating forlornly in the middle of it. And I think about Tom's hands on Julie's skin.

"Let me see," she says, standing and coming over to me. She tilts my head back so my face is under the light. Her fingers are cool and soft.

"Ouch," I say, flinching.

"Stay still, please," she says. "Have you cleaned these out?"

"In the lake. And the motel pool." She lets go of my head. "It's a long story."

"Wait here," she says, and leaves the room. I hear her rummaging around in the bathroom, and when she comes back she holds a brown bottle of peroxide in one hand and a couple of Q-tips in the other. "This will sting a little," she says. She rinses her hands off at the sink and then sets about cleaning my cuts. She was wrong, it stings a lot, but the feeling of her hand on the nape of my neck, holding my head steady, makes it worthwhile. I feel more relaxed than I have in days, maybe longer. I let my eyes close.

When she's finished, she takes her hand away, and it's like being shaken awake in the middle of a pleasant dream. She sits down. "What you said," she says, screwing the cap back on the peroxide bottle. "On the golf course? I keep thinking about it."

"I'm so sorry," I say. "I don't know what got into me."

"Lots of things got into you," she says. "That was partly my fault."

"No," I say. "None of it was." I reach for one of the lemon cookies out of nervousness, but once it's in my hand I don't want it anymore. I put it on the table. I clear my throat. "Things have been — difficult. At home," I say. "I should never have said those things to you. I was way out of line. I'm sorry."

She looks down, moving her hands over the faded red cloth. I can't tell whether she believes me or not, or how much she cares, either way. "It means a lot to hear you say that," she says.

I start to get up, but she puts a hand on my arm. "Logan."

I sit back down. "I don't even know where to begin," I say.

She says, "Try."

I pick up the cookie again, turn it over in my hand. "Julie and I had a fight."

"Okay."

I think of Julie. I think of Tom Zilinkas. I think of her dress. I think of his hands. I think of my baseball bat. I think of Owen. And then I think of Erica Pietryzyck. I think of Bill. I think of Julie again. I try to think of how I might convey any of it to Bennie in a way that makes any kind of sense.

"And?"

"And I don't know what else. Julie and I fought. I left. Here I am."

She shakes her head. I can tell she's disappointed, but I honestly don't know what else she wants to hear. I stand up from the table and drop the cookie into the trash.

"There's the old wedding quilt in the trunk, still," she says to my back. "You get the sofa, unless you and Owen want to share."

In the living room, I open the trunk. The menthol smell of mothballs wafts up into my nose. The quilt she's talking about, which my grandmother made my grandfather as a wedding gift, lies folded on the bottom. One more Pyle family treasure that's supposed to mean so much. I take it out and carry it into the living room.

"That's it for blankets," Bennie says in a flat voice. "I hope you're not too cold."

I turn to face her with the quilt in my arms. She's staring at me intently; in sunlight, I know, you can see flecks of gold deep in her irises, but in this light and from this distance they just look brown.

"You know where to find me if you change your mind," she says. She looks down. "I mean, if you want to talk."

"I thought we just did," I say.

She shakes her head again, almost imperceptibly, then dumps her tea out in the sink and fills the mug with water. She folds up the tablecloth, puts it in a drawer, and turns off the lights. She picks up her mug. Standing in front of the ladder, which leads up to the loft where she sleeps, she pauses, her free hand resting on the rail. "You're so much like him."

For some reason I can't look at her. I spread the quilt on the couch. "I'll take that as a compliment," I say.

She says, "Don't." Then she climbs the ladder, quite expertly considering she's using only one hand.

On the couch, wrapped in the wedding quilt, I toss and turn. The couch is about a foot shorter than me, so I can't stretch out, and there's the mothball smell, plus the place is so tiny, I swear I can hear every breath Bennie and Owen take. Hours pass. After what feels like a decade I sit up and check the antique ship's clock Bennie bought Gus one Christmas, years ago. It's almost one: still six hours, minimum, until it's light. Six hours before I can wake Owen up and we can get back on the road.

But where, exactly, do I think the road leads? Home is out — just thinking about facing Julie right now makes me want to be sick. And so are motels or hotels, or anywhere that requires money for us to stay. I close my eyes and think about waking Owen up right this minute, bundling him into the truck, and driving to Canada. I picture wide-open spaces and forests of tall trees, bright sun and dark shadows, Owen and me sitting on the steps of a cabin, his knee against my thigh. The front porch in my mind looks over a clear, fast-moving creek, where in the early evening fish fling themselves out of the water in gold and silver arcs, and families of moose come to drink. We're not a hundred miles from the border; we could be there in a couple of hours, max. Who would stop us? And if someone did? I'm his father, I would explain. He's my son.

But it's the middle of the night, and these are middle-of-the-night thoughts. I get up and go to the refrigerator, hoping to find something stronger than water to drink, but there's nothing. I fill a glass at the sink and sit down at the table, running my thumbnail along a seam between the panels, dislodging decades of crumbs.

29

I DON'T SEE Bennie until the next evening, when she comes in carrying a pizza box and a six-pack of beer. "I hope you guys like pepperoni," she says, kicking off her snowy boots.

Owen and I are in the living room playing Go Fish. He's been laying it on thick all day, dragging himself around the cabin like some kind of captive, and punishing me further by refusing to talk. "We do," I say, speaking for him. "It sounds great." I lay my hand of cards down on the coffee table and stand up. "Were you at the clinic?" I take the six-pack from her, trying unsuccessfully to gauge her current attitude toward me from the look on her face.

"Not today," she says, putting the pizza on the stove. "I do a CPR course at the Y, once a month." She seems distracted, turning the oven on, then opening the fridge, looking inside, and closing it again. She's still wearing her coat. She goes over to the ladder. From the loft she calls down, "I'll just be a few minutes. Put the pizza in the stove, if you don't mind."

I transfer six slices from the pizza box onto a cookie sheet I find in a drawer. The oven's practically an antique and takes a long time to warm, so I help myself to a beer and sit at the table to wait. From upstairs I can hear Bennie talking on her phone. "I was working all day," she says to whoever's on the other end of the line. "No. I mean all day. I just now took my first breath."

I get up and take a few quiet steps closer to the ladder, trying to hear more, but music comes on from up in the loft, I recognize

Joni Mitchell's *Blue*, and I quickly back into the living room, where Owen is wrapped in the wedding blanket, curled on the sofa, sucking his thumb.

I sit down next to him and put my hand on his back. "You hungry, champ?" He shakes his head. "Even for pizza? Bennie lugged it all the way up here from town." He shakes his head again. "You're going to have to talk to me sooner or later. You know that, right?" He shrugs. He's lying with his head close to the wood stove, and his cheeks are pink. "Do you have any idea what havoc that thumb's going to wreak on your teeth? Do you want to look like Bugs Bunny?"

"His teeth will be fine. Leave him alone," Bennie says, coming down the ladder. She's changed into a purple cardigan and blue jeans, and she has sheepskin slippers on her feet. Her phone is nowhere in sight. She comes over to where we're sitting and says, "I'm ravenous. All they had at the Y was chips from the vending machine. Who's ready to eat?"

I make Owen get up and come to the table, where he takes a seat between me and Bennie and stares without focus at the slice of pizza on his plate.

"Eat," I tell him, between mouthfuls. "It's going to get cold."

"I'm not hungry," he says.

"Lo, he speaks," I say. I push the plate closer to him. "I'm not kidding around. Bennie was nice enough to get us this food, and I want you to be respectful and eat it."

"I don't want it," he says, frowning and pushing the plate away.

I look at Bennie. "He's going through a meat thing," I tell her. "This isn't my doing. I'm sorry."

"I had no idea," she says, and starts to stand up. "Let me see if there are any pieces they forgot to put pepperoni on."

"No," I say. "Sit down. He can eat it the way it is, or he can go to bed."

"Are you sure?"

I say I am. "Did you hear that, Owen? Which is it going to be?"

"Bed," he says.

"Bed, then. There you have it. At least the man knows his mind." I start to get up but now Bennie stops me.

"How about I put him to bed? If that's okay."

"It's more than okay," I say, sitting back down.

By the time she rejoins me I'm on my second beer, but I've lost my appetite. She helps herself to a second slice of pizza from the oven and a beer from the fridge and sits down. I can feel her eyes on me, but I don't want to meet them.

She takes a long sip. "Are you always so hard on him?" she says, swallowing.

"No. I mean, yes. That wasn't hard." I wedge my thumbnail under the label on my beer bottle and try to peel it off but it tears. I roll the damp scrap of paper between my finger and thumb. "He pushes my buttons. It's hard to explain."

"He's four years old," she says.

"Almost five." Neither of us says anything for a while. I drink and she eats. "I'm doing my best," I say, finally. "I'm trying to do what's best for him, you know?"

"I don't know," she says, as if choosing her words carefully. "I don't, because you haven't told me a single thing."

I look down at my pizza. The slices of pepperoni have curled into tiny bowls of congealed grease. My stomach turns. "I'm not feeling so great," I tell her. "I think I might turn in myself."

It's in the smallest morning hours, and still very dark, when I find myself at the bottom of the ladder, with my hands on the rails and one foot poised on the bottom rung. I haven't slept. For hours I've been turning from one side to the other on the couch, unable to get comfortable or to quiet my thoughts.

I climb the sturdy ladder, whose rungs have been worn smooth by decades of Pyle hands and feet. At the top I stand up slowly, my body recalling how steeply the ceiling slopes before my mind does.

The bed is in the back corner now, by the window instead of in the middle of the south wall, where it had been since the beginning of time, and Bennie's moved the dresser and the chaise longue from the south side to the north. For some reason this, the new layout, gives me an unexpected burst of courage. I take a couple of steps. A rectangle of dim light from outside falls obliquely on the bed, and Bennie sleeps on her side in the center of it; I can just make out the curve of her hip under a thick white duvet. She sleeps on her folded hands, like a child, her dark hair spread out over the pillowcase. At the foot of the bed I pause a moment, holding my breath.

"Bennie," I whisper. "*Bennie.*" She doesn't stir. As gently as I can, I sit down and say her name again. "Bennie," I whisper a little more forcefully. "Hey, Bennie, wake up."

She sits bolt upright, her eyes wide with alarm. "What's the matter?" she says. "Is somebody hurt?"

She's wearing a white camisole with tiny straps. The moonlight coming through the window illuminates her bare shoulders and chest.

I look away, in the direction of her dresser, on top of which sits a dark-haired doll in a frilly dress. "Nobody's hurt. Nothing's wrong. I just wanted to talk."

"Jesus fucking Christ," she says, taking a deep breath and exhaling through her nose.

"I'm sorry." I turn to face her again. She has the quilt pulled up now, covering herself.

"Please hand me my shirt," she says, quite formally. I stand up and look around but don't see it. "There. On the chair."

I hand her the shirt, a denim button-down, and turn away while she puts it on. "I'm sorry again," I say to the doll.

"It's okay," she says. "So where's the fire?"

"I couldn't sleep."

"Well, I could," she says. She shifts over to one side of the bed. "Here, come on. Sit down."

I do. I sit on top of the covers with my back against the wall and my knees up. For a while I don't say anything and neither does she. Finally I say the sentence I've been rehearsing in my mind for the past few hours. "Julie and I had a — an altercation. A fight."

"You mentioned that," she says.

"No, I know." I pause. "But it wasn't a fight, really. I walked in on her with someone else."

"Okay," Bennie says calmly, turning onto her side again, resting her head on her arm.

I nod. "He's this awful guy, this real pig. Builds McMansions and shopping malls, drives a Hummer, that kind of thing. Thinks he owns the world. Like he's better than everyone else."

"What exactly did you see?"

"We were at his kids' birthday, and Owen got in a fight. They were upstairs. I heard them laughing. He had his hands on her. He's the worst kind of person, really, and Julie was — I went berserk. I said terrible things, cruel things, and then I left. I took Owen home and packed us some clothes and took off." I tell her all of it without stopping, practically without taking a breath — the offer, the lawsuit, the school, what I told Bill, what I told Stan, how I made Miss Pietryzyck cry. And the rest: the church, the convenience store, the lake, the boat, the bat, the night in the truck, the pool, the bakery, the phone, Julie. "And I'm so ashamed," I hear myself say, at the end. "I hate to imagine how scared Julie is, or what she thinks of me now — and Owen. I hate that I've put him through this. He's never going to forget it. I hate to think of all the damage I've done." After that, I close my eyes and cover them with my hands.

"Goodness," Bennie says. I feel her fingers on mine, gently prying them away from my face. "Come on," she says, squeezing my fingers in hers. "Look at me. No, at *me*. You made mistakes, but you made them out of love. You acted out of love. You have this enormous heart, it's like a sail, and sometimes that sail fills with wind and takes you where you don't mean to go. But a big heart is a big heart. Anyone who knows you, really knows you, will understand that."

I don't say anything.

"She will," she says, giving my hand another squeeze. "Julie will."

"I'm not so sure," I say.

"And Owen will," she says. "Kids are so resilient. He'll be fine."

"You really think so?"

"I know so."

Now I lie down on my side too, so we're facing each other.

She says, "Easy for the one with no kids to say, right? Here, come on, honey. You must be freezing. Get in." She tugs the quilt out from under me and I get under the covers, still in my T-shirt and jeans, and shift onto my back. I keep my arms at my sides but she doesn't. She comes close and puts her arms around me, rests her head on my chest. After a while, I let my fingers find a home in her hair. I'm not tired, exactly, but I close my eyes.

"You warm enough?" she says, after what could be minutes or hours.

"Warmer than I've been in months," I say.

She holds on to me. I hold on to her. We hold on to each other, I don't know for how long.

30

OWEN'S NOT FINE, it turns out; he's sick. Wednesday morning I wake up to him calling for me, and I hurry out of Bennie's bed and down the ladder, still in my clothes. I kneel beside the futon with my hand on his forehead, which is burning up, and tell him it's okay, I'm here.

"I'm cold, Dad," he says. His cheeks are flushed to a deep pink.

"I'll get a thermometer," Bennie says. I turn around. She's right behind me, wrapped in a red plaid flannel robe I recognize as my dad's.

I turn back to Owen and rest my hand on his cheek. "Does anything hurt?"

"I was swimming in the pool," he says. "And there were fish there. They were biting me on my legs."

"Okay, bud. I'm right here," I say. I turn around to see what's taking Bennie so long. She's in the bathroom, rifling through a shoebox she has balanced on the edge of the sink. "Could you hurry?" I call to her.

"I can't find the damn thing," she calls back. "I swear we had one. Hang on."

"Dad," Owen says, "what happened to the elephants? The ones in the lake. What happened to them?"

"Bennie?"

She comes out of the bathroom empty-handed. "I'll run down to town," she says. "It'll only take a few minutes. Let me put on some clothes."

She climbs the ladder, and the ceiling creaks as she hurries around overhead. I ask Owen if he's hungry or thirsty, but he shakes his head.

"Get some liquids into him," Bennie says. She's back downstairs already, pulling on her boots.

"I know what to do," I say, more harshly than I intend.

She slips into her jacket and spends a minute or two looking for her keys. Finding them on the counter, she says, "Call if he gets worse." Before she goes she comes over, leans down, and feels Owen's face. "One hundred and one," she says. "Maybe a hundred and two. I'll be back."

After she leaves I get Owen a glass of water and bring it to the bed. He drinks a few sips, then slides into sleep, which he drifts in and out of for the next hour. I sit close by, on a chair I've brought in from the kitchen. Each time he wakes up, he gives a small whimper, opens his eyes, and says, "Dad?"

"Right here," I tell him. "Your old man's right here."

Once, he wakes up suddenly and starts crying for real. I ask him what's wrong, but he's confused. He talks about the lake again. He asks if Grandpa's in the dirt. "With the gold," he says.

"It's going to be okay," I tell him, because I don't know what else to say. I can hardly stand it. I hear Julie's voice in my head: *If anything happens to him*. I hold his hot hand. "I'm right here," I say again and again. "It's okay." He shivers despite the two blankets he's under and drifts off. I get the wedding quilt from the couch and spread it over him.

The next time he wakes up he's more lucid. "I have to pee," he announces.

I carry him into the bathroom, pull down his underpants, and hold him steady on the toilet. While he's sitting, his eyelids droop. He falls asleep right there, on the seat.

I carry him back to bed and tuck him in, then check outside for Bennie's car. No sign of her. I sit back down and stare at his sweet face, willing him to get better. To be okay. I lay my hand on his forehead again and I tell him how sorry I am, for everything. I shouldn't have gone to Tom Zilinkas's house. I shouldn't have smashed up his boat. I shouldn't have said the things I said to his mom. And most of all, I shouldn't have taken him away.

Bennie bursts in just then, bringing a blast of cold air with her. "Better, or worse?" she says.

"I don't know," I say without turning around.

She comes over and sits on the futon. From a CVS bag she produces a digital thermometer, a bottle of Children's Tylenol, some neon-blue Pedialyte, and a stuffed toy duck. "I wanted a dog or a bear but this was all they had," she says, snapping the price tag off its yellow foot and setting it on the pillow, near his head.

"Thank you," I say. "Again." While she cuts away the thermometer's clamshell packaging with kitchen scissors, I pull my wallet out of my pants and fish out what cash there is.

"No," she says.

"Please. Here."

She frowns at the remains of the package in her hand. "I don't want your money. I mean it." She looks down at Owen. "Are you going to take his temperature or should I?"

I put the money away.

The thermometer says 102.4. "You should call her," Bennie says, standing up.

"It's not that high."

"She'd want to know," she says.

I can feel her eyes on me but I don't dare look up. I try to imagine a conversation with Julie that doesn't end with her getting in her car and coming up here, but I can't. "If it gets any higher, I will," I say. "I promise."

"Really?" Her voice has taken on an edge. "What's it going to take? A hundred and two point six? Seven? Eight? A hundred and three?"

I've seen this side of Bennie before, of course. She and Gus argued plenty. But then Gus was the target of her ire, not me, and if I resented her temper — or their arguing — it was because I knew that later, through the thin wall that separated my bedroom from theirs, I'd have to hear them making up.

"I'll handle this," I say, and look up at her. "Please, just let me handle this. Okay?"

She doesn't say yes or no. She goes into the kitchen and shakes a couple of Children's Tylenol into her palm.

I give the pills to him one at a time and convince him to take a few sips of the blue drink. For the remainder of the morning and the afternoon, he drifts in and out of sleep. I stay by the bed, trying to read an old Raymond Chandler novel from the shelf, but I can't concentrate. I must have read the same two paragraphs sixteen times. Around noon Bennie leaves again, to do what, I don't know, but when I hear the sound of her wheels on the snow-covered gravel outside a few hours later, I'm surprised by how relieved I feel. I watch her get out of her car; she's talking on the phone again, a look of deep concern on her face. I worry she's called Julie. Through the window I watch her pacing back and forth in the snow, nodding and gesturing with her mittened hand.

When she comes back inside, though, the grave look is gone, and the first thing she says is "Don't look so scared. It wasn't her. If I'd decided to do that, you'd know. Which isn't to say I've made up my mind, yet. Has he eaten anything?" I say no. "Have you?" I shake my head. She sheds her boots and coat again and starts banging around in the kitchen. I can tell she's upset, but I don't feel right asking what about. A few minutes later, she brings two mugs of steaming red soup and two grilled cheese sandwiches, on a tray.

It's becoming evening. I watch the clouds catch fire, then fade to gray through the windows while Bennie moves around the cabin, turning on lamps. I take Owen's temperature again. It's dropped to just over a hundred. "It's moving in the right direction," Bennie says, standing over me. Owen wakes up, looks at the duck near his shoulder, then at the two of us, and asks where he's been. "Right here, honey. Nobody's been anywhere but here."

I get him to eat some of the soup, now lukewarm, and a few bites of cold grilled cheese, and later Bennie gives him a bath while I change the sheets on his bed. After that she showers, and I read to him from *The Mayor of Casterbridge*, the most suitable thing I can find, while almond-scented steam seeps out from under the bathroom door, making the whole cabin smell sweet. His temperature drops further, to 99.9, and he goes to sleep.

In the kitchen, Bennie is heating up two cans of SpaghettiOs, and tonight she's opened a bottle of wine. "Not exactly gourmet fare, I'm afraid," she says. "Tomorrow morning, I'll shop." Without asking, she pours some wine into a juice glass for me, and I sit at the table while she opens a package of lettuce and shakes half into a metal bowl. She puts a cutting board with a tomato, two carrots, and a knife on it in front of me and says if I can wait a few minutes to eat, she needs to make a call.

She goes outside again to talk, and when she comes in, ten or fifteen minutes later, her face has high color from the cold. She doesn't look very happy.

"Is everything okay?" I ask.

"Fine," she says curtly, frowning into the pot of SpaghettiOs.

While we eat, she talks in a nervous, unfocused way I don't recognize. She starts stories and neglects to finish them, jumping from one topic to another practically without pause. It's clear something's bothering her, but I don't know whether or not she wants me to ask what.

While I'm rinsing the dishes, she says, "Have you called her yet?"

"No," I tell her.

"You need to," she says. "You need to let her know he's okay. That you both are."

"Thank you very much for the input," I say.

"You don't need to be an asshole," she says. "I'm on your side. I know you don't think so, but I am."

I don't know what to say to this. I pick up her bowl, which is empty, rinse it out, and put it in the dishwasher. I do the same with mine, and the pot. By the time I turn around, she's gone. The kitchen's empty. I sit alone at the table and finish my wine.

It's late — after midnight, maybe — when I check on Owen for the third time. He's sleeping soundly, and his fever is gone. I replace the thermometer on the bathroom sink and I'm about to go back to the sofa when I change my mind, climb the ladder, and lie down on Bennie's bed. She's wearing a dark-colored T-shirt, lying on her side, facing the wall, and she doesn't stir while I arrange myself on top of the duvet.

"What are you doing?" she whispers, once I'm still.

"I'm sorry," I whisper, close to her ear.

"What time is it?"

I don't answer. I lie down on my back, on top of the covers, aware that I should go back downstairs, and aware, also, of how much I want to stay here. I can feel the warmth coming off her, through the duvet. I can smell her sweet shampoo. I close my eyes. When I wake up, just before dawn, her eyes are wide open. She's propped up on her elbow, watching me. In the blue dark she reaches over and traces the line of my nose. She smiles a little sadly. "Your profile. It's so much like his, it's uncanny."

I wonder if I'm dreaming. "Like Owen's?" I whisper.

"No," she whispers back. "Like your dad's."

31

"ONCE UPON A TIME," Bennie says, "there was a man with two wives."

It's full light, now, and I'm lying in her bed, alone, listening to her voice float up from downstairs. It's morning. The clock on Bennie's nightstand says it's half past eight.

"The man was good, but the two wives were wicked," she's saying, "and they conspired to kill him."

"What's conspired?" I hear Owen ask.

"Planned. They *planned* to kill him." I sit up but hesitate before putting my feet on the floor.

"In the evenings, anyway," she says, "the man liked to sit on a buffalo skull up on a butte, to watch the sunset. One day, while he was out hunting, they went up to his butte and dug a deep hole, which they covered with sticks and grass, and then they put the buffalo skull back. That night, when the man sat on the skull, he fell into the hole. The wives thought he was dead, and they went back to their village and pretended to mourn. But meanwhile, the man was very much alive, stuck at the bottom of the hole. That night, a wolf traveling across the prairie heard his shouts for help, and he got his wolf pack together and they dragged the man out of the hole and brought him back to their den, where their chief, an old blind wolf with amazing powers, gave the man a wolf's head and wolf paws for hands, and all the strength and ability of the mighty animal."

"Really?"

"That's what they say," she says.

"Who says?"

"My grandfather. He's the one who told me that."

"What happened next?"

"I'll tell you later, if you eat some of that oatmeal. That was our deal."

I hear them move into the kitchen, and I scramble down the ladder and duck into the bathroom, where I wash my face, brush my teeth, and wet my hair, and when I come out, I pretend for Owen's benefit that that's where I've been all along.

He hardly notices. The two of them are seated at the table, each with a bowl of oatmeal. Owen is stirring raisins into his.

"Bennie showed me a picture of you with Santa," he says, holding his spoon in his fist.

I go over to him and feel his forehead. It feels fine. "Did she?" I glance at Bennie, but she looks away.

Owen nods. "You were trying to get away."

"I hated Santa when I was little," I tell him. "He scared me. All grownups in costumes did."

"Costumes?" he says.

I pour myself coffee from the pot Bennie's made and sit down.

Bennie stands up. "I'm heading into town," she says. "Will I see you two tonight?" There's something strange in her voice. I feel a little queasy.

I tell her yes, if that's okay.

She sets her bowl in the sink and says, "It makes no difference to me. Do what you need to do."

"What does that mean?" I ask.

"Exactly what I said. Stay if you want, or go. I'm off."

"I want to come with you," Owen says around his spoon.

"Me too," I say.

She still won't look me in the eye.

"How about we all go? A field trip. It'll be fun."

Now she looks at me. The expression on her face is vaguely pained. She turns to Owen, who's looking up at her pleadingly, his hands clasped under his chin. Shooting me a look of distinct displeasure, she says, "Okay, O. Get dressed."

Outside, the sky is overcast again, low and gray, and Bennie looks up at it, sniffs the air, and pronounces more snow is on the way. She crosses the yard quickly, heading for her car. I pick up Owen, who's dawdling by some icicles suspended from the eave, and follow her. Snow spills into my sneakers, and I do my best to walk in her tracks.

We ride down the canyon in silence. To our right is the river, to our left, a wall of sheer rock. Before long, as Bennie predicted, the snow starts. I watch the fat flakes falling into the river, which is choppy, the water dark as iron. It looks cold. I think about how every so often, you hear of someone taking a turn too fast and tumbling in. But Bennie is a careful driver, she always has been. She takes the curves slowly, keeping both hands on the wheel.

The supermarket, Albertsons, is in a strip mall called EastGate, named, evidently, for its position at what must once have been the eastern threshold of town — "once," as in, before developers had their way with the surrounding land. I can remember coming here with my father when I was a kid; none of this existed. A mile from the center of town, you were as likely to run into a bear as a person. But now, everywhere you look, something is being paved over or built or expanded or sold. The river must still be here, somewhere, but you'd never know. Instead, there's a bank, a Jiffy Lube, a Verizon, a Prime Donuts, a dry cleaner, and a Burger King.

"Who wants a Whopper besides me?" Bennie says, guiding her car into the drive-through lane.

I wait for Owen to answer, but he's silent. I nudge him, but he looks nonplussed. "Are you still feeling sick?"

He shakes his head.

"Doesn't a Whopper sound good?"

"What's a Whopper?" he finally asks. Bennie glances at me critically.

"I told you, this is not my doing," I say.

She smiles heartily for the first time all morning, which is a great relief to see. "Well, whoever's to blame, I think it's about time we fixed it," she says. At the speaker, she leans out her window and shouts our order into the microphone like a pro. "Three Cokes, two Whoppers, one Whopper Junior, and one large fries." I can tell Owen is excited. A few minutes later, she pulls up to the next window, where our food is already staining a white paper bag with grease.

I reach for my wallet, but she ignores the gesture and pays with her own twenty-dollar bill. "I owe you," I say. "Don't think I'm not keeping track."

We park in front of Albertsons and eat in the car while the windows fog. I'm not particularly hungry, for once, and I can manage only a few bites. Bennie eats enthusiastically but daintily, somehow, despite the unwieldiness of the Whopper, and Owen makes an impressive mess, evidently having conquered — or forgotten — his aversion to consuming flesh. He has ketchup on his fingers, and pink sauce all over his face. I say, "Can you thank Bennie for buying you lunch?"

"Don't do that," she says. "I hate parents who do that."

Chastised, I stare at the foggy windshield. It's snowing harder. When Owen finally finishes, I wipe him down with the thin, grease-soaked napkins from the bag, and we get out of the car.

We follow Bennie, who's walking toward the store at a clip. Inside, she is purposeful and efficient, pushing her cart up and down the aisles, pulling items off the shelves without ceremony: cereal, hamburger meat, bacon, flour, eggs, more SpaghettiOs, rice, canola oil, tin foil, wine, soap, frozen fruit. She doesn't agonize over brands or ingredients, doesn't buy anything organic, doesn't seem to ponder whether or not the product in question spent its days in a cage. Also, she doesn't look at me, not once. A couple of times her phone rings but she ignores it. The third time, she takes it out of her purse, looks at the screen, and puts it away. At the checkout line, she gives Owen a handful of quarters and tells him to pick something out from the machines.

"I have to tell you something," she says as soon as he's gone.

I'm holding a magazine about islands. My heart thumps. I put the magazine down.

"Vincent wants me to move in with him," she says.

I swallow hard. "He does?"

She nods. Her face is serious. She's holding on to the handle of the cart with both hands. "He asked me last week. Thanksgiving Day, actually. He wants to marry me."

"Really."

"Don't look so shocked. I'm not such a terrible catch."

"I'm sorry. It's not that. I'm just — " I have absolutely no right to feel as devastated as I do. I say, "I'm happy for you. Congratulations."

"Hold up. I didn't say yes."

"You said no?"

"I haven't said anything, yet."

"Hence all the calls."

She nods.

"Well, what do you want? Do you *want* to marry him?" I'm working hard to control my voice.

She looks at the food in the cart. "Most of the time I do, and then sometimes — once in a while — I don't."

I look past the checkout, to the vending machines, where Owen is bent over, peering into one filled with rubber balls.

The line has progressed. We move forward. My pulse is racing. I start loading items onto the belt. She hands me a carton of orange juice. "I'd feel a lot better if you said something, right about now."

I'm holding a loaf of wheat bread in my hand. I turn to face her. "And what exactly do you want me to say, Bennie? What is it, exactly, that you want from me?"

Her face turns pale. She looks down at her fingers, which are white from gripping the cart. "I'm sorry." She looks up at me. "I thought I was doing the right thing by telling you, but I think maybe I was wrong. Maybe all of this was. I shouldn't have let you stay. I should've told Julie that first day, on the phone. I should have followed my gut. I've made a terrible mistake."

Her words cut me. I don't agree or disagree. I don't say anything. I turn my back to her and take a package of razors off a metal hook. The package tells me the razors each have five blades. Why would any person need or want five blades? Nonetheless I put the package on the belt, which is dirty, smeared with something viscous and white. My stomach pitches. I look at Bennie once more. Gus's old coat practically swallows her up, and her expression is solemn, her dark eyes cast down. Still, she's so lovely.

"Cash or charge?" asks the cashier, a skinhead-looking kid with a blue tattoo on his neck.

"Charge," I say. Before Bennie can object, I take my card out of my wallet and run it through the machine. Miraculously, it works.

She doesn't thank me. She doesn't say anything at all. I step aside and she pushes the cart, now brimming with grocery bags, toward the doors. She goes through, while Owen waits for me by the vending machines. He has something in his hands: a plastic, neon-pink egg.

"What is it?" I ask.

"A surprise," he says.

My eyes jump from the egg to Bennie, who's outside, maneuvering the cart across the crosswalk, which is quickly disappearing under snow. "Come on," I say to Owen.

"I can't get it open," he whines. "Help."

"You can do it," I say.

"I can't," he says.

"I'll help you in the car."

Bennie is already by the LeBaron, loading bags into the trunk. "Come *on*," I say again, and step through the automatic doors into the cold. Behind me Owen dallies, locked in battle with the egg.

"Owen, get out here," I say over my shoulder, and step into the crosswalk. Bennie is almost finished loading the bags. I can see how upset she is by the clumsy, violent way she moves, and part of me feels awful; that part of me wants to tell her I'm sorry, and that I don't know what's wrong with me — that of course I want her to be happy, with Vincent or whoever, because I *do*, and that I can't seem to stop hurting people, no matter how hard I try. But watching her open the door and get into the driver's seat, another part of me is glad she's upset. That part hopes that someday someone tells her something that makes her feel as foolish and as lonely and as small as I do right now.

Owen is still standing on the sidewalk in front of the store. From across the crosswalk I shout at him, "Enough is enough, Owen. Get over here. *Now.*"

It's the *now* I won't be able to forget.

He looks up at me and steps into the parking lot at the same moment a mammoth silver 4 x 4 materializes, and as it slides over the snow-slick pavement toward him, I know exactly what's going to happen. I can see it happen in my mind, and in spite of this or perhaps because of it, I can't move. I stand there, frozen in place, watching two tons of metal slam into my son. Into Owen.

His head snaps back. His feet leave the firmament. He sails through the air.

The sky turns black. The world folds in on itself.

I scream, Bennie screams.

My life ends.

Everything ends.

32

EXCEPT THAT IT doesn't end.

The truck slides to a stop, its front bumper mere inches from Owen's hip. He stands there, stunned. The pink egg sits in the snow by his feet.

The driver tumbles out of the truck. She's a young woman, disheveled, with blue barrettes in her hair, hardly more than a child herself. She's talking nonsense. "Oh, my God, oh, my God. He came out of nowhere. I turned around to give Casey her giraffe and when I looked up there he was. Oh, my God, oh, my God." Snot drips from her nose. She swipes at it with her sleeve. Bile rises in my throat. Somewhere nearby, a baby cries.

Next thing I know I'm squatting in front of Owen, holding him by the shoulders. "Where's my egg?" he asks, dazed. "I need my egg."

"Fuck your egg," I say, and shake him once, hard. "Do you realize you almost just *died?* Do you *understand?* You didn't even look. You didn't even *look.*" My face is only a couple of inches from his. He struggles, trying to squirm away, but I hold him tight. "You have to pay *attention.* I won't always be here. Someday I'll be gone. Someday you'll be all alone, and the world — the world isn't going to look out for you. The world doesn't give a shit about you. The world isn't going to keep you from getting hurt."

His face has lost its color, and his eyes are wide. "You're hurting me," he says. Tears spill down his cheeks. I squeeze him tighter.

"Do you understand?" I shout again. "Tell me you *understand*."

"Easy now," says a voice. There's a hand on my shoulder: Bennie's. I don't turn around.

"Owen, look at me," I'm saying. "Look at me and tell me you hear me. Tell me you'll never do that again. Promise me. Promise me."

He doesn't promise, though. He's crying too hard to talk. He's crying so hard he can barely breathe.

"That's *enough*," Bennie says, pushing me out of the way. She bends down and takes him in her arms, and he buries his face in her hair and sobs. She carries him to her car while I watch. After he climbs in back and she closes the passenger-side door, she turns and looks at me.

My legs won't move. They feel like concrete. "Come on," she calls, waving. My throat is too tight to make any words, and there's a loud ringing in my ears. I shake my head, trying to make it go away. She shakes hers in response, gets in the driver's side, and drives over to where I'm standing. My legs are stone. She rolls down her window and says, "Get in."

I can't. I can't move. I can't talk.

Owen cries, curled up in the back seat. She looks at him, then me. "Get in," she says again.

The ringing doesn't stop. I say, "I can't."

"You can."

"Go," I say.

"What?"

"Go."

"Where? What?"

Now the words come. "Bennie, go. Take him home. Take him away from me."

"Logan," Bennie says.

"Dad?"

I can't bear to look at him.

"Don't do this," Bennie says.

"Go," I roar for the last time. "Both of you. Get out of my sight."

Bennie shakes her head silently, putting the car in gear. When it catches, she turns and looks up at me. "This is wrong," she says.

I push back from the car, and she drives away.

33

MINERS WORK AROUND the clock, so finding a bar that's open this early in the day isn't hard. The first one I come to, Percy's, occupies the southwest corner of Hayward and Main. The name and an arrow flash in green neon, pointing down a set of concrete stairs, which I descend.

The room is dark and empty. At one end sits an old jukebox with an Out of Order sign taped onto it. A Miller High Life sign plus a few outdated posters — one of a woman on a Porsche, one of Brooke Shields, one of horses galloping — constitute the décor. I sit on a stool. A big man with a bandanna on his head puts a cocktail napkin in front of me and asks me what I want to drink.

I order a beer and a shot of bourbon — I don't know why bourbon, I've never been able to stomach the stuff, but that's what I say. He says, "Coming right up," and turns away. I turn my attention to the TV in the corner, which is showing a competition for the world's strongest man. A brute with bulging veins lifts a block of concrete. Another pulls the cab of a truck by a chain. The bartender puts my drinks in front of me. His eyes are uncannily blue. I swallow the bourbon and start in on the beer.

"Another round," I say when the bartender comes back. He raises an eyebrow but does as I ask.

"How's your day going?" he asks, setting down my second beer.

I swallow the second shot instead of answering him. I'm three drinks in, almost four, before my hands stop shaking. After six I feel like I can breathe deeply enough to fill my lungs with air.

There are no other patrons. I drink steadily and somehow it becomes afternoon. I can tell from the changing quality of the light coming through the single window by the door.

I drink more. A young couple wanders in, drinks a beer, pays their bill. Two old guys in ball caps set up shop at the end of the bar. The bartender changes the TV channel to Fox, which is covering a mudslide in the Philippines. A reporter in a raincoat holds a microphone in one hand and tries to keep her hat on her head with the other. I start thinking about Bennie, and it hurts. I see Owen, sobbing, his face in her hair. Then I think about Julie. I think about her voice on the phone, the fear in it, and then for no reason I can name, I think about the night we met: I can see her now, standing in front of her apartment in her black dress, digging in her purse for the keys. From behind, I put my hands on her waist. She's startled. "Hold still," I say into her ear. I whisper, "Trust me." She closes her eyes and leans into me. I move my hands up and down her sides, holding on to her ribs, feeling her lungs fill with air.

With each drink I feel worse, but I keep at it. And why shouldn't I? Julie surely hates me — as she should. Owen's afraid of me. And the look in Bennie's eyes, outside the grocery store? Pure disdain.

The light in the room contracts, then expands. I turn around to watch another couple come in from the cold. The woman unwraps a knit scarf with a zigzag pattern from around her neck. She has a pretty face but the boy she is with is pimpled. The old men at the end of the bar sit silently, nursing pints of pale gold beer.

When I try to order yet another round, the bartender frowns and slides me my bill. I don't care what it is. I hand him my card.

The snow has stopped. It's late in the day, almost evening. The sky is dishwater gray.

I turn left out of Percy's and walk north, through desolate downtown, stopping in a seedy package store for a pint of whatever, which I've made it almost halfway through by the time Main Street runs into the railroad tracks. I wait for a train piled high with coal to pass, and then I follow a dirt path down to the river, which snakes along the eastern edge of town. I pass the hospital where Gus was born, with its big, white, light-up cross, and I drift, without quite intending to, into the part of Tobey where Gus grew up.

At his high school I stop and lean on a chain-link fence, watching some kids with their bottom halves encased in black garbage bags slide down a hill. It's twilight now, cold. I start walking again to stay warm. I find Gus's old street and walk the length of his block, but I can't find his house. I walk up and down the block again, and then again, but his house isn't where it's supposed to be. In its place there's the burned foundation of a house and some loose police tape, flapping in the wind. How could this have happened? Shouldn't someone have let me know? I sit on a curb across the street and stare at the empty lot until a woman in a housecoat and curlers steps onto her stoop, frowning at me and holding a phone. I stand up.

I start walking again, and maybe it's the cold, but I have the sensation that my feet aren't hitting anything, that I'm floating a few inches above the ground. Everything is bathed in moonlight. Everything looks silver. Nothing looks real. I look up. Stars streak across the sky, leaving trails of purple and green. Sometime later, I find myself on the steps of a church.

It's Our Lady of the Mines — Gus's church — and inside I stand at the back, waiting while my eyes adjust, making certain I'm alone. I am alone. I walk to the front, my wet sneakers squeaking on the polished stone floor, and I sit in the first pew, the very same spot where I sat four months ago. I close my eyes and let my head fall back.

That morning, the priest said love is stronger than death. He said love bears all things, believes all things, hopes all things, endures all things. He said that while we are certain to feel sorrow, we shouldn't weep. I didn't weep — not there. Bennie did. She sobbed unselfconsciously through the whole service. I can see her now, the tears dripping off her jaw and landing on the program she held with two black-gloved hands, in her lap. Julie cried too, but silently. I can see her also, standing when the priest said to stand, kneeling when he said to kneel, searching dutifully through her hymnal for the hymns, pausing now and again to press a balled-up Kleenex against her eyes.

And I can see myself. I'm up at the podium, holding on to my notes. My eyes are dry, but my hands tremble and the pages I hold are damp. In a shaky, uneven voice I read the lines Gus loved, the Whitman — lines I'd read to him so many times while he lay in bed that I knew them by heart: *I bequeath myself to the dirt to grow from the grass I love. If you want me again look for me under your boot-soles. You will hardly know who I am or what I mean, but I shall be good health to you nevertheless, and filter and fibre your blood. Failing to fetch me at first keep encouraged. Missing me one place search another, I stop somewhere waiting for you.*

I wake up in the dark with a headache, a pain in my neck, and an embroidered kneeling cushion under my cheek. I sit up and return the cushion to its hook. There's noise coming from somewhere behind me; I'm no longer alone. I make my way back toward the doors. In a small chapel to one side of the nave, an elderly couple kneels in front of a table covered with flickering candles in red glass jars.

Outside, it's dark. I don't know what time it is. The sky is riddled with stars. I start walking on Route 13, the road that leads up the canyon, out of town. With my hands in my pockets, I walk and walk. I pass the cemetery where Gus is buried but I don't dare stop. I can't even look. Cars zoom by me with their high beams on. I stumble along the road's slanted shoulder, keeping my eyes on Orion's belt. It can't be more than ten or fifteen degrees out. My thoughts slow until my head feels empty. The road finds the river. I keep walking, up the canyon, against the current. In the black water the stars sparkle: sky and earth, merged. I find a penny in my pocket. I make a wish.

34

IT DOESN'T COME true. I wake up alone in the front seat of my truck, shaking from the cold. My mouth feels like burlap and tastes sour. I sit up and blink, trying to get my bearings. I clear a circle of window and see the cabin, covered in snow and bathed in moonlight, all its windows black. I don't know how I got here, or if no one's home — which I can see from the empty driveway that they aren't — why I didn't go inside. I look at my watch, whose glow-in-the-dark hands point to two A.M. I step outside and trudge through the snow to the house.

As soon as I try the front door, I understand: she locked me out. "Goddamn it," I say aloud, kicking a stone at the bottom of the steps before heading to the back. I'm not surprised to find the same situation there. I stand, shivering, in the snow, watching the river, wondering what I'm supposed to do.

I don't relish the idea of breaking in, but I can rationalize it: Bennie has left me little choice. I search the riverbank for the proper stone, and finding one roughly the size of an apple, but with a point at one end, I go to the side of the cabin where there's a low window, and I tap the stone's prow against one of the panes until it breaks. Only when I've knocked the glass into the cabin do I realize my oversight; though the window sash is low, I still can't reach the lock, which is at least a foot too high.

I carry the rock around to the back, where I break one of the panes in the door, which is what I should have done in the first place, and then I cover my hand with my coat sleeve, reach inside, disengage the deadbolt, and turn the knob.

When I walk in, glass crunches under my feet but I don't care. I'm freezing. I turn on some lamps, stuff as many logs as I can into the wood stove, and with numb fingers strike five or ten matches before I get a spark. When the fire's started, I find a couple of plastic shopping bags under the sink, plus the duct tape Bennie used the other day, and I fashion two rough patches for the windowpanes I broke. The results aren't pretty, but they'll have to do. Under the sink I find a dustpan and a whisk broom, and I sweep up what I can see of the glass.

The work makes me warmer, but it's still cold enough in the cabin to see my breath. Laying my hand on the wood stove, I discover it's still ice cold, so I open it back up and add some pieces of old newspaper, but for some reason the fire won't light. I keep trying, feeding in matches one after another, but the flame keeps fading out. Finally I give up. I go into the kitchen and put a kettle of water on the stovetop to boil. While I'm waiting, I remember the brandy in the wall.

It doesn't take long to find; the square of wood gives under pressure from my palm, and the not-so-secret door springs open, revealing a single shelf with the bottle, still half full after who knows how long. I take it out and carry it to the table with the Mason jar Gus always used as a glass.

The stuff tastes like hell, but if memory serves it did back then, too, and the taste passes quickly, leaving intense warmth in its wake. I pour myself a second serving and slug it down. After that I stand over the oven and warm my hands. I take one more sip of brandy, a long one, straight from the bottle, and I think about all the lips that have touched that glass — lips that no longer exist. I think of Gus's lips. I think of his face. His hands. I think of him in his coffin, of his coffin in the cold, cold ground, and I shiver. I carry the bottle into the living room and sit down.

The photo albums are still out from when Owen was looking at them, and now I take one onto my lap and leaf through the crackling, plastic-lined pages, studying the faces of the Pyle dead. I'm looking for something, I don't know what. I pause at a shot of my grandfather, Paul. He's standing, unsmiling, outside a brick building, in an army uniform. He was a sweeper in the dry mill at the mine, starting when he was seventeen, and he died of mesothelioma (*asbestosis*, they called it then) two weeks before he turned sixty-four. Each year on his birthday, Gus took me to his grave, where he always left a sprig of holly and an airline-size bottle of Early Times. I look closer at the photo, searching for something familiar in Paul's features, but I come up blank. I turn the page. Here is one of Paul as a young man, shirtless and lean, grinning and kneeling by a river somewhere, holding an enormous, silver-skinned fish.

I'm putting the album away when a photo falls out and lands on the floor. I pick it up. It's the one Owen was talking about, the one of me on some dime-store Santa's lap. I hold it under the light. I'm screaming, fighting to get away, but the blue-eyed Santa's holding me by the forearms. Gus adored this picture. He thought it was hilarious. At dinner parties when I was a kid he would take it out and show it to his friends, and later, when I was a teenager, he would show it to mine. I never understood why; I assumed he got some sordid kind of pleasure out of humiliating me. But tonight I notice something new: Santa's watch. It's gold. I hold the photo up to my face. I've never really looked before, but tonight, for the first time, I see that the Santa is Gus.

I guess I fall asleep there, on the couch, because sometime later I wake up shivering again, my plastic-bag patches snapping in the wind. I sit up, and in the gray half-light of dawn I see snow blowing around the room. I get up and stumble into the kitchen, where I find the tape again and repair the patch on the door. Then I gather the blankets from the futon where Owen slept and wrap myself in them, breathing in the remnants of his scent while I try to sleep.

But of course I can't. Every time I close my eyes I see that truck barreling around the corner, Owen in its path. I open my eyes. All

I can think about is what a mess I've made of everything, of all the people I've hurt, of all the people I've let down. Julie. Owen. Bennie. Bill. Miss Pietryzyck — *Erica*. Stan. The dog — Jerry. Even the dead vermiculite miners. I even feel bad about them.

Outside the wind howls. I hear noises like voices, like laughter, like crying, like knuckles knocking against the windowpanes even though I know no one's there.

I get up. Wrapped in the blanket, I go into the kitchen and drink some orange juice from the carton, standing in the refrigerator's hard white light.

The sun is just beginning to rise. Through the trees I can see the slightest hint of dawn in the sky. I run a hot shower, as hot as I can stand, and I scrub my skin until it hurts. I wash my hair with Bennie's shampoo. When I'm finished, I stand naked in the steamy room, searching for my reflection. In the thickly fogged glass, I look more like a ghost than a man.

Still naked, I climb the ladder and hide between Bennie's clean, cold, blue-and-white-striped sheets.

35

"You're unbelievable," says a voice.

I open my eyes and see the light in the room has changed. Bennie is standing at the foot of the bed, directly in front of the window, so I can't see her face.

"What time is it?" I ask. "Is it morning already?" The smell of wood smoke hangs in the air.

"It's almost night. Four thirty."

"You came back," I say, sitting up. But my head hurts too much, and I lie down again and close my eyes.

"I live here," she says, and sits on the bed. She's wearing her coat and a knit cap with earflaps. She's brought me a glass of water, and she holds it out. I take it and set it on the nightstand. "You look terrible," she says. "Almost as bad as my house."

Flashes from last night come back to me: brandy, smoke, broken glass. "I'm sorry," I say.

"What happened down there?"

I shake my head and reach for the water. When I've drained the glass, I ask her if Owen's okay.

"Physically, yes."

I look at the window. The sun is low, about to disappear behind the ridge. "It's good that he's safe. It's good that he's with Julie."

She seems about to say something but at the last second changes her mind and presses her lips together. The light slanting in through the window illuminates her face. It finds the gold cross around her neck, the tiny gold flecks in her eyes. "I got really worried about you," she says in an unsteady voice. "I had this awful feeling. I drove back here way too fast. The whole time I was thinking I shouldn't have."

"Driven so fast?"

"Come back."

"I'm glad you did," I say.

She looks down.

The next time I come to, it's dark. Bennie sits next to me, this time holding a steaming mug in her hands. She sets it on the nightstand and turns on the lamp. The clock says it's after nine. "Chicken soup," she says. "Give it a few minutes to cool."

I try sitting up again. My head hurts less than it did before. When the steam from the soup reaches my nose, my stomach groans. "About the window," I say. "And the door. I'll have them both replaced tomorrow, first thing."

"And the rug?"

I ask what she means, and she tells me there are singed spots all over it — where I tossed the matches, I guess. "Plus you left the stove on. You're just lucky you didn't burn the place down."

"Jesus. I'm sorry. Then that, too."

She shrugs. When she moves her necklace catches the light. "I never liked that rug anyway. It was your dad who was dead set against all things new."

"Still. I had no right," I say. I pick up the mug and raise it to my lips; the broth is hot and salty, like tears.

She watches me. "They're just things. They aren't what matters."

I set the mug back down and look at her. "I've really fucked everything up, haven't I?"

"Yes, you have," she says.

"I meant that more rhetorically."

"Well." She reaches over and brushes my hair out of my eyes with her fingers. They feel cold. "You need to go home. You know you do."

I look into the mug. "I don't think I can."

"You can," she says.

I shake my head. "You don't understand. Everything's ruined. Owen's terrified of me. And I bet Julie would be happy if she never saw me again. I wouldn't even blame her if that's how she felt."

"You know it's not," she says. She pulls her feet up on the bed and crosses her legs. "Julie loves you. And you love Julie. And most of all, you both love Owen. That's reason to go back in itself."

"Fine," I say, unable to keep the petulance out of my voice. "I'll go tonight. I'll go right now, if that's what you want."

Her fingers are woven together. She looks at her thumbs. Her hair falls forward. "This isn't about what I want."

Before I can think better of it, I reach out and touch her head, tracing the pale line of scalp where her hair is parted. She doesn't look up. I can hear her breathing. She says, "If I tell you something embarrassing, do you promise you won't laugh?"

"I promise."

She's still looking down. "I had such a wicked crush on you, that first summer."

My heart thumps. I don't say anything.

"You were so handsome, and sweet, and when you hurt your leg — It's not funny." She bats me on the leg. "You promised."

"I'm laughing at *me*," I say. I stop smiling. "I was so in awe of you. I would have gouged out my eyes if you'd asked me to. But you knew that."

She shakes her head. "I didn't. I had no idea, I swear. I always thought you just tolerated me. I mean, you were polite and everything, but if you had your druthers, I wouldn't have been around." She pauses. "I was the interloper. I mean, it was just the two of you for a long time, before."

"It wasn't that." I clear my throat, gather my courage. "I was in love with you. You'll say I wasn't really, or that I was only seventeen, but it was real. It caused me a lot of pain." Downstairs, the fire crackles. "I loved you, and I hated you for it — and for loving Gus. He always got everything he wanted — or it seemed that way to me. I know it doesn't make much sense."

"It does," she says. "In the way that how we feel doesn't always — or it doesn't have to — that's what I mean. And you know what? Gus felt the same way about you. He never quite came out and said it, but I could tell."

"I don't understand," I say.

"It's simple. You had so much. From where he stood, you had everything. Your mind, and your strength, and your health, and then Julie and Owen, so much promise, and this whole wonderful life ahead of you — you had your youth, I guess it comes down to. No matter how badly he wanted it, he couldn't have that." She looks like she's thinking hard. After a long moment, she says, "Julie doesn't like me, does she? She never has."

I start to protest, but I stop. "It isn't your fault" is all I say.

She smiles a little sadly and reaches over and covers my hand with hers. "What I said the other night? It's the truth. You're so much like him — and I don't just mean your nose."

I consider this. "I've always thought we were so different. We always have been."

"Yes and no," she says. "I'm thinking about how you are in the world. And your sense of humor. And what makes you happy — and sad. And then there's your big heart — don't even get me started on that." She looks down. "All those things, I know they're abstract, but they're important. They're what make up a human being. And they're the things I loved him for, and they're in you, too. Is what I'm saying so hard to understand?"

I shake my head. I'm afraid if I move my hand she'll take hers away, so I stay still.

She laughs, or maybe she's crying a little, it's hard to tell. "You need to go home," she says.

But I'm not ready, yet. "What I said to you the other day, in the store?" I say. She looks at me and waits. She bites down on her lip. "I shouldn't have. I want you to be happy. I do. And I'll be happy if you marry Vince — or whoever — if you are. Happy, I mean."

"You don't have to say that." She sniffles. "You don't have to say anything else." She is crying, after all. Tears slide down her cheeks. I reach over and wipe one away with my thumb. She doesn't pull away. "You have to leave," she says. "Now." I don't say anything. "You know you do."

"I'm afraid," I say.

She says, "You should be." She squeezes my hand once, and then she lets me go.

In the dark, I gather my things and leave while Bennie sleeps. Backing out of the driveway, I pause a moment with my foot on the brake to look at the cabin one more time. I wonder if I'll be back here; maybe I'll bring Owen someday after all, take him hunting or teach him to fish. But it's hard to imagine. In fact, I can't imagine coming back here, ever, for any reason. Still, my imagination — I'm learning — is a deeply flawed instrument, one that has failed me before and is almost certain to fail me again.

When I flip on my high beams, I think I see a figure in the window upstairs: a flash of pale behind the black glass, there and then gone. I glance over at the passenger seat, where Gus's father's bottle of brandy is propped against Owen's stuffed duck. One last look at the window, which is black again, and then I pull out onto the road.

At the bottom of the canyon, where the road forks, I turn left, toward town, instead of right, toward the highway. The sun is getting ready to rise, and the first shadow of daylight tints the eastern sky. By the time I pass through the cemetery's open gates and find the arbitrary rectangle of earth where my ancestors have been laid to rest for the last century and a half, the sky is streaked with wide ribbons of gold and red.

It's a frigid morning. The moment I step out of the truck and onto the snow, the cold infiltrates me, burning my nostrils, all the way down into my lungs. I put up my hood and zip my coat all the way, but I don't have gloves so I carry the bottle in my bare hands, stepping around the various Pyle headstones until I find myself standing in front of Gus's grave. His is the newest one. The ground hasn't yet found its level, and in front of his headstone, the earth, covered with fresh snow, makes a vaguely casket-shaped mound.

Hesitantly, I step closer, and closer still, until — I suppose — I'm standing right on top of him. I study the inscription, "Heart of Gold," and I think about what Bennie said. I try to think of similarities between the two of us, things we shared, things we both loved: the smell of pine tar, baseball on the radio, cherry pie. But these are superficial things. I close my eyes and try harder: eggs over easy, Johnny Cash, the Fourth of July, swimming in cold water. And then another thing we both loved, a bigger one, dawns on me: Bennie. Finally, this morning, I understand.

I open my eyes just in time to see a hawk swoop down and snatch something small and brown from the snow, a few feet from Gus's stone. The hawk's gone in an instant, but it leaves a perfect imprint of its wings behind. I wish Bennie could see it. She would say they look like angel's wings, and she'd probably insist it was a harbinger of good things to come.

It's time for me to go home. I kneel down in front of the stone and dig a hole in the snow with my bare hands. I dig until I get to grass, and I put the brandy bottle there, at the bottom, as close to Gus as it will go, and then, with hardly any feeling left in my fingers, I fill the hole back in.

Part V

36

WHY ARE DOORS so much harder to open than they are to close?

It's Saturday, a few minutes before eleven, sunny and cold, and I'm standing outside the Aquatic Complex, gathering the wherewithal to go in. Warily I scan the parking lot for Julie's car but don't see it, and I take a sip of the coffee I bought at the Shell station on my way into town. It's not even a little warm anymore, and as I go over and toss it in the trash, I notice that the thermometer on the sign has been filled in completely with red, and the thermometer-creature has been altered so he's saying, "Thanks a million, folks," and proffering a hearty thumbs-up.

"Logan? Is that you?" says a voice. I turn around. It's Jennifer Huber-Green, holding Arturo by the wrist and looking concerned. "Everything okay? We haven't seen you since the party. And Arturo said Owen missed school."

"He had a cold," I say.

She raises an eyebrow, like she's deciding whether or not to believe me, or maybe like she doesn't believe me at all, and she's deciding whether or not to say so. Either way, I'm grateful when Arturo starts tugging on her arm. He says, "Mom, I'll miss the relay. Come *on*."

"Yes, *sir*," she says. To me she says, "You coming in?"

We all proceed into the lobby, where Arturo splits off to change into his trunks. I tell Jennifer to go into the gallery without me, and when I follow a couple of minutes later I choose a spot high in the bleachers, at the very back. The first thing I do is scan the pool for

Owen. As usual, he's easy to find, clinging to a yellow Eden kick-board, making his way across the shallow end. His progress is slow, but the expression on his face is determined. I knew I missed him these last couple of days, but the emotion I feel now, seeing him, is like a wave breaking over me. I sit down, loosen my scarf, and unzip my coat, breathing in the chlorine-saturated air and watching him kick his way from one side of the pool to the other. When he reaches the wall, he grins and pumps one fist in the air, looking up into the bleachers for his mother, who stands up and waves at him with both hands.

Julie: here she is, sitting alone at the far end of the second row. Clearly she didn't see me come in. She blows Owen a couple of kisses and sits back down. She's wearing her glasses and she has a pen in her hand, and I can see, on the seat beside her, her cell phone and a thick manila folder, which she picks up as soon as Owen and the other kids start climbing out of the pool. I hang back and watch her work, gathering my nerve while the other parents file out. In the slow-moving crowd I spot Donna Zilinkas but no Tom, and I quickly look away.

After five or ten minutes, Julie and I are the only two left in the gallery, and I'm contemplating my approach when Owen appears on the other side of the glass, still in his swim trunks, and sees me. His face contorts with delight; he grins and waves, and Julie turns around.

The expression on *her* face I would not describe as delight. Her eyes are small, narrowed, and her mouth is a straight line. I wave to Owen and pantomime that I'll see him up front in a few minutes. Then, heart pounding, I descend the bleachers. By the time I reach Julie, she's gathered her belongings and is standing up.

"Hi," I say.

"What are you doing here?" she says, and starts toward the door.

I follow. "Julie."

She turns around and says, "What." The fury in her voice stops me cold.

I clear my throat and swallow. "Can we talk?"

"No," she says, and turns away. This time I let her go.

After a couple of minutes I follow her through the doors and into the lobby, where the parents' committee has set up what appears to be a Mexican-themed reception. Jennifer Huber-Green stands behind a red-clothed table in a sombrero, wearing an apron with a sombrero on it, grinning and handing out cups of juice.

I see Julie in the corner, hunched over, plugging her ear with her index finger and talking on the phone, so I station myself by the locker room in hopes of intercepting Owen, and a couple of minutes later he comes bursting through the door and hurls himself into my chest. "I missed you, bud," I say, hugging him hard. "You have no idea how much."

"Ow, Dad," he says, "that hurts."

Over his shoulder I see Julie see us. She pockets her cell phone and crosses the lobby in quick, even strides. Her expression is still stony, but her eyes look fierce. I hold on to Owen until she reaches us, and then I stand up, take hold of his hand for strength, and tell her in as normal a voice as I can muster that I'll bring him home.

"No, you won't," she says. Her voice is sharp and restrained.

"Excuse me?" I say.

"I said, *No, you won't.* You're not taking him anywhere." She turns to Owen. Unsmilingly, she says, "Come on, monkey. Let's go home."

My throat tightens as Owen drops my hand and picks up his swim bag off the floor. I try to catch Julie's eye but I can't. I say her name.

She looks up at me and blinks.

"I know you're angry."

I'm not finished talking — I've barely even started — but she cuts me off. "Goddamn right I'm angry," she says, reaching for Owen. She's not talking so quietly anymore. A few nearby parents turn to look.

"Calm down, please," I say in a low voice.

"Calm down? Calm down? How dare you," she says. People are staring now. She takes hold of Owen.

They head for the doors, leaving me alone in the sea of overtly interested Eden parents. To prove I'm not intimidated, I take a doughnut from one of the tables and wash it down with some of Jennifer's juice.

For the next hour or so, though, I drive around town, thinking, circling our neighborhood and passing by our home, imagining what awaits me inside. Every time I decide I'm ready to go in, something stops me, and I take a left instead of a right, or a right instead of a left, or I keep going straight instead of making the turn. I cross the river and weave through downtown. I haven't even been gone a week, but everything looks different. It's officially become The Most Wonderful Time of the Year; big plastic snowflakes swing from the streetlights, and wide red ribbons have transformed the telephone poles into presents. On Main Street I encounter the ice-sculpting festival, the annual event with the dubious mission of uniting undergraduates with power tools and beer, and from my truck I watch a couple of girls in wacky, Christmas-themed attire try their hand at the Arc de Triomphe.

I'm in no mood for merriness. I decide to find Bill and see if he'll talk to me — he has to be easier to appease than Julie. I drive to the silo but it's locked up and my keys are at home, so I walk around to the front, where a handwritten sign in the darkened window says, "Closed until further notice, the Management." I look around; Bill's motorcycle isn't in the lot. I get back in my truck and sit in the parking lot there, staring at the river. A lone fisherman stands about halfway out in waders and a heavy jacket, casting his line. It's late afternoon by now, and the winter light is harsh and lovely, the water flat. The man catches nothing, doesn't even get a nibble as far as I can see, but again and again he reels the line in and tosses it out again, in that unhurried manner that certain fishermen possess. The light begins to change. Eventually he leaves, fishless, and watching him make his way up the rocky bank to where he's parked behind the supermarket, I wonder if he's disappointed, but something in the way he carries himself, the way he loads his gear, still unhurried, into the back of his truck, tells me he's probably not. I watch until his tail-lights disappear. It's almost dusk. It's time for me to go home.

First, I drive to Turtle Mountain and buy all the foods Julie prefers, and some fancy wine and some tiger lilies, white and orange, the kind she likes best. There's a long line at checkout, plus some festival-generated traffic coming back through town, and by the time I pull up in front of the house it's nearly dark. I stand on the stoop with three bulging bags in my arms plus the flowers and use my thumb to ring the bell.

Owen lets me in. "Hey, buddy," I say, handing him the flowers. "You want to do me a favor and deliver those to your mom?"

He carries them into the living room. I take the groceries into the kitchen and listen for her reaction, but I can't hear anything so I put the perishables away and go into the living room myself.

Julie sits at the far end of the sofa in sweatpants, slippers, and one of Gus's old shirts. Her knees are drawn up, and the thick folder from the pool sits open on the cushion, near her hip. The flowers I bought lie on the coffee table, still in their white paper cone. Jerry is curled on the floor in front of the fireplace, and to my great surprise he lifts his head and thumps his tail against the floor when I come in.

"Look at that. Somebody missed me," I say, squatting by him and scratching him behind the ears.

"Dogs have no sense of time. You could have been gone ten minutes or ten years," Julie says without looking up. The TV is on, but she's not watching it. She uses the pen in her hand to write something down.

Owen stands in the doorway, looking uneasy. He glances from me to her, and then at the TV screen. It's a show about space. He puts his hands in his pockets and rocks from his heels to his toes and back again a couple of times, a gesture so unchildlike my heart hurts. "Do you think you could give us a minute, bud?" I say. "Maybe take Jerry out in the yard?"

"It's too cold," Julie says.

"It's not so bad. The sun was out all afternoon."

"I said no," Julie says. To Owen she says, "It's okay. Sit down. Watch the show."

"Julie," I say.

Now she looks up at me. Behind her glasses, her eyes are rimmed in red.

"Go upstairs, Owen, just for a couple of minutes," I say. "I want to have a conversation with Mom."

"Don't," Julie counters. "Sit." He obeys.

I don't know what I expected, but somehow it wasn't this. I stand there for a long moment, waiting to see if she'll look at me again, but it seems the answer is no, so I gather the flowers off the table and carry them into the kitchen, where I trim the stems and arrange them in a tall glass vase, then set them on the table in there. Then I put the groceries away and start cooking supper. I'm trimming the fat off some grass-fed organic beef when I hear Julie's voice behind me.

"What's that?" she says.

I turn around. "Dinner," I say. "I'm making chili."

"I'm not hungry," she says.

"It's only five thirty. It'll take a while."

"I don't want any," she says, making a face at the meat. Crossing her arms over her chest, she inspects the lilies. If it's possible, she looks even skinnier than she did before I left. "You didn't clip the stamens," she says. "You always forget."

"I'll clip them."

"If you don't clip them, the pollen gets everywhere. I keep telling you that."

"Okay," I say.

"And for the record, you shouldn't buy tiger lilies. You shouldn't buy fresh-cut flowers at all. They're basically soaked in poison, and they pay the people who grow them nothing. And did you ever consider how much fossil fuel it takes to get them here?"

I put down my knife. "Julie."

She looks up at me.

I wipe my hands on my pants. "I'm sorry."

She doesn't answer.

"I really am," I say.

"For what?" she says.

"For everything. For Thanksgiving, and for the things I said, and for not telling you about the offer, but mostly for taking Owen. I know how you must have felt, and I feel terrible about that."

Her expression is flat again. "You have no idea how I felt."

I say, "Okay, then tell me."

"You broke *my* heart," she says.

A lump pushes into my throat. "No. Jules. It was only a couple of days. I never meant to — "

"Stop. You'll only make it worse. Please."

"But I need to explain. I need you to listen."

She glares at me. "If you care about me at all, you'll stop right now. I'm not kidding."

"Mama?" Owen's standing in the doorway, sucking his thumb and tugging on his ear.

She turns to face him, and her demeanor changes completely. She smiles. "Sweetpea," she says.

"I'm ready to go to bed."

"It's not even six o'clock," I say. "It's not a school night."

"He's tired." Julie crosses the kitchen and picks him up. "It takes a very sensible little boy to know that."

I rinse my hands at the sink and dry them on a dishtowel. "I'll take him up," I say.

Julie stops me. She doesn't even bother to say no, she just carries him out of the room.

I hear the bath water running upstairs, and I get myself a beer. From the kitchen table I can hear Owen splashing in the tub, the two of them laughing, and then afterwards, the sound of the drain. Their footsteps move into our bedroom, and I hear the gentle rise and fall of Julie's voice, reading to him. And then I hear nothing. I wait for the sound of her feet on the stairs but it doesn't come. I keep waiting. I drink another beer. I finish assembling the chili. Around seven, I make a sandwich. I watch some TV. Eight becomes nine, and she's still up there. It's after ten by the time I admit to myself that she's not coming down.

37

SUNDAY DAWNS COLD and clear. I wake up early in the sun-filled sewing room after a few hours of fitful sleep. Downstairs, Owen's stationed in front of cartoons and Julie is up, too, working away already at the desk under the stairs. When I say, "Good morning," she offers no reply.

I pour myself coffee and carry it into the living room, where I ask Owen if he wants to join me for a swim.

"It's Sunday. They're closed," he says without looking up.

He's right, of course. I pick up his empty cereal bowl from the coffee table and take it into the kitchen, where I stand in front of the glass doors, looking out. A couple of squirrels are chasing each other up the apple tree, whose branches are bare except for a few remarkably stubborn pieces of fruit.

"Hey, Owen," I call into the living room. "I'm embarking on a home-improvement project. Want to help?"

"What kind of home-improvement project?" he shouts back.

"I'm going to build you a swing. I'm going to hang it from the apple tree. Come on, get your coat."

"It's too cold," Julie says from her desk.

"It's not, it's sunny. Look for yourself," I shout back.

She doesn't look. "Could you stop shouting, please? I'm trying to work."

I bite my tongue. From the front hall I get my coat, and some work gloves from the closet upstairs. I pass Julie coming and going but she keeps her head down. In the kitchen I put on my boots and then I go out back and push open the door to Gus's shed.

I haven't been out here since before Gus died, nobody has, but aside from some cobwebs and a layer of dust, it looks exactly how it did when he was alive: meticulous, every single thing in its place. A calm feeling comes over me, now, looking around. There is comfort in order. This was a concept, it occurs to me now, that he was constantly trying to convey.

The white-pine board I bought expressly for this purpose, five years back (the October before Owen was born, and before Gus got sick), still leans against the wall. I pick it up, dust it off, and lay it across the twin sawhorses that have sat stacked in the corner for almost as long.

On the rear wall hangs Gus's collection of saws. I can remember standing right here, nearly three decades ago, while he instructed me on the relative merits of the ripsaw versus the crosscut versus the jigsaw versus the hack, explaining the physics of each and its particular dangers, then naming all the various parts and having me say them back, when all I wanted in the world was to hold one of the sharp-toothed beauties in my hands.

Now I take the crosscut saw off its nail and lay it on the workbench, then measure out three feet of wood and trace a straight line using Gus's square, which hangs on a nail over the bench. I make the first cut slowly and carefully, inhaling the sweet lemon smell of the sawdust. I guess I shouldn't be surprised at how sharp the blade is, even now, how easily it glides through the wood.

I've worked up a sweat. I take off my jacket and toss it over the horse. Once the seat has been cut, I bevel the edges and each corner. In a drawer under the bench I find Gus's supply of sandpaper, arranged (of course) in order, according to grit. I work my way through all the grades, the way he taught me, starting with rough and progressing to fine.

Now, the holes for the rope: Gus kept his drill locked in a big iron safe under the window, which I squat in front of now, wishing I'd thought to ask him the combination. I try his birthday first, and then just the year he was born, and when that doesn't work I try Bennie's, and then the house address, moving the dial to and fro to no avail. As a last resort I try my own birthday — 9-13-74 — and the lock pops open. What do you know.

I take out the drill and the box of bits and set them on the bench, and then I go back in for the hole saw, which I can also remember him lecturing me on how to use. It's exactly where it's supposed to be, of course, and though I'm new to it and a little awkward, I manage to attach it to the drill and cut two satisfactory holes, one at each end of the seat.

I lay the saw blade outside on the grass to cool, and when I come back in, I scan the shelves for some sealant. On a high shelf I spot some Surekote. With a paintbrush I find in a drawer marked "Paintbrushes," I cover the swing with two coats and set it up in Gus's vise to dry.

Back in the house, I go down to the basement and move aside boxes of baby clothes and books and outdated appliances and sports equipment we never use until I find the coil of rope I bought five years back, still in the plastic bag from the store. I take it out and inspect it, inch by inch, for fraying. Finding none, I hoist it onto my shoulder and climb the stairs.

38

THAT NIGHT I reheat the chili and set the kitchen table for two while Julie puts Owen to bed. She comes downstairs in gray U of M sweats and sits in a chair without speaking to me.

"Did he go down okay?" I ask, setting a steaming bowl in front of her.

"He's fine," she says. I've poured us each a glass of overpriced organic wine from Washington State, and I taste mine.

"I know you're still upset," I say.

"I can't have this conversation right now. I'm exhausted," she says, and I believe her. Her eyes are bloodshot, and there's no color in her face.

"Then when?"

She takes a tentative bite of her food, swallows with apparent difficulty, and puts down her spoon.

Working to control my voice, I say, "Unless I'm wasting my time. Maybe working things out isn't what you want. Maybe you want to be with Tom Zilinkas. Is that it?"

"Don't be an ass," she says.

"Look, I screwed up. Bigtime. I know I did. But you've barely been around lately, and I miss you, we both do. And I'm busting my ass to take good care of Owen, I really am, and it feels like all I do is chase you around, and then I have to find out from Miss Pietryzyck — from *Erica* — that you've gone and switched Owen's class, just like that. Did you ever stop to think how that made me feel?"

"Logan," she says.

"Wait. I'm not done. And then, next thing I know, there you are, on the bed, with that pig? I just went ballistic, Jules. It was like everything exploded. I'm not justifying what I did. I hope you don't think I am. I'm only trying to explain."

Slowly she takes her napkin from her lap and wipes her mouth. "I'm pregnant," she says.

I'm sure I've heard her wrong. "What?"

She nods silently.

"Oh, my God," I say.

"I'm not sure what *he* has to do with it." She lays the napkin on the table. "I'm exhausted, I told you. I'm going to bed." She starts to get up but I catch her wrist.

"You can't just drop that kind of news and leave. You can't. It's not fair."

She twists her hand away. "Since when did 'fair' become part of the equation?" She carries her bowl over to the trash and tips the chili in. Her posture — her whole demeanor — emanates defeat.

"Are you even — " I take a deep breath. "Aren't you happy?"

She turns to face me. "I don't know what I am, honestly. I'm tired."

"Well, I'm happy. I'm thrilled," I say, even though I know I probably shouldn't.

She sets her bowl in the sink. Still facing the window, she says, "Considering the circumstances, do you actually think bringing a child into this house is the best idea?" It takes a minute for what she's suggesting to sink in. Before I can respond, she says, "I'm sorry, but I'm trying to be realistic. I'm trying to consider the child."

I don't know what to say. My hands tremble, so I clasp them together. "Julie, please. I told you I'm sorry. What else can I say? I love you. You have to believe me. You have to give me a chance."

She turns to face me. "I need to know what happened up there. With Bennie."

"Nothing happened," I say.

She doesn't seem to hear me, though. "You need to tell me, in the plainest terms possible, what it is between you and her. Because ever since I met you, it's been there. That very first night at the party, when your dad brought her up on the stage, I knew it, even if I didn't know exactly what it was that I knew."

"Julie, no. It isn't like that. I know I've hurt you, but you have to believe me. It's you I love."

And then, just like that, she starts to cry. Real sobs. Tears stream down her cheeks.

"Julie, baby, no," I say. I go over and try to touch her, but she pulls away.

"Can you imagine how I felt, when it's *her* who brings Owen home? Knowing that's where you went? *That's* where you took him? It was the cruelest thing you could have done."

I reach for her again, and this time she lets me hold her. Maybe she's too worn out to resist. I tell her I'm sorry again. She says nothing. She just cries.

After what feels like ages, I step back and put my hands on her shoulders. Her nose is running and her eyes are bright red. "I love you. It's not Bennie I want. It's you. Us. More than anything. How can I make you see that?"

She wipes her nose on her sleeve and studies my face. She sniffles. "If you stand here and tell me you mean that, and if you look me in the eye when you say it, then I'm prepared to believe you."

I look her in the eye. "I mean it."

She makes a small nod. "Okay," she says.

"Okay? That's all?"

"That's all," she says, and then she leaves. I hear her footsteps on the stairs and in the bedroom, and then the familiar clank of water waking old pipes, overhead: Julie, running water for a bath.

I can't sleep. In the sewing room I lie on my back with my eyes open, studying the clouds I painted on the ceiling for Owen, all those Octobers ago. This was supposed to have been his room, but he never spent a single night in here. When we brought him home, we were way too nervous to let him sleep away from us, so we had his bassinet right next to our bed, and for the first couple of months, Julie slept with her fingers resting on his chest. I remember looking over and seeing her arm draped over the side. All night long, she'd wake up every few minutes and check to make sure he was breathing, even though the hospital had sent us home with a machine that kept track of that, plus his heart rate and the oxygen level in his blood.

Then, also, Gus was in decline. He and Bennie spent the winter fighting over whether he should see a doctor, and he spent as many nights here — in the sewing room — as he did in their bed, with her. By summer, this room was unofficially his. Bennie had taken to sleeping in the guest room, still stacked with moving boxes Julie had yet to unpack, or more often, wrapped in a blanket on the sofa downstairs, and she insisted we take the master bedroom, which we did. Owen stayed where he was — in my boyhood room, next door.

I think about him in there, now, and about Julie in our bed, all alone. I close my eyes. It's in *this* bed, in this very spot, that Gus took his last breath, and I wonder, tonight, if some piece of him still lingers — if the soul hangs around eternally in places a person experienced great joy or pain, like Bennie believes it does. Or if, like Bill said the other day, gone is gone. I turn onto my side but I can't get comfortable. I think about Bill, about the store, about the land. I think about the tiny new life inside Julie. I think about Tom Zilinkas. I think about Owen. I think about Stan. I start to get that feeling in my chest. I close my eyes, but the harder I try to sleep, the more unlikely sleep becomes.

I get up. At the desk under the stairs, I turn on the out-of-date desktop Julie and I share, and I open up my e-mail. I read Valentine's note again, then once more, and then I begin to type. *Dear Professor Valentine*, I write. My heart thumps a couple of times, but I ignore it. *Logan Pyle here. We've never met, but contrary to what you might think, I haven't fallen into a sinkhole, or disappeared from the face of the Earth; I actually exist. I'm ALIVE. Do you have any idea how spectacular that feels, to type? And how about this one: I am going to finish my dissertation by June. I imagine this sounds absurd to you, and probably impossible, but defying expectations is something at which we Pyle men have excelled over the years. I look forward to speaking with you so we can discuss. Sincerely, Logan Pyle.*

I read it over. The only change I make is adding "Augustus" to my name. But that's all. I don't read it over again. I hit "Send."

After that I call Bill. He doesn't answer his phone (it is the middle of the night, after all), and honestly I'm a little relieved. "I'm sorry for the other day," I tell his voice mail. "I was an asshole, and in retrospect I have to admit you made some strong points. You're my best friend and I feel like shit about pretty much every single thing I said, and the truth is I miss the hell out of you already. So call me back, okay? If you do, we can talk about the store. No promises, but I'm willing to talk."

After that I call Stan. "It's four o'clock in the morning, kiddo," he says. "Somebody better have died."

"It's okay with me," I tell him. "The exhumation. Just tell me where I need to sign."

"Holy crap, kiddo," he says. "This is great news. Are you sure?"

I tell him I am, and he says he'll have the papers ready tomorrow, first thing. Before we hang up he asks me what it was that changed my mind.

"Somebody did die," I say. "I guess I just took a while to understand that it wasn't me."

39

First thing in the morning, I drive to the Zilinkases' house and park behind a yellow-painted truck, out of which two burly, tattooed men are attempting to unload a grand piano. For a few minutes I watch them struggle, moving the lacquered black behemoth a few inches at a time down the ramp, stopping every few seconds to rest.

I check my reflection in the mirror. My cuts from the glass are still evident, if healing, and I have dark circles under my eyes from how little I've slept. I look pummeled and ragged, like I've been in a fight, which I guess, in a way, I have.

It's Donna who answers the door. She wears oversize sunglasses and a clingy, pastel-pink jogging suit. Diamonds the size of cocktail onions sparkle in her ears. I clear my throat and do my best to stand tall. "Good morning, Donna. I'll bet I'm the last person you want to see."

"Sorry. That spot's already taken," she says. Her voice is high, like a child's, and I realize this is the first time I've actually heard her speak — aside from the moon bounce. She glances out at the piano situation and frowns. "It's a Steinway, from 1923," she says — presumably to me. "Tom's grandfather bought it in Chicago. They had it in Denver, where they lived. His mother was very musical. She passed away a few months ago, his father is moving to a condo, and Tom insisted on having it shipped."

I clear my throat. "I know it's early," I say. "I was hoping to speak with Tom."

"He's not here," she says. She crosses her arms over her chest. I ask when she expects him back, and she says, "Not for at least another couple of days. Not if he has any sense — which is debatable, at this point." She smiles weakly. "I'm sorry. Where are my manners? I haven't had my coffee yet." I notice she speaks with a slight southern drawl. "I'm not myself before coffee. Did you want to come in?"

Uneasily I follow her through the foyer. Her giant white sneakers squeak with every step she takes, crossing the black-and-white marble floor. I glance up the spiral staircase, and I start to get upset, remembering the last time I was here. I tell myself to breathe. I think about Julie. I remind myself why I've come.

In the kitchen, Donna makes a beeline for the coffeemaker. From a glass carafe she pours out two cups and adds cream from a white porcelain pitcher shaped like a cow. I accept the mug she hands me and try the coffee. It's very strong.

She says, "He's up at the lake. He can't come home until I say it's okay." Her skin looks pale, and rough in spots, and I realize how much makeup she must usually wear to look the way she usually does.

I swallow more coffee and say, "I see."

"It'll be all right. He knows what a shit he's been. He'll buy me something extravagant, and make a laundry list of promises, and we'll forget the whole thing. That's how the lake house came to be, and these earrings — it's not entirely terrible, when Tom screws up." She produces a stiff smile. She's still wearing her sunglasses. With shaky hands she lifts her coffee to her lips. When she puts it down, she says, "I apologize." She props her sunglasses on top of her head. Her eyes are puffy, and the whites look pink. "We hardly know each other. You must think I'm a complete nut."

Something about her does seem unhinged, it's true, but I say, "It's okay. I'm not exactly the poster boy for sanity either, these days." She looks curious.

"That's why I'm here," I say, gathering my courage. In my head I've rehearsed my apology — and my proposition — at least fifteen times. But one of the piano movers comes in just then, and he informs Donna that the piano qualifies as a double-oversize item, hence there will be a double charge for getting it into the house. "The money doesn't matter," she says. "Just get it done."

Once he's gone, I say, "It's about Tom's boat. And his offer on my land. I was hoping he and I could work something out."

"It's a shame, what happened to that boat," she says.

I clear my throat again. "I know. It was a mistake," I say. "I wasn't thinking clearly. But I have every intention of — "

She interrupts me. "A tree branch falling, smashing up the windshield like that? What are the odds? Henry Pierce, our caretaker, called it an act of God. Henry's a very superstitious person. He thinks everything is an omen or a sign, or fate. Tom doesn't go in much for God. He had the boat insured to the gills. He's already gotten it fixed. It didn't cost him a dime."

"I'm glad to hear that," I say, trying to read the expression on her face.

She puts her sunglasses back on. "Sometimes these things just happen," she says. "There's no point in searching for an explanation. You just have to move on. That's what I told Tom."

"Does he agree?"

"Tom is a businessman," she says. "He's a very practical person. Wait here." She leaves the room. While I'm alone I look around. A bowl of bright green apples sits on the center island. There's not a bruise on one of them, and I wonder if they're fake. I reach out and take one in my hand, but I still can't tell.

Donna comes back, and I put the apple down. She's carrying my Louisville Slugger. "Cecelia, Henry's wife, likes to sit out on the dock with her lunch. She spotted this bobbing in the reeds." She holds it out to me. "Tom never even got to see it — or the boat. He was in L.A. Which is too bad. He gets a kick out of antique sports things."

I'm overjoyed to be reunited with my bat. I want to hug it, but I refrain. I run my fingers up and down the shaft, feeling the smooth grain of the wood. "I thought this was a goner," I say.

"Henry fished it out. He thought it might be valuable." She gets the coffee carafe again and pours herself a second cup. She offers me more but I refuse. My blood is bounding through my veins as it is.

"Tell Henry thanks, really," I say, thumbing the burned, black letters that make up my name. "It's not valuable. Or it is, but only to me." This gets me thinking about Tom's offer again, and maybe it does the same for her, because she opens a drawer, gets out a piece of paper, and writes a phone number down. "This is the number at the lake," she says. "If you want to talk business, you should give him a call." She holds the piece of paper out and smiles kindly.

I don't take it. "I'm not sure what I want, to tell you the truth."

"Okay," she says, and withdraws her hand.

Something about her makes me want to explain. "I mean, I need the money, we do, really badly." Before I think better of it, I say, "We're expecting a baby in July."

A different smile spreads across her face, now — a genuinely joyful one. "A baby, good for you. A *baby*. That's the nicest news I've heard in a while."

"But I don't know what to do. I mean the land Tom wants to buy — it was left to me by my dad. I care what happens to it."

She nods somberly and reaches over and touches my arm. "You hold firm. Money's only money. Giving up something that matters to you?" Her eyes flit around the room. "That's a real shame."

We walk back into the foyer, and she opens the door. It's very bright outside. "You seem like a nice person," she says, turning to face me. "Julie too. I probably shouldn't say this, but for what it's worth, that business — you know, what happened upstairs?" I nod, but that's as far as she gets. "You know what? Forget I said anything. I've said too much already. It's a bad habit of mine, sticking my nose where it doesn't belong." She shrugs. "It drives Tom crazy, but I can't help it. I've always been this way. My mother used to say that if I didn't mind my own business, somebody was going to sneak into my room in the middle of the night and cut my nose *off*." She laughs a little sadly and rests her hand on the doorknob, and we both look outside.

For reasons unclear, the movers have turned the old piano onto its side and left it on the lawn, like a tipped cow.

"It doesn't look very dignified that way, does it?" Donna says, and I agree. "You know what's really sad? They dragged it all the way from Denver, and none of us has the first notion how to play."

40

LATE THAT AFTERNOON, as the light changes, I check to see if the swing's seat is dry and find that it is. I remove it from the vise, carry Gus's ladder out from behind the shed, and set about hanging the swing from the tree.

It's a straightforward job. First I put two long eyebolts in my pocket, and then I climb the ladder and screw the hooks into the bottom of the anointed branch. I cut two thirteen-foot sections of rope and tie each one to a carabiner from the store with a sturdy bowline knot. Then I climb the ladder again and clip the carabiners into the hooks. Last comes the seat.

I'm coming out of the shed with it in my hands when Owen wanders out of the house, Jerry in tow. "Hey, bud," I say. "You're just in time."

"For what?" He frowns at the wood in my hands.

"I built you something," I tell him. "Come here. I need your help."

"Really?" He follows me back to the tree, where the two ropes hang limp, like dead snakes. We both look up. Through the ragged grid of black branches the sky is dark blue, almost violet, and from the west a steady wind blows.

"You warm enough?" I ask him, and he nods his head. He's just had his bath, and under his down vest he's got his PJs on, the ones with the guitars. His hair is combed neatly across his forehead, parted on the side.

I get down on one knee and thread one of the ropes through one of the holes I made in the seat. "How was school?" I ask.

He kicks at a root. "I got changed to Elm."

"Is that so?" I keep my eyes on the stopper knot I'm tying. "So what do they do that's excellent in Elm?"

"They have a wooden horse you can ride," he says tentatively. "And a big bowl of marbles with swirls inside."

"Who doesn't like swirls?" I say. He has his hands in his pockets. "Come here. Hold this." I hand him one side of the seat. "Now make sure to hold it tight. That's right. Good job." I finish tying the second knot, stand up, and tell him it's okay to let go.

"What now?" he says.

Up in the house, the kitchen lights come on. Through the windows I can see Julie, leaning over and peering into the fridge. She studies the contents, frowns, stands back up, and closes the door.

"Dad," Owen says. "I said, 'What *now?*'"

I tug on each of the ropes, hard, for a few seconds, letting the branch suspend my weight. Satisfied, I tell Owen to climb aboard. He looks up at the branch, and I do too.

"I'm scared," he says.

"That's okay," I tell him.

He considers this. Gingerly he sits on the seat, taking one of the ropes in each hand and gripping it tight. I stand back. Using his toes, he pushes off the ground, gently at first, and then with more force. I step up and give him a light push on the back, and soon his legs start pumping. He gains height. He begins to laugh, softly at first and then louder. It's the best sound I've heard in a while.

"You're a natural," I say, when he's through. I look over his head, at the windows. Julie's waving to me. "You better go in," I say.

"What about you?"

"I have to clean up first," I say.

He doesn't go anywhere. He looks up at the house, then back at me. "Is Mama still mad at you?"

"I think so, yes," I say.

He frowns. "Is she mad at you because of me?"

"No." I shake my head and say it again, more forcefully. "*No,*

259

okay? She's mad at me because of *me*. It's more like — Listen: she loves you very much. We both do. When you love someone so much, so deeply, you get really scared when they go away. And being scared makes people angry. It sounds weird, but it's true."

He seems to accept this. "How long will she be mad for?"

"I don't know, champ," I say. "Maybe for a while." He looks up at the house once more. "You really should go in. Wait." I reach over and mess up his hair. "That's better. Now you look like my child." Swallowing the lump in my throat, I watch him trudge across the grass and up the steps, where Julie ushers him inside. With her hands on her hips, she looks out at me for a moment, through the glass. She raises a hand, holds it there a moment, and then turns away.

In Gus's shed, I straighten and neaten and clean, telling myself it's not that I'm afraid to go in, but that I want to honor Gus. I tell myself the least I can do is keep his favorite space on Earth in the condition he labored tirelessly to keep it in while he was alive, and as I work I start to believe it's true. I sweep the sawdust off the floor and the workbench. I clean, dry, and rehang his saws. I soak the paintbrush I used in a jar of diluted turpentine. I replace the can of Surekote on the shelf. I even clean the windows, inside and out, with Windex and a soft rag. Last, I restack the sawhorses in the corner, just the way he left them.

The clock on the wall says nine forty. I look up at the house. The kitchen light is still on, but it's the only one. Owen's certainly asleep by now and chances are Julie is, too. I look around; there's nothing left I can clean. I'm putting the drill back into the safe when my fingers touch something unexpected — paper. An envelope. I take it out. It's heavier than a letter, and bulkier, and where an address should be, my name is written in Gus's unmistakable, back-slanting hand. I sit down on the freshly swept floor and open the seal.

Inside I find a folded piece of paper, and inside that a small, blue velvet pouch. First I unfold the paper — Mayfield and Pyle letterhead, of course — and find a handwritten note: *If you found this, kiddo*, it says, *chances are you're building something or fixing some-*

thing or making something with your hands. And that means I did <u>*something*</u> *right, as your pop. I'm no dummy, kid. I know you disagree. I know you have your problems with my choices, as your dad. But if you haven't already, you'll learn, just like I did, that we all try our best and we all fail. It's written into the rules of the game. And someday, more likely than not, Owen will regard you with similar skepticism, or dare I say, disdain. Only in his case, I know for a fact he will be wrong.*

Don't bother arguing with me. One benefit of being dead is that I get the last word.

Love, Gus.

I put the note down and pick up the blue pouch, loosening its silken laces. When I turn it over in my hand, a watch falls out — Gus's watch. I flip it over and read the inscription on the back to make sure. There it is: "AJP 6-6-62," the day he graduated from high school. I move it from one hand to the other, feeling the heft of it in my palm. Finally I put it on. I fumble some, fastening the old-fashioned clasp, but I get it closed and stand up to admire it under the light. The watch looks delicate and unfamiliar on my wrist, but the gold — well, there's nothing in the world like gold. It gleams as if it's lit up from within.

I close the safe, turn out the light, and lock the shed. On the other side of the yard I sit down on the swing. The branch bows under my weight, but it holds, and I push off with my feet, moving tentatively at first, just like Owen did, and then gaining speed. The branch creaks but it doesn't break. It's more than strong enough. I hear the last of the apples thump against the ground. I glide higher and higher. I put all my faith in the tree.

Acknowledgments

I am enormously grateful to my agent, Lisa Bankoff, for being great at her job and for believing in this book right away, and to my editor, Andrea Schulz, who is thoughtful and wise, and who made the book much better. Also: Dan Kirschen at ICM and everyone at HMH including Christina Morgan (who came up with the title), Barbara Wood, Rebecca Springer, Carla Gray, and Summer Smith, all of whom I feel very fortunate to have on my team.

Thanks to the Corporation of Yaddo and Vermont Studio Center.

Thank you to my invaluable early readers (and wonderful friends), Katie Brandi and Curtis Sittenfeld. And to Hillary C. Adams, Shauna Seliy, McKay Jenkins, and Glen Gold: I'm grateful to each of you for your hours, your enthusiastic support, your smarts, and of course your fine friendship over the years.

I've been lucky to have great teachers along the way: the late Hank Harrington, Don Snow, Fred Haefele, and Kevin Canty, in Montana; David Leavitt and Padgett Powell in Florida; and Tom Roy, who convinced me to come to Missoula in 1998 and more recently answered my questions about crocuses. And most recently, Bob Bausch, whose Hope and Belief (and daily emails) were integral to this book's completion.

And last but not least, my family: Andrew and Henry; Jamie, Dudley, Edmund, and Jakey; Mom, Dad, Bruce, and Steph. Thank you all for everything. I don't know where or who I would be without you.